Tom Woolberson

&

the School for Watchers

K.J. Brookes

SRL Publishing Ltd

SRL Publishing Ltd
Office 47396
PO Box 6945
London
W1A 6US

First published worldwide by SRL Publishing in 2020

ISBN: 978-191633733-6

*To my wife, Amanda, who is the kindest and most gentle person I
know*

Praise for K. J. Brookes

Vivid detailed imagery of the setting, the author's writing is exceptional. I can't stop reading now.

I loved this brilliant story. Well written with a cast of compelling unforgettable characters.

Chapter One
Dead from the Beginning

Tom Woolberson was only fifteen years old when his life ended. It was through no fault of his own, or the fault of anyone for that matter. It was simply something that happened, and he had been powerless to control it. Of all the ways he could have gone, lying on his bed playing the computer was not the way he would have chosen for himself. It was rather embarrassing really when he found the time to think about it. He had been mindlessly minding his own business when suddenly, everything went blindingly white, then silent, and then black - like somebody had hit pause on his life and tinkered off to the bathroom.

It was only when the lights came back on again that he realised that something quite momentous must have happened, but he wasn't quite sure what it was. The first thing that he noticed, was not that his game had ended or that he'd been pulverised into compote. In fact, the first thing he noticed was that his feet were now wet. What a strange thing to notice. He looked down at them and saw that he was standing, ankle deep, in horrible wet marshland. To say this came as a surprise was nothing compared to what he would realise next. When he finally finished grimacing at his feet, he looked up again and saw what could only be described as the most mundanely alien surroundings imaginable.

To describe something as *mundanely alien* is rather paradoxical; but that is the only way he could think to describe it. You see, it wasn't the endless marshes that worried him, but rather the sheer flatness of the land that gave him cause for concern. There was not a single thing in sight except for sodden mush and bloated rain clouds. Like some dystopian perversion of a familiar Yorkshire countryside. The land was completely flat to the extent that it looked like it'd been drawn with the aid of a spirit level by some highly astute land surveyor to ensure of its perfect flatness. There were no hills or slight inclines or dips or hollows or even a frickin' tree to break the absolute uniform plainness of this strange new place that he'd found himself in.

It wasn't until thirty seconds later when he realised that while he'd remained still, he'd been slowly sinking into the marshes and was now almost knee-deep in the thing. With some effort, he managed to shake himself free.

He walked for what felt like days (but was perhaps only an hour) until finally he came across what appeared to be some sort of building. As the dark and ominous clouds around him slowly started to disperse, they revealed a perfect screen of blue. That's when he saw it. The blurred oblong shape in the distance. Finally, a building among all this wanton flatness! It shimmered and swayed hypnotically against the glassy backdrop behind it. Tom squinted his eyes again, forcing them into focus, and could make out what appeared to be some sort of exceedingly tall edifice set against the endlessly clear expanse. As it slowly came into focus, he saw it looming above him. The colossal black tower.

*

It stood lone on the horizon extending endlessly into the sky. It was thin and most definitely black (or at least a very dark grey in colour). It appeared to be made of stone, which brought Tom a dash of comfort thinking that soon he would find his feet somewhere solid and dry again. Getting closer, the morsel of comfort vanished as he saw that this building was anything but welcoming.

It materialised like a menacing castle in front of him. The exterior was harsh and beaten, as if it had endured centuries of extremely bad weather (and if today's conditions were anything to go by then he was quite sure that it had done). The stones of the façade were huge, surprisingly so, which made Tom wonder who or what had built this foreboding fortification, that stood now a mere five hundred feet in distance.

As he approached, he could make out a large doorway at the entrance – 'enormous' in fact was a more befitting word for this particular door, he realised quickly. It was a monstrous wooden gate, arched at its peak with heavy looking brass hinges strapped across the centre. There were large steps leading up to the entrance and Tom approached them with increasing apprehension as he stepped into the immense shadow cast by the tower.

He ascended the steps slowly, cherishing the brief moment of ecstasy that came with finding his feet on solid ground again. Unfortunately for Tom, any relief he felt was quickly replaced by blinding terror and an immediate urge to flee. This was because the door, that was now only ten feet in front of him, had begun to creak open, and standing there before him was the most utterly terrifying figure imaginable.

At least eight feet tall, covered completely by a black hooded robe, that revealed no signs of what might be hidden underneath, the figure gazed down at him and

Tom felt himself fall backwards, landing hard on the cold floor.

"Enter," spoke a grim voice from above him.

The word crawled over him like a million scuttling insects poured from this shadowy spectre's featureless visage. His first instinct was to get up and run, but he found himself entirely unable to move – he was frozen in fear like a plank of petrified wood. Before he could muster a syllable in reply, the enormous door swung open and the giant spectre disappeared into the shadows, leaving Tom sprawled chaotically on the floor.

His lower back was beginning to throb as he unceremoniously pulled himself to his feet again. He stared through the open doorway, then taking a deep breath, he followed 'It' into the tower - momentarily impressed by his own reckless daring.

The air inside smelt dank and dusty, like it had hung there for millennia and began to mothball and fester. There was a staircase in front of him that spiralled up through the centre of the floors above, twisting like a malevolent snake through the building. Two wooden spheres were perched atop the banisters at the base of the stairs, staring at Tom like the patient eyes of a predator, daring him to ascend.

The flagstone floor was cold and hard, as were the walls and the ceilings, made with the same weather-beaten stones that lined the exterior. He was surprised, but relieved, to find that the enormous hooded figure had now vanished completely. Choosing not to start a search party, he turned instead to the stairs. There were no other doorways or passages around him except for this staircase - so it must have gone up? (Or so he'd thought at the time).

Tom made his way towards the stairs and, with only

4

a moment's hesitation, began to climb. He rounded the first corner and could see the beginnings of the floor above. Hesitantly (but with increasing curiosity) he took the last few steps and entered out onto the first floor. Strangely enough, his trepidation seemed to thaw considerably at what he saw there.

In front of him, towards the back and propped against the cold stone wall, was a tiny wooden booth with a very small, very flustered, looking man perched on a chair behind the smallest desk he'd ever seen. The man (who reminded him immediately of Elmer Fudd – the cantankerous yet endearing adversary of Bugs Bunny) hadn't seemed to notice his arrival. He appeared to be too busy to have any concern whatsoever for the goings on in his surroundings. Instead, he was deep in concentration, muttering a low string of inaudible profanities under his breath, one hand frantically rummaging through mountains of paperwork while the other scribbled furiously at the desk. The scene would have been comical under any other circumstances, except, at this particular juncture, Tom felt that humour had abandoned him entirely.

Letting the relief wash over him at the sight of another person, he rushed over to the booth and began to explain himself.

"Name?" barked the man.

"Excuse me?"

"Your name. I need your name," the man repeated.

"Oh, it's, uhh, Tom Woolberson," Tom managed with a start.

"Born day?" barked the man.

"I'm sorry?"

"Born day! Your born day please!" Barked the man again, without looking up at him.

"Oh, err… I was born on the… twenty third of…

5

March… err… two thousand and… four," he said after a brief pause in which he entirely forgot his own birthday.

"Cause of death?" asked the man.

"What?" Tom coughed loudly as he choked on the mouthful of air that he'd been in the process of inhaling.

"I need your cause of death, now come on I don't have all day!"

"But… I'm not d-d-dead?" Tom stuttered. He had of course been entertaining this thought ever since first finding his feet in the marshes outside, but having it spoken aloud was something different entirely. Unfortunately, the blatant incredulity in Tom's voice had only proved to irritate the man further.

"I don't suffer time wasters son. Please answer the question!"

"I'm not dead. I can't be…" he said frantically, feeling his mind start to reel wildly out of control.

"Cause of death?" barked the tiny old man again, looking tremendously agitated now.

"I… eh… I don't know…" Tom managed, looking deflated.

"I'll just put *to be determined* then. Please make your way to the seated area to your right to await 'enrrrrolment'." He trilled the 'r' while he fixed Tom with a murderous glare.

Tom walked away from the tiny booth feeling like he'd just been hit over the head with a tiny, but very real, cricket bat. He saw to his right a narrow hallway lined with wooden chairs. Seated in those chairs, to his surprise, were dozens of kids that (like him) looked rather misplaced and anxious. They seemed to range in ages and nationalities like they'd been pulled at random from a giant tombola drum containing the world's entire population of minors. There were some older looking kids who were clearly in their late teens (brooding types with no interest in conversing with those they saw as younger and inferior); there were some girls near the back that must've been no older than eleven or twelve (who were whispering frantically, noses centimetres apart); an Indian boy (who was solemnly assessing his own folded hands); a few tall Scandinavian looking kids (who had placed some distance between themselves and the chattering girls); and one small Chinese boy (who looked particularly nervous) sitting in one of the seats closest to him. He walked up to the first free chair he could find and collapsed into it.

He tried to remember the last memory he had before waking up in this place. It had been just a normal day. Normal Tom Woolberson. There was nothing particularly remarkable about him. He was of medium height and build, brown hair swept up out of his face, small nose, blue eyes, broad shoulders like his dad, long legs like his mum - he supposed he would've been classed as reasonably attractive if he were being completely honest with himself (mostly because of his excellent hairstyle), though it was in a way that was appealing to mums and aunties, rather than to any girl he'd shown interest in.

As far as he could remember, he'd woken up like he always did in his house where he'd lived with his parents since he was born. He'd spent the day in his room playing the Xbox. Dad was at work as always (big law firm in town), and mum was out with Aunt Sue (shopping or something equally as uninteresting), and he'd spent the day alone – which had been his only option as his friends had all abandoned him. So, how had he ended up here? As he'd already established, he had no memory of leaving the house that day – surely, he'd remember something as significant as his own death? But there was nothing… nothing that he could remember happening that might've

7

led to this now exceedingly bleak situation.

Just then a door opened down the hall and a girl with bright red hair, who must have been around his age, burst out and started making her way down the corridor towards him. She was a little ditsy and seemed to stumble rather than walk.

"Sorry!" she yelped as she stepped on the toes of the boy beside Tom and he winced in pain. "We're not really supposed to use these restrooms, but I couldn't find any free one's upstairs."

Tom looked around, wondering if she were talking to him now that the other boy was folded over in pain. She had pale blue eyes and her red hair fell in soft curls to her shoulder. She was pretty, he noticed, but in a peculiar kind of way that wasn't immediately obvious to those who looked at her. She was wearing such an odd selection of clothes that all attention was drawn away from her pretty face anyway.

She wore a knitted blue jumper which surely must've belonged to an older sibling or parent as it was at least three sizes too big for her and was pockmarked with holes; a bright red corduroy skirt that clashed horribly with her hair; knitted polka dot tights, that looked as itchy as they were inexplicable; and a pair of large black Doc Martin style boots. She sat down in the seat next to Tom and turned towards him with an exaggerated look of sympathy on her face.

"Don't worry, we've all been there."

"Ermm sorry?"

"We've all been there," she repeated.

"Been where?"

"Been where you are now of course! Sitting here looking just like you. Like your whole world just crashed down around you. Let me guess, you woke up and all you

8

could see were marshes and dark scary looking clouds, right?"

"Eh, yes, actually," Tom replied.

"Well you're here now and there's no going back I'm afraid," she said matter-of-factly. "It's not so bad believe me. My name's Mary," she offered cordially, "Mary Elizabeth Habersmith".

"Oh, err… I'm Tom," he said, "Tom Woolberson."

"*Wool*-berson? Like a sheep's wool? That's a very unusual name," she mused.

"Err… yeah I guess," muttered Tom, looking rather taken aback and resisting the urge to mention that her name wasn't exactly run-of-the-mill either.

"Well Tom Woolberson, I'm pleased to meet you," she said, holding out her hand. "What is it that brings you here then exactly, if you don't mind me asking?"

"You mean how did I die?" Tom said, surprising himself as he shook the girl's hand.

"Yes, that's precisely what I mean," she beamed.

"Well… I don't know exactly," Tom managed. "I was just in my room… then, I must have fallen asleep… then I just sort of… woke up here."

"How mysterious!" she said conspiratorially. "Maybe you were murdered in your sleep?"

Tom gaped at her, dumfounded.

"I'll show you the ropes if you like?" she said, seeing his reaction and swiftly changing the subject.

"Yeah ok," Tom replied, looking at his feet again.

"What is this place anyway?" He wasn't sure why but talking to this strange girl with the odd tights and the curly red hair was starting to make him feel slightly better (despite the surprise news that had just been unceremoniously dumped on him by the tiny man in the wooden hut).

"Think of it as a *school for dead kids*," she said, glancing at Tom with a wry smile.

"You're dead t-t-too... I mean you died too then?" stuttered Tom haphazardly.

"Well yeah, duuuuuh," she said. "We're all goners in here. Not one single living soul around. Where did you think you were anyway?" she chuckled.

"Good point," said Tom. And now that he thought about it, it did kind of make sense. Except for the dying part of course, which he still couldn't get his head around.

"So, you met the Headmaster then?" she asked.

"The who?"

"The Headmaster... You know, upsettingly tall with the black robe on an' all."

"Is that who 'It' was?" Tom croaked.

"Yeah that's the Headmaster – he welcomes all the new students. 'Azrael' is his name... Doesn't speak much. He used to be 'Death' you know, but he retired and now he's taken the role of Headmaster as a sort of ceremonial position, I guess. He doesn't do any of his old duties anymore, that's for sure. Apparently, he was the longest serving Angel of Death there's ever been! He even escorted Jesus to the afterlife if you can believe that! That's what I read anyway... I've never actually spoken to him. He gives me the creeps to be perfectly honest with you."

Just then another door opened down the hall and a shrill voice reverberated off the stone walls around them.

"TOM WOOLBERSON!"

"You better go," Mary said, looking back down the hallway. "Wouldn't want to keep her waiting, if you know what's good for you. It was nice to meet you Tom... I'll look out for you after orientation," and with that she skipped off in the other direction towards the stairs.

Tom watched her round the corner and disappear.

He noticed a few of the other boys staring at her curiously as she left.

Pulling himself together as best as he could, he headed off down the hallway towards the shrill voice that had emitted from one of the rooms there. When he arrived at an open door, thirty or so metres down the corridor, he leaned around slowly and peered across the threshold, unsure of whether to knock or announce himself – as it turned out, neither was necessary.

Chapter Two
Orientation

Inside the dark room lit only by candle light, sat a tall thin bespectacled woman who was dressed from head to toe in green. She wore a silk green shawl around her shoulders under which a green blazer topped what looked like an entirely green pant suit. She wore sensible looking green shoes and even wore a polished emerald beret on her head. She sat at a desk in the middle of the room - which was apparently the 'Enrolment Office' according to the sign on the door.

Around the tiny office were dozens of heavy looking filing cabinets, some of which hung open revealing hundreds of dusty folders and providing multiple tripping hazards for anyone not paying attention to where they were walking. On the desk in front of the woman sat the strangest assortment of items he'd ever seen. There was what looked like an enormous set of antique metal binoculars. There were dials and levers on the side of them and several sets of lenses of gradually increasing size attached to the front. Next to the binoculars was a dusty looking magnifying glass with a battered looking wooden handle and lying across the table was what looked like a baseball bat, but on closer inspection he realised it was some sort of brass telescope with intricate etchings of winged angels along the barrel.

"Well come in then!" said the woman. "Let's not wait

for hell to freeze."

Tom crept nervously into the dark room, stepping over a drawer fully extended from the filling cabinet to his right.

"Tom Woolberson?" she asked briskly.

"Eh yes ma'am," Tom fumbled.

"Well take a seat Mister Woolberson and we shall get you enrolled." She spun in her chair to the cabinet behind her and immediately started rummaging through an open drawer.

"My name is Uriel and you may call me the same," she said over her shoulder. "Mister Enoch informs me that you are unaware of how you came to be with us today?"

"Who?" Tom said, sounding rude despite himself.

"Mister Enoch I said, Mister Enoch. Do try and keep up now, Tom".

"Oh, err... yes then. I mean, I don't know," Tom said finally; assuming Mister Enoch must be the small flustered man in the booth by the stairs.

"Well not to worry," she said. "That is easily fixed!"

She swung back around on her chair and opened a drawer by her feet, pulling out what appeared to be a large glass fish bowl.

"Right," she said, "this should only take a moment, but I will require you to come a little bit closer so you can see."

Tom grabbed the bottom of his chair and shuffled it a few inches closer.

"Mister Woolberson... Of forty-four Needless Road, Steppsworth, Bridlington, England, United Kingdom, Europe, Northern Hemisphere, Planet Earth. Correct?"

"Err... that's right," Tom said. Needless Road was indeed the road on which he'd lived. The history behind the bizarrely named street had stemmed from one

13

decidedly bitter town planner who had fought against its inclusion in the blueprints for the town deeming it 'unnecessary', seeing as the street parallel was already providing a suitable diversion for traffic away from the main road. Unsuccessful in his attempts and near furious at the extra expenditure, he decided to show his irritation in the moniker that now adorns the street sign at the end of the road.

Uriel reached again into the drawer at her feet and this time pulled out a large green bottle corked at the top and sloshing with liquid inside. She uncorked the bottle with an almighty tug.

"Now, Mister Woolberson, straight to the point if you don't mind – terribly busy - the matter of your departure from the land of the living."

Tom's eyebrows furrowed, still not completely at ease with his untimely death being mentioned so brazenly. She poured the clear liquid from the bottle into the large fish bowl.

"Lucky for you I happen to be the sharpest sighted spirit in the history of existence," she stated hurriedly, eyeing Tom's shrinking demeanour.

She reached across the desk and picked up the dusty looking magnifying glass. Then she pushed the goldfish bowl across the table towards Tom and walked around the desk, so she was stood directly behind his right shoulder.

"Ok then, Mister Woolberson," she said, holding the magnifying glass up in front of them and peering into the liquid at the bottom of the bowl, "show time!"

Confused, Tom leaned forward expecting to see a slightly magnified bowl of clear liquid. However, what he saw in the magnifying glass made his breath catch in the back of his throat and his hands clasp tightly around the

14

bottom of his chair. It was as if they were falling through the air towards Earth, thousands of feet above the ground, plummeting through the clouds towards the green landmass below. He could see the outline of Great Britain as the clouds dispersed, and as they fell further, he could see green fields and small towns and the coast around Bridlington where he lived. He could see boats out to sea and the beach and the pier with the big ferris wheel he hadn't been on in years. Closer still, he could see the church on the hill in the village of Steppsworth where he lived and the houses on his street and the roof of their house and his dad's second car in their driveway. They went right through the roof of his house as if it were never there and into the upstairs hall and through the door into his bedroom, where Tom could see himself lying on his bed playing the Xbox, wholly oblivious to being observed.

"There we are," said Uriel with a satisfied glance down at Tom. "Thanks to my trusty looking glass here, we are able to see into the past and the present. Comes in handy with matters like these."

Tom was staring at himself lying on his bed, unable to look away from the face that was so familiar to him. It seemed different somehow - his features were backwards as if being viewed through someone else's eyes as opposed to seeing his own mirror image which he was used to. Everything was flipped. Seeing himself this way made his grip tighten in suspense and he could feel his palms starting to sweat on the chair beneath him.

"Half past eleven in the morning and you have yet to leave the comfort of your own bedroom, Mister Woolberson! Heavens, the more I get to know humans the more I understand why Noah was permitted only animals on his boat!" she fumed with apparent distain.

She directed her attention back towards her looking

glass and motioned for Tom to do the same. The Tom on the bed had his teeth bared in concentration and he watched himself bite down on his lip, as something evidently happened on screen to merit an increase in focus. Suddenly, the room exploded with light and sound and dust and chunks of concrete and fire and the view within the magnifying glass was completely obscured.

"What happened?!" Tom cried, springing from his chair and slamming his hands on the desk. "Where did I go?!"

Uriel looked down at Tom with a look that could almost have been mistaken for pity if it hadn't been so laden with irritation.

"Keep watching the glass," she said biting her lip, the way Tom had in the glass a few moments before.

As the dust in the glass began to settle, a scene of total destruction was visible on the site that had been Tom's bedroom. There was no longer any sign of Tom or his bed or the ceiling or even his Xbox; but as his eyes scanned the room intently, desperately looking for the source of the chaos that had just engulfed him, they fell upon something that hadn't been there moments before... something that didn't belong. Something sitting among the rubble, toppled onto its front and covered in dust. Something that looked curiously like... a row of seats... from... from... an airplane?

"Whozzat!?" Tom blurted, jumping out of his chair again. "How'd that get there? What happened to my room?"

He fell back into his seat, both stunned and stupefied, his face twisted with incredulity.

Uriel turned the magnifying glass in her hand, so the rear was now facing the goldfish bowl. Suddenly the image started to change, and their view of the room started to recede up through the destruction and rubble, through the newly formed hole in the roof and up into the sky, coming to a stop a few dozen feet above the house, giving them a view of the full-scale destruction that'd befell the Woolberson estate. The entire east side of the house was collapsed and in ruin and the broken fuselage of a large passenger plane laid spread across the scene. It lay in three pieces; the wings no longer attached. There was fire and smoke and burning embers scattered amongst the rubble and to Tom's horror he saw the twisted and charred remains of passengers sprawled on the ground. In the middle section of the fuselage, there were passengers still strapped to their seats - hanging grotesquely like ventriloquist dummies in some macabre vaudeville.

"Ok I think that's enough," Uriel said curtly. "Tragic. Always so terribly tragic," she said as she quickly stowed the magnifying glass and fish bowl away in the drawers by her feet. Tom sat in stunned silence. *An airplane crash? On his house? Had an airplane just crashed into his house?* He couldn't believe it… it was, in itself, utterly unbelievable.

He couldn't believe that this was how he had died - casually reclining on his bed minding his own business then obliterated by an aluminium tube of commuters. What an utterly implausible way to go! He thought about his parents. How lucky it'd been that it was only him in the house at the time. Where were they now? They must've been in pieces (although not as literally as he was most likely) – the life they knew in ruins (again). Taken from them in one fell swoop of a jumbo jet. He thought about his grandparents and his cousins and friends and all those faces he would never see again. Tears brimmed in his eyes and Uriel coughed awkwardly.

"Now now, Mister Woolberson. It happens to all humans eventually. The world breaks everyone, and

17

afterward, some are strong at the broken places… Just look at where you are now! The line you were born into qualified you for admission into this prestigious institution. Some of the greatest minds in the history of your race teach here!" She spun in her chair again and extracted a folder from the cabinet behind her. "Now here I have the essentials," she said emptying the contents of the folder onto the desk. "This is your timetable," she said passing Tom a thin papyrus scroll of paper, "and here is your map," she said passing Tom another scroll. "On here you'll find the common rooms for each of the Houses, as well as the locations of the various departments and anywhere else you might need to go."

She eyed Tom cautiously. "Now do be careful, it is very easy to get lost if you don't know where you're going. There are many (many!) floors and most people prefer to take the elevators, but you may use the stairs if you wish, although I don't recommend it – unless of course you enjoy experiencing a severe bout of vertigo. There are places, obviously, that are off limits to students, and these are marked on the map in red."

She gave Tom a stern look over the scroll. "And here is your new student allocation of 'shekels'," she said as she emptied a small draw-string purse onto the table, revealing a handful of battered looking silver coins. "This is the currency we use at this school; it can be spent on new clothes or food, or scrolls and ink, or any number of luxury items you can use in your free time. This should last you for the first month, after which you'll find there are many ways in which you can earn your own."

"Now you will find that communication at this school is a lot more fluid than what you've been used to back on Earth. We do not have the hinderance of endless dialects and languages – instead, you will find that everyone here speaks the same language, which is *Angelican*, and which you'll be pleased to hear you are already fluent in as we've been conversing in it since you arrived in my office."

Tom stared at her blankly while he processed this bizarre revelation.

"Thankfully, I see you died while wearing clothes so there's no need to issue you with the emergency pyjamas." she motioned to a cupboard behind her. "However, if you wish to purchase any new garments you will find there is a tailor on the seventy-sixth floor who will do a fine job with any orders you put in, for a fair price... And now I do believe that is everything you will need for the moment, Mister Woolberson."

She stood up from her desk and ushered Tom towards the door.

"Next, you are required to attend orientation with all of the new students on the twenty-third floor, where you will meet our three Heads of House and find out which House you will be calling home for the duration of your stay here with us."

Tom made his way out of the door feeling rather dizzy.

"I wish you luck, Mister Woolberson. I'm sure your time with us with be fruitful."

And with that she closed the door leaving Tom standing in the hall staring blankly at the wooden doorframe. He heard whispers from a few of the boys seated in the hall behind him.

"Wonder what happened to that poor sod?" Said one boy to another with a barely concealed snigger.

Chapter Three
Earth, Water and Fire

Tom looked at the map and saw the typical '*You are here*' marker next to the Enrolment Office on the first floor. Along the corridor he saw there was an elevator. He headed towards it and ignored the ogling looks from the other kids in the hall. He pressed the arrow call button on the wall next to the elevator and it dinged immediately, opening the doors in front of him.

The elevator was surprisingly pleasant compared to what he'd thus far seen of the building. Polished cedar rails and oak panelling on the walls decorated with gold finishing. It looked like the type of elevator you might have found in an upmarket Manhattan apartment building used by rich socialites and rapacious debutantes. His eyes widened in disbelief when he saw the number of buttons on the wall. There were buttons for floors from one to five hundred stacked neatly on the wall like silvery brooches on a shiny metallic overcoat. Next to each button was a little silver label telling you what was on that floor. Then there was the small sign above the buttons that read, *for floors 501 and above – please use the upper elevator (off limits to students!).* Tom shook his head again in amazement before pressing the button for the twenty-third floor.

Moments later the elevator doors pinged open to reveal a lavish golden library. Like the elevator, the room was rich with opulence. Gold handled staircases spiralled through the three floors of the room which was curved into a giant oval. The balconies of the floors above ringed the room like golden bracelets, and the walls were lined completely with shelves upon shelves of books, that had golden ladders propped against them on railings, so they could slide around the bookshelves like Angela Lansbury in Bedknobs and Broomsticks. The hall was filled with youths of all ages; some seated in chairs facing the stage at the front and some had formed little groups and were standing off to the side, chatting and laughing nervously. An impressive array of paintings and portraits adorned the segments of the walls that weren't overtaken with bookshelves. He recognised the style of some impressionist paintings to his left from his time in A-level art and design, but he didn't recognise any of the paintings themselves.

"What? Do you think they stopped painting when they died?" laughed an older boy standing near the elevator who noticed Tom staring. He had a bronze 'prefect' badge fastened to the lapel of his smart looking brown suit that was cut in a nineteen-sixties style. "This school is home to the greatest collection of art the world has *never* seen," he said with a haughty smirk walking towards Tom and holding out his hand. "I'm Giles," he said.

"Oh, err… Tom," Tom replied, shaking the older boy's hand.

"Some of my favourites are in this room you know," Giles said, with an admiring look around the hall. "That's a Caravaggio over there, and that one's a Degas of course, and those ones at the back are Rembrandts. I was an art student at university when I died. Car crash. Turns out our designated driver was a bit of a pill head - if that's what you want to call a guy who chokes back two

21

handfuls of Nembutal then gets behind the wheel of a car and drives straight over an embankment and into a ravine. Anyway, I'm up here now and I'm a prefect, so don't let me catch you out of line," he said with a playful grin.

Just then a woman walked out onto the stage and the chattering groups around the wings gradually fell silent and turned to the front.

"Ladies and gentlemen if you would take your seats," she called over the shuffling crowd. She was very beautiful Tom noticed, although she hid it well. Her blonde hair was pulled back tight against her scalp and her features were sharp and piercing. Her lips were set into a stern pout and her penetrating gaze made her look rather frightening – like an eagle fixated on its prey. She looked to be no older than thirty, but she carried an air of authority that was immediately present, and Tom noticed that Giles had stood to attention as if the drill sergeant had just entered the barrack's dorms.

"You better take a seat," Giles said looking down at Tom.

Tom ran to the back row of seats closest to the elevator and jumped into the nearest one.

"My name is Gabriel," began the frightening looking woman. "Welcome to your orientation. Anyone who talks or interrupts without first being spoken to shall be escorted to the dungeons on the thirteenth floor so quickly they'd need treatment for whiplash if they still had a neck prone to such ailments."

The last few mutterings around the room fell silent.

"That's better," she said. "Now, I understand many of you will still be confused about why you are sat in this room with me today. I assure you it is an honour and a privilege to be one of the chosen few among us. For those whom the school has appeared have been specially

selected to enrol here and will be nurtured and guided by
some of the greatest minds to have walked the Earth, and
by some who have never set foot there. You should count
yourselves extremely fortunate that I may address you
here today at *St Michael's School for Watchers*."

"Wotchers?" A boy in the back row along from Tom
blurted before catching himself at the last moment.
Gabriel eyed him menacingly. Tom looked around and
saw more than one confused expression as the crowd of
new students stirred uncomfortably in their seats.

"Because of your age, you possess the required
mailability that we look for here at St Michael's. This
prerequisite aside, it is the lineage within each of you that
has granted you entry into our grand institution. At St
Michael's you will be afforded the opportunity to reach
your true potential and ascend beyond the makings of the
merely mortal. Some of you of course, will fail. It is as
inevitable as man is fallible."

Tom felt an uneasy knot twist in his stomach.

"This school was founded long before your recorded
history began. Those who teach here have been hand-
picked for their knowledge and their various talents. At St
Michael's you shall meet the greatest of your kind and you
shall learn from them as they have learned from us. When
your time with us comes to an end, those lucky few who
have lived to their greatest potential shall rise 'On' and
ascend to the Realm of the Watcher. The land of the
Seventh Heaven. The place my brethren and I call home."

"Now, obviously there have been some big changes
for each of you in the recent present and it will take some
getting used to before you are entirely at ease, but I'm
sure in time you will feel as comfortable here with us as
you once did on Earth."

There was a noise from the left of the stage, and
Tom could see a large door open. Gabriel turned to her

side and spread her arms in welcome. The two men who came out of the door were tall, muscled and equally as striking as Gabriel. They walked out onto the stage and stood at her side. The man closest to Gabriel was the taller of the two. Tom could see some of the girl's eyes widen as the man surveyed the room and smiled coolly. He was extraordinarily handsome. His tussled blonde hair was swept back and looked effortlessly perfect; his folded muscular arms looked like pythons constricted menacingly across his chest. He was the archetypal Greek Adonis; Michelangelo's David in the flesh and he cut a very imposing figure. The man next to him was slightly smaller though still large by terrestrial standards. He had short greased black hair and piercing eyes which made him look just as frightening as the woman.

"May I introduce my brothers - Michael and Raphael," she said ushering to the two men in turn.

"With myself we make up your three Heads of House. Michael," she said gesturing to the taller man, "is Head of The House of Revelation; Raphael," she said ushering to the smaller man, "is Head of the House of Deuteronomy; and I am Head of the House of Numbers. Each of you will be placed in one of these three Houses where you will remain for the entirety of your time at St Michael's. Your house will determine what you learn as each Head has selected their own teachers based on the qualities revered by that House. Your House will also determine the people you will meet and the places you will visit as well as the obstacles you will have to overcome. Each House is magnificent and challenging in its own unique way and each has bred heroes and champions to be worshiped and admired."

Tom looked around the room, starting to feel the panic rise in his throat again. It was like his first day of school back at Bridlington High, except twisted and warped like in some bizarre dream. He felt suddenly important – '*chosen*'. He had no idea what this 'lineage' was that she was talking about, but he couldn't for the life of him remember a single notable thing he'd done to merit being chosen by some omnipotent league of 'Watchers'. In fact, he could think of a lot more bad things than good things he'd done in his life. Like what he did to his brother for instance… He flushed, ashamed of that thought, but quickly shook it off as Gabriel continued.

"We shall now begin the selection process and you shall discover which house you are to call home during your time at St Michael's. The prefects will sort you into an orderly line and each of you will get the chance to select the House to which you shall belong."

Chatter erupted around Tom as people pushed back chairs and scanned the room expectantly. One of the prefects towards the front – a tall girl, with glasses and a distinctly bossy demeaner, shouted across the room.

"EVERYONE PLEASE FORM A LINE BEHIND ME!"

Tom jumbled out of his chair and saw Giles to his left ushering students towards the front. He scrambled in that direction and was pushed out of the way by a bulky kid with curly ginger hair and freckles. Eventually the room quietened, and a semi-orderly line was visible twisting like a snake around the large hall. Tom found himself only a few places from the very back, but he didn't mind. He was in no rush to go into the tepee like tent that had appeared at the front of the line and which students had now started taking it in turns to enter.

After what seemed like hours, Tom was finally approaching the front. He perched up on his tiptoes and tried to get a glimpse of what might be inside the tent, but all he could see was the back of the head of the student at the front of the line. The room had emptied and there were now only a few straggling students left and the bossy looking prefect who stood at the entrance to the tent. At last it was his turn. He approached the entrance and the prefect pulled back the curtain for him and gave him a taunting sneer.

"Choose wisely now," she said through rusted train-track braces.

He stepped across the threshold - it was dark, and he almost tripped over some curtain that was rolled up on the floor. The tent was lit by a single burning torch that hung on the wall to his left. The ground in here wasn't the cold stone floor he had left behind in the hall; it was something different entirely. There was grass as if they had pitched a tent over a field, and there were thick branches on the floor as if they had just fallen from a tree above. There was also the sound of running water and to his amazement he saw there was a small stream winding through the tent. Next to the stream was a wooden bucket filled to the brim with water. He saw the three Heads of House standing at the back of the tent looking down at him expectantly. Tom looked up to them waiting for instruction but none of the three Heads spoke a word. Gabriel, who stood at the centre of the three, was holding a round wicker basket in her hands. Gently, she removed the lid with one hand and tipped the contents onto the grass below. Tom stumbled back in horror, his arms grabbing the material of the tent to keep from falling over. Out of the basket slithered a large brown snake, its thin tongue darting repeatedly from its mouth and its unblinking yellow eyes focused intently on Tom. It slithered across the grass towards him, backing him into the far corner and blocking his only exit. There was no escape. Tom clung to the thick material of the tent - there was nowhere to run. He looked to the three Heads in desperation, but their cool gazes simply surveyed him with mild curiosity. Slithering closer still, Tom realised he was completely trapped – the back exit to the tent was blocked by the encroaching serpent. The snake hissing loudly, arching its back ready to strike. This was it. The snake would attack at any second. Without thinking he lunged for the burning torch that hung a few feet away from him and pulled it from the wall. Turning on his heels he swung his arm wildly at the snake, which hissed louder still but slowly began to retreat across the grass towards the three Heads. Tom clung to the torch tightly; he felt the fire from it burning his forearm as he swung at the snake, but by now he knew that he had won. Gabriel lowered the basket to the ground and the snake slithered back inside obediently, lowering its head as the lid closed shut and it disappeared from sight.

"You have chosen the House of Revelation," Gabriel said, gesturing to the burning torch in his hand. "Michael was chosen by God to bear the element of fire, therefore in his House is where you shall stay."

Tom looked up at Michael whose stoic profile gave no signs of having heard his own name. The three Heads as one stepped aside revealing the back of the tent and Gabriel swung her arm and motioned for Tom to exit. He walked past them feeling rather sheepish and exited the back of the tent where he found another prefect waiting for him - a goofy looking teen who wouldn't have looked out of place as an extra on Stranger Things. His long mullet was decidedly eighties, as were his sweatbands and his yellow Marty McFly Nikey high tops.

"Revelation then, eh? What's your damage? Bit of a pyromaniac are we?" he said with a snigger. "I'm in Deuteronomy. Went for the branch. Nearly took that things head off with one swing! It was gnarly. Our Head's

Raphael - his element's Earth. I guess like, that includes trees and rocks and everything."

He walked Tom out the back doors of the library and back into the dark hallway. There was another elevator just to the right of them. The prefect hit the call button and turned to Tom again.

"Revelation are up on the three-hundredth floor - gaudy bunch. You should have gone for the branch!"

The elevator doors pinged open and Tom walked in.

"I'm Davon by the way. Take it easy little dude," he said, grinning as the doors closed.

Chapter Four
The House of Revelation

The entire three-hundredth floor was designated to the House of Revelation. The halls were lined with enormous renaissance style frescos of fiery angels and hideous demons. Massive wings and talons clutched together in heated battles set against scorched skies of black and electric blue. Tom recognised Michael's face in some of the paintings – he was holding a flaming sword held high above his impressive wing span; a triumphant cry etched onto his face as he stood over the crumpled body of a writhing Satan.

The Revelation common room was a vast hall set with chesterfield armchairs, ottoman couches and pouffes - none of which were matching but rather like they'd been amassed haphazardly over the centuries and thrown into the collection. There were marble sculptures placed around the room that looked like they'd been swiped straight from the Louvre or the Uffizi – more priceless originals Tom guessed. An enormous marble fountain sat at the centre of the room. It had winged cherubs jetting water from flutes and reclining angels bathing in the waters below. A few of the students were perched at the side of the fountain, flicking water back and forth and laughing. The common room itself looked like an Italian piazza set inside a giant artisan coffee shop.

Students from similar times seemed to have joined

little cliques, and you could almost tell which era each clique was from based on their matching attire. There was a group of preppy looking boys to the right of the fountain that were quite obviously American and looked like they might have come from the same time as the prefect who had shown him to the elevator - they were wearing popped collar polo shirts and slacks – one boy was even wearing sunglasses despite the fact it was dark and they were indoors. He threw him a dirty look and a two-finger salute when he noticed Tom staring. To his relief he spotted a familiar face sitting in an armchair near the back of the room. It was Mary who he'd met in the hallway outside the Enrolment Office. She was staring inquisitively at the boys by the fountain – a look of gentle abstraction mixed with minor annoyance splayed on her face. He made his way through the imposing array of statues and chairs to take a seat on a couch across from her.

"Hi!" she said cheerfully, having spotted his approach.

"Hey!" Tom said, dumping his scrolls on the couch next to her.

"I was hoping you'd choose Revelation!" she beamed. "We could use some new faces around here – apparently no one fights snakes with fire anymore," she said matter-of-factly. "What class have you got first?"

"Eh…" Tom rummaged for the timetable he'd been given by Uriel and Mary sprang out of her armchair and took a seat next to him on the couch.

"Let me see," she said, grabbing the timetable out of his hands. "Excellent!" she exclaimed. "You've got Laws of the Universe second period with me at ten o'clock."

"Isn't it getting a bit late for class?" Tom said, wanting to yawn but finding the impulse oddly muted.

"We have all our classes at night here. During the day is free time."

"Oh, that's strange," Tom said, slightly disappointed that he wouldn't be getting to a bed anytime soon.

"Not that strange. Ghosts do haunt at night after all." She made a 'woooo' sound and shook her arms in what must have been the worst ghost impersonation he'd ever witnessed - they both erupted in laughter.

"I've got 'Ancient History Revisited' first. What's that like?" Tom asked.

"It's actually not bad," she said, approvingly. "It's like the entire history of the world except what actually happened, instead of just the revisionist nonsense we were taught down on Earth. History's been written and rewritten so many times, don't you know? And it's always written by the victors who rarely give accurate accounts of what actually happened. Most of the history you know will be heavily biased and painted in a way to make one group of people seem peaceful and progressive and make another group of people look like bungling philistines."

"Oh, that's pretty cool I guess," Tom replied, unsure of how to respond.

"Anyway, who would have thought it - you still get school when you're dead!" Mary chuckled.

"How did you… y'know? If you don't mind me asking," asked Tom, with a shy glance in her direction.

"How did I die you mean? Well, it wasn't the most exciting death there's ever been that's for sure," she said nonchalantly. "Quite boring and ordinary really… I was sick ever since I can remember. Ever since I was just a baby I think. Cystic Fibrosis it was called. It's when your lungs get really full up with mucus and it's really hard to breathe. Every morning my mum had to hit me on the back for a full thirty minutes to clear my lungs for the day. I couldn't do much running or playing like a normal

31

kid. It got worse instead of better as I got older then eventually one day I couldn't clear my throat and I blacked out and that was it. I woke up here. It was quite horrible really. In a way I'm miles better off up here as I feel healthy as a horse! See!" She jumped off the couch and span on her heals smiling, then made a show of doing star jumps while Tom laughed encouragingly.

"We probably shouldn't be laughing," Tom said tersely.

"Why not?" Mary replied. "It happens to everyone eventually doesn't it? And look where we are. Not everyone gets to come here and learn from actual angels! We're the pick of the litter!"

"What do you know about them anyway?" Tom asked, suddenly curious.

"Plenty! But don't worry you'll learn all that in Ancient History Revisited - speaking of which, that's almost nine o'clock! You better get going."

Tom pulled out his time table.

Ancient History (Revisited) 9-10pm – Room 3B
142nd Floor – Professor Suetonius

He folded the timetable and stashed it away in his pocket.

"I'll catch you later then I guess," he said.

"See you second period!" Mary beamed as Tom pulled himself from the couch and started making his way back across the common room.

Chapter Five
The Devil in the Details

Five minutes later, Tom was down on the one-hundred and forty-second floor staring at the door handle for room 3B. He had just built up the courage to reach for it when someone else's hand beat him to the punch. He turned and saw a skinny kid around his own age with long black bangs that hung in his eyes obscuring (what must've been) most of his vision. He was wearing a black windbreaker jacket – typical festival attire (an innocuous impersonation of Liam Gallagher, Tom suspected).

"They don't open themselves you know," he laughed.

"Oh… err… sorry," said Tom. "I was just about to get that."

"Don't worry about it. I'm Finn. You're new here right? What's your name?"

"I'm Tom," he replied.

"You look like you might actually be alright, Tom – a rare thing around here."

"Oh, err… thanks I guess."

"First class then is it?" the boy enquired.

"Yeah…" Tom said, feeling nervous despite himself.

"Don't worry, the whole things a breeze. Stick with me and you'll be right as rain."

"Thanks," Tom said, slightly encouraged.

"Anyway, we better get a seat before we're stuck

33

right at the front," Finn said, pushing through the door and revealing the classroom beyond.

The room was arched like a university lecture hall except the seats were replaced with white marble tiers reminiscent of an ancient Roman Senate building. It was lit by candles that were placed intermittently along the tiers and by a large candle-lit chandelier that hung from the ceiling. The teacher stood at the large chalk board at the front and was wearing what appeared to be a long white toga. He looked Greek, or possibly Italian. His tanned skin accentuated the deep wrinkles etched onto his face.

Finn noticed Tom ogling the strange apparel. "That's Professor Suetonius," he whispered. "He's from ancient Rome. We can barely understand him - which is fine as he talks a load of nonsense anyway."

They grabbed two seats on an aisle near the back of the classroom. The other kids sat around were the same strange mix that he was getting used to seeing around the school. The kids sat directly along from them were prime examples; there was a tall blonde boy with long wavy hair who was wearing tan flares that hailed from a more disco-centric era than the one he'd come from; there was a slick kid with a rockabilly greaser style which was either extremely contemporary or extremely dated – he thought maybe the latter; and then there was the usual cliques of pretty girls who were reserved for only the most popular jocks, but for shy loners like Tom, were perpetually unobtainable - he sighed at the thought of reliving the trauma of high school social politics all over again. Incidentally, he found himself catching the eye of a pretty blonde girl who sat down last near the front, but she looked away quickly. She was by all accounts the most flawlessly good-looking girl he'd ever seen. Not that it mattered, as she'd never go for his type anyway, but he was sure there'd never been anyone like this back in Bridlington. She was the kind of pretty you only saw in magazines once the picture had been edited to the extent that all the model's flaws and imperfections were removed, leaving a figure unattainable enough to give any fourteen-year-old girl an eating disorder. He could have sworn her hair moved in slow motion as she whipped it back and stashed her bag under her desk (was she filming a commercial right now?). Tom felt suddenly very shy and quickly started fiddling with his fingernails as if oblivious to the girl who had just sat down.

"That's Alice," said Finn leaning over the marble towards Tom. "I'd get over it quickly if I were you. You're in Wonderland if you think you can land that one - she's as stuck up as they come."

Tom glanced to the front hoping to catch her eye again.

"If you're having trouble with girls, I've got some advice for you," he said, slouching back on the marble. "Be a goth…"

"What? Why?" asked Tom, breaking from his reverie.

"Be a goth… You always see really hot goth girls with well below average guys. There's no league system in the goth universe. Everyone is in everyone else's league. As long as they're a goth, it doesn't matter to them - goths aren't picky. You know I'm thinking of becoming a goth myself. The only problem is, I don't have any eyeliner…"

Just then Professor Suetonius slammed his chalk duster sharply against his desk.

"Quiet please," he said, in heavily accented Angelican.

The chattering slowly quelled and Professor

35

Suetonius began.

"For any new studaants with us today, aye emm
Professor Suetonius, and aye will be your Ancient History
Revisited teachuur. Aye will start at thee very beginning
for the benefit of our new guests before we return to our
usual lesson."

There was an audible groan around the room and
Tom felt himself sink lower into his seat.

"At thee very beginning there was God. Then God
of course created thee angels. First, he created Lucifer
who was thee eldest and wisest of all thee angels. Then he
created Michael, then Gabriel, then Raphael, then Uriel,
then Raziel, then Remiel etcetera etcetera. After he
created thee angels, God created Adam. Then he told
thee Angels that they must worship Adam as they
worshiped him. Of course, Lucifer the eldest angel was
not happy about thees and rebelled against God. He
asked Michael to rebel with him and when Michael said
'no', so began the great war een heaven. Lucifer and hees
dissenting angels battled against Michael and hees band of
angels that were loyal to God. Until finally, Lucifer – who
had become thee 'Great Dragon' - was defeated and cast
out of heaven. Doomed to spend an eternity in hell with
those angels who had followed heem."

He looked around the room ominously, before
continuing.

"In Hell, these angels would go on to become Satan's
great generals, each commanding legions of demons.
Thee treacherous Baal for instance - the king of Hell and
Satan's most trusted general. The body of an arachnid and
the head of a man, a cat and a toad."

One of the boys in the back aisle blew a loud
raspberry, and the girls at the front burst into fits of
giggles – even Alice joined in (to Tom's dismay).

"Thees is not a joke!" Barked Professor Suetonius from the front. "These creatures are real, and you should be deadly afraid of them if you know what eees good for you. Thee modern Catholic Church on Earth has finally accepted the exeestence of these blasphemes beings that have stared them in thee face for centuries. The knowledge that was long forgotten has resurfaced. Een thee year of our Lord two thousand aan five anno domini, his Holiness Pope John Paul thee second decreed that every diocese on earth must appoint an offeecial exorcist to deal with the growing threat of demonic possession."

The room quietened again, and he continued.

"Belial!" he boomed, scribbling a quick sketch onto the chalkboard. "He is thee dancing lion who has five legs but stands on two like a man. A prince of evil and adversary of God; he is the great tempter who tempted the children of Israeel to their deaths. He exeests only to bring wickedness and guilt to thee sons of man. Then there eees Liviathan!" he said, scribbling again. "The great serpent monster of thee sea. The demon of envy. One of thee seven Princes of Hell. Her sharp claws and rows of razor-sharp teeth have devoured the sheeps of man whole."

"The what, Sir?" Interrupted a boy sat near the door.

"The sheeps! The boats! He ate the sheeps whole," Professor Suetonius repeated.

A few of the girls at the front giggled into their sleeves.

"Then of course, thee ruler of Hell. Thee Great Dragon, Satan heemself."

The class seemed to calm at the words and listened keenly.

"Be sober, be vigilant; because your adversary thee Devil walks about like a roaring lion, seeking whom hee may devour. Sometimes he weel take human form so he can hide among us. Pretending to be one of us. He walked among men with Isaiah and Ezekiel who watched him fall from heaven like a flash of lightening; he has ruled nations as the King of Tyre and of Babylon and as thee Emperor Nero whose number was seeex, seeex, seeex! He is intelligent - he knows more theology than all thee theologians combined. Those who have not yet ascended to thee realms above are vulnerable to hees attacks - *you* in this very classroom are vulnerable to hees attacks!"

Tom sensed the tension in the room around him - every last set of eyes was locked on Professor Suetonius as he spoke.

"Once the most beautiful of all angels until he was cast from thee heavens into the lake of fire, hees true appearance is now a mystery. It is said hee may take any form he wishes to ensnare those unlucky souls who cross hees path. He was thee ancient serpent that whispered in the ear of Eve as she sat under the Tree of Knowledge in thee Garden of Eden, fooling her into taking a bite from thee forbidden fruit. He was there when Jesus Christ was arrested and sentenced to be scourged and nailed to thee cross between two thieves until a soldier's spear pierced his side and took his life; he walked the streets of Paris when the Black Death ravaged the earth and the piles of dead grew higher than thee buildings; he was there in London when thee great fire came from thee bakers house in Pudding Lane and crumbled the great city to ashes; he was in Salem when thee young girls were pulled from their homes, their tongues cut from their mouths and then burnt at thee stake in screaming agony! And he was there in October when the red Bolsheviks spread revolution across thee frozen city, burning thee royal palace to the ground and murdering the Romanov's in

38

cold blood."

He stopped and slowly cast his gaze around the candlelit room. The class had fallen silent and all eyes were locked on him as he assessed them.

"Do *not* be ignorant of Satan's devices my children," he said. "He wants each of you for his own."

Chapter Six
Black Holes and Revelations

After class, the students filed back out into the dark hall and quickly dispersed. Finn and Tom were the last two to leave.

"Well that was eh... interesting," said Tom.

"Oh yeah, he loves to give the new kids a good scare," Finn sneered. "A proper lunatic that one. Where does he come up with that stuff? The body of a spider and the head of a toad and a... what was the last one?"

"A cat I think."

"Well he's pulled that one straight out of his arse. Next, he'll be telling us about a demon with the body of a dog, the legs of an elephant and the ears of a rabbit."

Tom guffawed loudly, attracting a few curious glances.

"Which house are you in anyway?" Finn asked.

"Revelation," Tom replied.

"That's a shame. I'm in Deuteronomy. Our common room is rubbish and there's barely anyone decent in the entire House. Mostly just eighties losers that've been stuck here for ages and can't stop talking about Poison and Motley Crue. If I hear one more guy singing 'Home Sweet Home' I swear I'm gonna torch the place."

Tom snickered awkwardly.

"Two years I've been in this dump. If I'd known I'd have to go to school after I died, I would have lived an eternity as a vegetable on life support. Never forgive my mom for switching it off."

"What happened to you?" Tom asked, suddenly curious.

"Diabetic coma," he said flatly. "I'm a type one. Used to have to stick a needle in my arse three times a day just so I could eat a mars bar and not keel over dead. Apparently, God intended my arse to be a pin cushion. Anyway, I was on this skiing trip with school in France and I must have hit my head. Skip two days and two helicopter rides later and I'm in the ICU with something called 'ketoacidosis'. No idea how long I was out but they must have thought I was a goner as I woke up here instead of in a bed with fifteen tubes in me. Still slightly bitter about the whole thing but I'll be damned if I ever touch another needle again. What class you got next?"

"Err… Laws of the Universe," Tom replied, pulling out his timetable.

"Me too. God it's boring! Even worse than that droll we just sat through. Why they're teaching advanced physics to teenagers is beyond me. Don't think I've made it through a whole class without falling asleep."

Finn led Tom to the elevator around the corner and hit the button for floor four hundred and twenty. Next to the button the little silver label read *Astronomy*.

"We're way up the tower for this one," he said, reclining against the smooth wooden banister in the elevator.

When the door pinged open, Mary was stood waiting for Tom – her knitted polka dot tights attracting curious glances and a few sniggers from passing students.

"Hi Tom!" she beamed at him.

"Oh, hi," he said. "This is err… Finn. Finn this is Mary…"

"Oh, hi Finn," Mary said, less than thrilled to see

Tom's elevator companion.

"Yeah, hi 'Mary'," Finn jibed, rolling his eyes and raising his eyebrows in mock horror at the sight of her tights.

"You two, eh… know each other then?" Tom asked awkwardly.

"Yes, I know Finley," Mary said flatly.

The three of them made their way quickly to the classroom which thankfully was just down the hall - Finn hung back a few paces as if not wanting to be seen with Mary and her unique choice of legwear.

The classroom where Laws of the Universe was held was spectacular to say the least. Upon entering, Tom's eyes were immediately drawn upwards and he gaped at the spectacle displayed overhead. The night sky expanded endlessly above them and the light from billions of stars and galaxies shone through the domed glass ceiling and illuminated the classroom. Tom stood slack jawed in wonder, gazing at the majesty of the universe above. He'd never considered himself much of a 'star-gazer' per se, but this view into the heavens was simply magnificent. Blue and pink spiralling galaxies swirled elegantly amongst star clusters and technicolour space dust. The room was irradiated with starlight; it shone down spectacularly bouncing off the white faces of the handful of students sat inside the small room. Finn, whose enthusiasm seemed to have abandoned him entirely, glanced up briefly and rolled his eyes again, clearly unimpressed by the galactic lightshow above.

"Isn't it beautiful," he mumbled sardonically.

The three of them took their seats at the desks arranged in a circle around the centre of the room. Tom was quietly pleased to see that Alice was among the few students sat around the table. She was engrossed in whispers with one of the other girls he recognised from first period. The teacher, who Tom hadn't noticed until now, made his way into the centre of the circle. He looked vaguely familiar, but Tom couldn't quite put his finger on where he recognised the man's face from. He was middle-aged judging by his long grey hair that fell in light curls to his shoulders, but he had a distinctly young face that stood in sharp contrast to the hair. He was 'easy on the eyes' as his mum would have said. His clothes looked like costume from a Jane Austin period drama that he might have flicked past once on the television. He smiled around the room at them warmly and Tom felt an immediate fondness for the man.

"Welcome!" he said. "I see a few new faces among you tonight – I am Professor Newton, and this is Laws of the Universe!" He spun on the wooden heels of his buckle shoes and raised his arm to the glass ceiling.

"In this classroom, we shall harness the heavens! Dissect the stars! Glimpse the galaxies! And slice open the very fabric of the cosmos itself! You will learn the true nature of our universe and you will learn the answers to the questions that have troubled man for millennia! Each of you will be privy to the secrets of our own creation! The secrets of matter and time and of *His* 'Grand Design' – the blueprint for all of existence!"

Finn nudged Tom in the ribs and nodded towards Alice, who was watching Professor Newton in awe.

"Looks like you've got some competition mate," he sniggered.

"Today's lesson will focus on gravity," Professor Newton continued. "Gravity is the glue that holds the universe together. It was myself who got the first bite of the proverbial 'apple' - if you will pardon the pun, but my esteemed colleague and good friend Professor Einstein was quite correct in his assertions – General Relativity

43

does indeed provide a satisfactory representation of the movements of the heavenly bodies, and their relationships in regard to space and time. The larger the object, the greater its effect on space and time."

He ran his fingers through his grey hair and continued.

"If you can picture a large sheet of rubber; this sheet represents 'spacetime'. General Relativity states that the fabric of 'spacetime' is nice and flat if there's nothing there to warp it. So, if we were to roll a marble across this rubber sheet it should travel in a nice straight trajectory across the plane. Now imagine you placed a pebble in the centre of the sheet of rubber - the pebble will create a small indentation in the rubber which is representative of mass warping spacetime – the effect is very small however as the pebble doesn't have much mass. Now if you can imagine dropping a bowling ball (or the Sun) in the centre of the sheet of rubber; the effect is much larger. It will create a huge indentation in the sheet of rubber which is the same effect heavenly bodies such as planets and stars have on the spacetime around them – they cause it to curve massively. If you then roll some marbles across that sheet of rubber, they will immediately fall into the indentation created by the bowling ball which is the same as the planets in our solar system falling into orbit around the sun, because of the warping of spacetime its huge mass creates."

Finn stifled a yawn and fell back into his seat. "Nap time," he sighed.

As Professor Newton continued his lecture on gravity, Tom drifted off into his own thoughts. He glanced across the room at Alice and wished he could get to know her. Where was she from? How long had she been here? Was she nice or totally stuck up like Finn said?

He didn't care. He'd been totally distracted with thoughts of her since first period had started. All thoughts of plane crashes, winged angels and of his parents had left his head completely – the strange workings of the teenage mind.

"So, you see, the time distortion caused by a blackhole is so great that as you cross the event horizon into a black hole, the curvature of spacetime becomes infinite and time will slow down to such an extent that it stops completely!" Professor Newton continued animatedly. "Which brings me to my next point, inside a black hole."

He bent down and grabbed something off the desk nearest to him.

"Take this sheet of paper," he said holding up a blank sheet of yellowed parchment. "Now, as we did with the rubber sheet, imagine that this sheet of paper is spacetime. The two ends of this sheet of paper," he pointed to each end in turn, "are great distances apart. But if you were to fold this piece of paper in the middle then the two ends will touch and the distance between them is reduced to nothing. This is what happens at the singularity. As you enter a black hole your mortal body is stretched infinitely through the Einstein-Rosen bridge and you will exit at the exact opposite point of the universe - *billions* of lightyears away! This method of travel has of course been used extensively throughout the history of the universe…"

Chapter Seven
The Five-Hundredth Floor

Forty-five minutes later when the class filed out of the small room back into the dark hallway, Tom noticed Alice hanging back to talk to Professor Newton privately. Looking back over his shoulder curiously, he noticed Professor Newton hand something small to Alice before his view was obscured entirely by the closing door. The exchange had been quick, but he'd caught it. Mary looked back and saw Tom straggling behind.

"Come on, Tom! Let's get back to the common room. I want to make the most of free period."

Ten minutes later they were back downstairs sitting in three large armchairs at the back of the Revelation common room. Finn had tagged along reluctantly and had signed in as a guest, though it was obvious he was still uncomfortable being seen publicly with Mary (who in turn was making every effort to pretend Finn didn't exist).

"That was *so* boring," Finn said putting his legs up on the arm of his chair. "Why don't we do something cool for a change instead of moping around here."

"Like what?" Tom asked.

"Let's get out of here for a while."

"You can leave?" Tom asked, suddenly curious.

"Yes, but only if you're stupid," Mary fired back.

"Oh, you're just scared," Finn jibed. "I've left tonnes of times. Look at me, I'm fine, aren't I?"

"Debatable," Tom heard Mary whisper under her breath.

"What's outside anyway? All I could see were fields and clouds. Not very interesting," Tom said.

"That's just around the school," Finn replied. "There's a whole world up here ripe for exploring. Way better than back down on Earth. Come on, are you in or not?"

"It's dangerous out there, Finn!" Mary tried again.

"Oh, come on we won't go too far! Don't be such a loser." He jumped up out of his seat and started across the room for the door. Tom looked hesitantly at Mary. He certainly didn't like the idea of danger or getting into any serious trouble when he'd only just got here.

"I'll only go if you come," Tom said tentatively.

"Well I'm not going," she said flatly. Finn was already at the door now and Tom looked over to him anxiously.

"Oh, fine!" she said finally. "But I'm only coming to make sure Finn doesn't get you killed."

"I thought we were already dead?" Tom laughed nervously.

"You know what I mean," she said. "There's worse things than dying. You'd know that if you'd been paying attention in Ancient History Revisited..."

"I've only had one class!" Tom replied, defensively.

"Well, Finn certainly *hasn't* been paying attention, that's for sure."

She looked to the door reluctantly, then with a long sigh that said, *'I'm going to regret this'*, she ran to the door after him.

*

"How exactly *do* we get out of here?" Tom called

47

after Finn, as they rounded the first bend on the way towards the elevator.

"Well…" said Finn, "there's the same way you came in obviously, but that isn't a good idea – especially if you don't want to be caught by the Headmaster who makes a habit of patrolling that door."

Tom shivered at the memory of the terrifying robed spectre known as 'the Headmaster'.

"So, what then?" Tom asked.

"We get inventive," Finn grinned, winking at him. Mary rolled her eyes.

"We're going to get caught you know," she said. "Leaving the school is forbidden unless accompanied by one of the staff."

"Oh, quit your habering, Habersmith," Finn spat at her. "I am one of the staff. I'm just not on the payroll yet."

"What floor then?" Tom asked, stepping inside the flush wooden elevator, which as usual arrived surprisingly quickly.

"We're going up," he said with a mischievous look at Mary.

"Up?" she said. "How exactly are we supposed to get out of here by going up?"

"Ye of little faith," he said stepping into the elevator behind them.

He hit the button for the five-hundredth floor and reclined against the banister. Next to the button the little silver label read 'Restricted'. When the door pinged open thirty seconds later, they alighted the elevator cautiously.

"Technically," Finn began, "floor five hundred is off limits to students, but I know for a fact that most teachers go down to the break room for free third period. Sooo with any luck, we should be in the clear."

He led the way along the dark corridor slowly – Tom held his breath to reduce any noise they were emitting. There were no paintings on the walls up here like there were on the other floors. They were bare, which augmented Tom's increasingly unsettling feeling that they shouldn't be up here. He looked back nervously at Mary whose face held a look of both fear and irritation, which he would have found impressive if he weren't so scared of getting caught. Just then, a door further down the hall in front of them burst open and they all froze in fear, pressed hard against the stone wall. A small man exited the room and without looking in their direction, made his way immediately in the opposite direction. The three of them let out a combined sigh of relief.

"Who was that?!" Tom whispered frantically.

"I've no idea," Finn said, turning back to look at him anxiously.

"I thought there was meant to be no one up here!" Mary shot at Finn harshly.

"I said no teachers. I've no idea who *that* guy was!" he fired back.

They continued down the hall even slower now, making each step forward hang in the air before them like three cartoon villains from a Scooby Doo mystery, (this thought occurred to Tom who stifled a laugh before Mary prodded him sharply in the back).

"Not much further now," Finn whispered back, motioning to the gleaming metal of the elevator doors ahead. That's when they heard it.

"Ahhheeemmm!" A gruff voice bellied from behind them.

They stood frozen in place, too scared to turn around and see who had emitted the appalling sound. It was Raphael. Tom recognised his muscled physique immediately from down in the library earlier that day. He was stood, not ten feet behind them, assessing them fiercely. His lank black hair was dragged back tightly and pulled his sharp features into a frightening scowl.

"Who are you?" he said threateningly, staring down at Finn.

"Eh... it's me sir... Finn... eh... Finley Hansen..."

"You're trespassing," Raphael said sternly. "It is forbidden for students to enter the five-hundredth floor."

Tom stared at him, still frozen in place. Finn stood frozen too, unable to muster another word after the exacting reprimand by the Head of House.

"Please sir..." Mary began, to the alarm of both Tom and Finn.

"Quiet!" interrupted Raphael. "You shall come with me."

He turned his back on them and began walking back down the dark corridor from where he'd come from. His dark cloak whipping behind him with each large stride. Tom looked at the other two – both of their faces were as pale as milk bottles. This was exactly the situation he'd wanted to avoid. Reluctantly, the three of them started down the hall after him.

Chapter Eight
Mastema

"Admit it Finn!" Mary seethed. "You've never been to the five-hundredth floor before. You have no idea what's up there."

"Fine, I admit it," Finn conceded. "But my friend George did tell me that there's an exit to the outside up there. I wanted to see it for myself."

"And you were willing to risk us in the process!?" Mary chided through gritted teeth.

Finn shrugged and Mary rapped him hard on the shoulder.

"Ouch!" he protested.

"Serves you right," she scolded

"Where is he taking us?" Tom whispered, interrupting their fleeting altercation.

"To Mastema…" Mary breathed, turning back to face him and revealing the gaunt expression that had engulfed her face.

"Who?" Tom whispered back.

"The Punisher," Finn grumbled from behind. "She's in charge of discipling students."

"Not someone you want to get acquainted with," Mary interjected.

"Hideous she is," Finn continued. "I knew a guy who was sent to her once. Never the same again. It was like he'd been lobotomized the way he talked after."

Tom grimaced.

"You've never been sent to her before then?" Tom asked, already guessing the answer.

"No, I've never been in this tight a corner before – caught red handed by a Head of House. What was he doing here anyway? Usually the Heads stick around for orientation then they're off. Leave the school, no idea where they go. Just our bloody luck."

"This is your fault Finley!" Mary shrilled. "We never should have been up here in the first place! And now to top it all off, we're going to be late for class!"

"So sorry to tarnish your flawless record your majesty," Finn jibed. "Anyway, it'll be fine I'm sure. We're probably just going to his office. Detention. Yeah detention, that'll be it - quick slap on the wrist and one evening's detention. We'll be laughing."

Tom didn't feel so sure. And he could tell by Finn's nervous laughter that he didn't either.

*

The elevator doors pinged open to reveal the Thirteenth floor – *The Dungeons*. Not one of them dared breathe a word on the ride down. The Dungeons were just as horrible as you might imagine them to be. The air felt hot and putrid and the walls looked damp and oily.

"Could do with a lick of paint," Finn tried feebly, but Raphael's expression was cold and as hard as the stone walls as he led them through the narrow aisle between the grotty stone cells, all currently without occupants. Mastema's office was at the far end of the 'cell block'. When they reached it Raphael didn't knock, but instead pushed through the door with an almighty clank and ushered the three students into the gloom.

There were no candles lighting this office. No windows displaying the heavy rainclouds that hung just out of reach. Instead the darkness enclosed you like the clasps of a coffin lid. Not a single beam of light could breach the impenetrable darkness they were left in when the heavy door slammed closed behind them.

"Mastema," declared Raphael stridently. "I have three students who need your attention. Trespassing on the five-hundredth floor. I trust you will know what to do."

And with that short declaration, Raphael turned and pushed back through the heavy door, allowing a brief glimmer of light to illuminate the figure that lurked in the corner of the room.

Tom squinted to try and make out anything around him, but the room was so dark he could barely see Mary or Finn. He only knew they were still beside him by their breathing which had quickened considerably since the door closed again. A foul smell filled his nostrils, the smell of rot and decay.

"Trespassing?" Came a delighted whispered voice from the corner.

Tom stopped breathing. The question hung souring the air.

"Trespassing on the five-hundredth floor? Oh my… what to do."

Tom felt Mary shuffle uncomfortably to his left.

"Do you know who I am?" It whispered out of the darkness, the voice sickeningly sweet.

"Yes ma'am," squeaked Mary.

"That is very good indeed," came the voice from the corner. "I do so enjoy my reputation. Now what to do with you three… I wonder… I wonder…"

There was a strumming sound against wood that reminded Tom of spider legs scuttling across a desk. The sound sent a shiver down his spine.

"Tell me, do any of you have any debilitating fears? Any severe allergies? Any painful past memories too dreadful to bare? No? Oh, how disappointing…"

The figure emerged from the corner sluggishly and Tom could make out the faint outline of a tall, skeletal shape. It bent towards a desk and struck a match revealing its emaciated frame. The revolting green-tinged skin was paper thin across its bones. Its back was hunched away from them; each vertebrae of its spine was visible, protruding unnaturally through the skin like jagged green mountains.

It turned towards them, match in hand, and lit the wick of a wasted candle on the desk. Bending down towards it, Tom could now see the true awfulness of what was in the room with them. A Cheshire cat grin spread across her face as she stared at them with glee.

"Oh, I know!" Mastema breathed through her rotted teeth. "A visit… Yes, a little school trip! Oh, it will be such fun! The four of us together!"

"Where are you t-t-t-taking us?" Finn managed shakily.

"Why spoil the surprise? Such fun it will be!" she beamed back at them. Her neck was horribly disfigured, which made her head cock awkwardly to the side as if she were peering around a corner at them.

"Come, my dears! We shall travel together! Down, down, down we go! All the way down!"

She lurched across the room awkwardly and Tom got an awful whiff of her decaying skin. It was like a corpse, buried six feet in the dirt, had been dug up and was now walking animatedly around, oblivious to the fact that it should have been dead and buried. She passed within inches of the three of them and Tom had to actively resist the urge to vomit. Terror and revulsion were brewing in equal measure in his stomach.

"This way, my dears!" she said, opening the heavy door with clear difficulty as her disfigured neck allowed for only the tiniest of shoulder movements. She led them out of her office back into the slimy corridor lined with cells. She hobbled awkwardly, shifting her weight from leg to leg, as if her hips were calcified at the joints, bones fused together, or as if she were shaking off the last of the rigor mortis that had long since set in. It was extremely peculiar to watch. The movement was akin to a puppet, controlled by unseen hands that pulled strings attached to each of her bony limbs.

At the end of the long row of cells there was what appeared to be an old service elevator. Instead of the shiny metal doors of the elevators in the rest of the tower, this one had a rough iron grate in place of a door, revealing the cramped compartment inside. Mastema reached the elevator and, with a crooked, emaciated arm, pulled the grate open.

"Inside please!" She beamed at Tom through rotted teeth.

Inside the service elevator there was no impressive panel of buttons like the rest of the elevators. There was no polished wooden hand rails or luxurious oak panelling. Instead there was a rusted lever with a yellow plastic cap. Mastema pulled the iron grate closed and then with great effort, thrust the lever back and the elevator began shaking to life. It descended slowly below the line of the dungeon floor and Tom could see the cold brick of the tower through the grate door. As they got lower, the brick was replaced by wet bedrock on which the tower must have been built, millennia ago. The bedrock outside the grate seemed to go on forever as they descended in total silence – the only noise, the shaking of the grate as it vibrated with the lift's movement. Tom looked over at Finn and Mary nervously but neither of them made eye contact. Mary looked as though she'd lapsed into a waking trance, her eyes glazed and unblinking, and Finn, trying to keep his cool demeanour, was clearly struggling with the effort. Eventually the wet bedrock outside the grate ended and Mastema pushed the lever down and the old service elevator grumbled to a halt. In front of them was an underground lake inside an enormous cave system that stretched off into the blackness; a dark world located miles beneath the school.

Mastema ushered the three of them out of the service elevator and then standing at the edge of the lake, threw each of them a hooded red robe which she pulled from the brown buckled case she'd carried down with her.

"Put these on my dears!" she grinned.

"Why?" asked Finn anxiously.

"For protection. Protection of course my dears! These robes allow the wearer to travel unseen! Which is going to come in handy where we're going, oh you will see!"

As each of them donned the robe uneasily, Mastema began hobbling towards a long wooden boat, which was shaped like a sort of gondola, docked close by.

"All aboard!" she said turning to them. Her grotesque smile visible beneath her own red hood.

Chapter Nine
Mount Purgatorio

Inside the boat, once the moorings were untied, Mastema reached for the long wooden oar that was propped across the cramped wooden interior. Using it like a barge pole, she pushed them off from the shoreline and the boat started to gradually drift out onto the water. She remained standing at the end of the boat and started to row, slowly, taking her time to dig deep into the water with each awkward lunge of the oar – her head moving in unison with her arms, as if her collar bone were fused to her chin. It was almost like a boat trip that one might enjoy on a lake on a particularly pleasant summer's day, except this particular trip was most certainly not pleasant and their gondolier was the most grotesque, unsightly creature any of them had ever seen.

Thirty minutes later they were deep inside the caves, their progress across the lake exasperatingly slow. Above them, ominous looking stalactites hung perilously close to their heads, like daggers threatening to plunge into them at any second. The roof of the cave was uncomfortably low, and Tom was beginning to feel claustrophobia set in as they progressed deeper and deeper. The ceiling seeming to close in with each passing minute. They journeyed in total silence as none of them had dared utter a word. Finn who was at the back of the boat had started dragging one of his hands in the black water beneath him.

"I wouldn't do that if I were you m'dear," Mastema said menacingly, noticing his hand in the water. "I wouldn't want to guess at what might be lurking in these waters. Old as time itself they are. It would be such a shame if you were dragged overboard and never seen again. It would ruin our whole trip I'd imagine." She grinned a horrid toothy smile, then turned her gaze back to the caves in front. Finn whipped his hand out of the water with an almighty jerk, splashing both Mary and Tom in the process.

Eventually the roof of the cave started to recede and gave way to a completely black sky. No stars, no moon, not a single inflection penetrated the darkness. It was like a black dome above them. Tom wondered if in fact they might still be underground but now the ceiling of the colossal cave (or whatever they were in) was so high that it just appeared as a perfect sheet of darkness above them. The three of them silently took in their new surroundings, the lake still stretched on, for as far as they could see, but now, either side of the shorelines were visibly edged with mountainous peaks stretching high into the darkness. Most unsettlingly of all was the fact that the peaks of the mountains appeared to be on fire. They could see the light from the flames illuminating the shores and the water around them. Thick smoke was circling in the air and they began coughing in unison as if the mere sight of the smoke had triggered the reflex.

"Not far now my dears!" Mastema trilled, admiring the burning elevations as she steered the long boat in the direction of the western shoreline. A few minutes later they felt it beaching onto the sand with a hard jerk that threw the three of them from their seats. Dishevelled, they pulled themselves up and jumped from the boat into the shallow waters - their long red robes pulling at them as the water saturated the fabric. As they waded towards the shore, Mastema motioned towards the rockface which was now only a hundred feet or so away. The rock before them grew into a towering mountain, its enormous shadow stretching far out onto the lake.

"Mount Purgatorio," she said, twisting her disfigured neck to look up at the looming statures of the mountain. "The great baptism by fire."

Tom twisted his own neck upwards and gasped. Like the others around it, the mountain was on fire. It stretched endlessly up into the darkness, its jagged peaks sharp as knife edges. Near the top of the mountain there appeared to be a bridge connecting it with an exit from the colossal cave. A gleaming light glowed from the far side of the bridge, revealing a small arched doorway cut into the rock.

"The bridge," Mastema said, grinning at Tom serenely.

"Where does it go?" Tom asked, now craning his neck to within millimetres of its natural limits.

"The bridge leads to the stairs, then the stairs, they lead the worthy to paradise my dear. Of course, first they will have to suffer through the excruciating torture of ascending the mountain, naked as the day they were born, limbs broken and skin torn to shreds, but eventually, if they are worthy, their souls will be cleansed."

Tom gaped in fascination. The bridge, which he could just make out in the upper reaches of the mountain, looked narrow and highly unstable like one footstep might crumble the whole thing and send whosoever stepped on it tumbling into the abyss. It looked so narrow in fact that the likelihood of falling over the side was probably greater than actually being able to make it across. It couldn't have been more than a foot in width.

"But that path is only for those wishing to be

cleansed my dear. Those who have rejected all spiritual values and have yielded to their more bestial appetites are destined for another path."

"What path?" Tom asked, staring now at Mastema who's hunched form had settled beside him.

"All in good time my dear, all in good time!" she said, as she limped away towards the rockface.

Arriving at the foot of the mountain, Tom leaped back in horror – there was a man sitting alone, perched on the rock, watching him with casual interest. Once he had gotten over his initial shock, he could see the man appeared to be relatively unthreatening. He was elderly and looked quite frail and had a long-grizzled beard that hung down in tresses to his stomach. The skin of his bald head was burned a deep olive brown. He wore a yellow hooded robe, not completely dissimilar to their own red ones. Mastema approached the man, with the three of them following apprehensively in tow.

"Mastema," the stranger said pulling himself to his feet.

"Cato, my dear friend!" she shrilled back to him, her grotesque smile managing to convey a measure of civility.

"You bring souls to be purged?" he said, gesturing to the three red hooded forms following her. "Yet they wear the robe of Saint Patrick? Why adorn them with such treasures?"

"Simply borrowing I assure you and we are merely visiting today, Cato my dear." Mastema replied pleasantly.

"I see," Cato muttered, looking disappointed.

Mastema twisted her crooked neck around to look at them. "Cato is the guardian of Mount Purgatorio, if you wish to ascend this mountain, you must first receive permission from him," she grinned. "It is said that the mountain was created by the displacement of rock caused by the impact from the fall of Lucifer himself! Isn't that right, Cato?"

She swung her neck back around to face Cato who nodded his agreement.

"Those who do not receive admittance into the kingdom above are shipped by boat to this very mountain," she continued. "These arrivals can then request to ascend the mountain to purge their earthly sins - though very few make it to the bridge my dears…" She looked up to the highest reaches of the mountain, the grotesque grin playing on her black lips. "Most spend an eternity in perpetual torment!" she beamed. "Trying to reach the thing that is always just out of reach. Those few sinners that make the bridge must then be granted permission to cross of course, which is no easy ticket," she continued, clearly delighted by the prospect. "By the Angel Remiel no less – who has the most delightful temper! I do so enjoy his company!"

Tom shivered at the thought of this angel, already acquainted with just how fearsome they could be.

"The mountain has seven terraces. Each terrace represents one of the Deadly Sins – and each is just as delightful as the last! With your permission Cato, I wish to take these students on a brief tour – perhaps just to the first terrace, or perhaps a little higher. I think the experience will be very… enlightening!" she said turning back to Cato, flashing a grotesque grin of rotted teeth.

Cato turned and assessed them with an unforgiving glower.

"Very well. If they can make it that far," he said, seeming to perk up slightly. "Those cloaks should hide them from any unwanted attention, though there are no guarantees. Nothing can hide the most wicked of souls from some things on this mountain." He fixed his gaze firmly on Tom and a knowing grimace crept slowly across his lips.

"You are most kind, my dear Cato," Mastema crooned.

Cato nodded again, then to Tom's bewilderment, walked directly towards him brandishing a concealed object from his robe. Confusion quickly turned to horror as Tom saw the concealed object was in fact a small but very deadly looking knife that he was now pointing directly at him. He recoiled, letting out an inaudible yelp as he stepped back, tripping on the tail of his robe. Cato held the knife above him, hesitated for the slightest of instants, then lowered it slowly onto his own outstretched hand, cutting his thumb to reveal a tiny droplet of blood. He held the bloodied thumb up towards Tom's forehead.

"Hold still child," he said coolly.

Pressing his thumb firmly against Tom's forehead, he used the blood to draw a shape which Tom couldn't see. The old man smelt like soot and ash. Tom looked frantically towards Finn and Mary, but their bewildered expressions offered little explanation. Cato then, walking towards Mary next, repeating the process with her and then with Finn, and when he'd finished, Tom could see that he'd drawn a red letter 'P' on each of their foreheads.

Satisfied and offering no explanation for his actions, he bid a brief farewell to Mastema, then turned and hovelled back towards his perch at the foot of the mountain.

"After you my dears," Mastema said to them once Cato had gone. She motioned towards a small path next to where Cato had sat that began the ascent upwards.

Resigned, Tom took the lead and led the group onto the path and up towards the edges of the mountain. The path, which had started so agreeably, turned quickly against them, taking a dramatic incline, transforming their civilian stroll into a slow arduous climb, which necessitated using their hands on the nearest rocks to heave themselves up at places. It didn't take long before Tom was gasping for breath. Cato and the foot of the mountain were far out of sight and the lake they rowed in on was looking increasingly distant. The further they climbed the hotter the air seemed to feel. It felt heavy and oppressive and their sharp breaths burned the backs of their throats as they limbered on.

"I guess this is a bad time to mention that I'm afraid of heights?" Finn quipped, with a pleading look at Tom.

"Oh, how wonderful!" Mastema squealed up at him. "I was so hoping that might be the case with one of you. How fortunate!"

The path had narrowed to a thin passage, bordered at one side by perilously sharp rocks and at the other by a daunting drop off the side of the mountain. Tom began side-on and moved his way carefully across the thin path, using his hands to grab the rockface to save from falling over the edge. Looking down, he saw his hands were cut and bleeding. He rubbed the blood on his robe and grimaced in pain as the rough material penetrated his paper-thin lacerations. It felt like rubbing an open wound with sandpaper. Mastema smiled seeing his discomfort.

Chapter Ten
The Purge of Finley Hansen

Soon the first terrace of the mountain was in sight, thirty feet or so above them. As they moved closer, Tom could hear a faint noise like the high-pitched ringing of a bell in the distance.

"Oh, how I've missed the sounds of the purge!" Mastema crooned to herself.

They rounded a bend on the thin path and saw the entrance to the first terrace risen before them. Two grand statues were carved into the rock at either side of the entrance. To his surprise, Tom recognised the face of Gabriel carved into one of the statues. Her sharp features and penetrating gaze were unmistakable. She was kneeled in front of a woman, her huge wings stretched above her. Despite her frightening gaze instilling in Tom the same fear he had felt during orientation, she appeared to be kneeling in submission to the woman in this statue.

"Yes, The Annunciation…" Mastema offered, motioning to the statue on the left. "Not one of my favourites. A depiction of the humility of our dear Head of House." The way she said this, it was clear she held a brewing contempt for the woman.

"Ahh now this one is much better!" she said turning to the statue on the right. "A recent addition to the mountain, I believe."

Tom turned to the opposing statue and it was clear

why she preferred this one.

"The Kiss of Death," she proclaimed proudly. "What awaits those that resign the purge."

The statue was quite disturbing. It depicted a man, collapsed to his knees, unconscious by the looks of it, wearing nothing but a loin cloth over his groin. Holding his shoulders between its bony fingers was a winged skeleton, which was kissing the man on his cold dead cheek, before lifting him away (from the land of the living presumably).

"Our dear Headmaster!" Mastema crooned. "In his younger days of course. He's much less busy now he's retired."

She led them through the rock statues out onto a large plateau. The terrace was arranged into a circular arena with a pointed boulder at its centre. Moving around the boulder, Tom saw the source of the noise that was now almost deafening. There were men, thousands of them, crumpled under the weight of the huge rocks they carried on their backs. Their spines were bent to breaking and their legs quaked violently as they took step after agonising step around the boulder. Their screams, which echoed around the basin arena, seemed to merge into one appallingly high-pitched note - a ringing - the sound was almost unbearable. Tom clasped his hands over his ears as they moved closer.

"The souls of the prideful," Mastema smiled sadistically, glaring out across the plateau. "Arrogant, exhausted, wretched souls. Now they carry the burden of their sins on their backs. Each must carry the stone for a time equal to their time on Earth - a fitting punishment for such scum." She turned and spat a green sinewy glob of phlegm on the ground.

"Come, we must walk around to continue."

She led them towards the circular arena but came to

an abrupt stop after only a dozen paces. Hidden in plain sight was an enormous fissure through the rock - a deep crack through the mountain, at least eight feet across, that dropped down into shadowy darkness below.

"We must jump my dears!" Mastema declared - the awful grin returning to her face. Without a moment's hesitation she launched herself across the gap, her disfigured body twisting awkwardly in the air before her feet touched down and found their footing on the other side. Tom jumped next . Lifting his robe at the hems, he sprung himself across the gap, landing hard on the other side and toppling onto his stomach. Mastema erupted with cackling glee.

"Marvellous boy! Simply marvellous! Who's next?"

Picking himself up, Tom turned to look at Mary, who was lining herself up for the jump. She was surprisingly acrobatic and made it with a casual grace that made Tom's own effort look embarrassingly amateur in the process. Even Finn looked marginally impressed, though Tom saw him roll his eyes quickly afterwards.

"Your turn my dear!" Mastema shouted across to Finn, but Finn wasn't moving. He was assessing the jump with increasing trepidation, his hands set firmly in the pockets of his robe.

"Come on Finn! It's not hard!" Mary shouted over at him.

"I… I… can't!" Finn shouted back.

"Come on Finn!" Tom urged. Mastema was gleaming at Finn with a troublingly delighted look in her eye.

"Why can't you my dear?" She bellowed across to him.

"I… I… just can't ok!" he shouted back.

Hearing the finality in Finn's tone, Tom grudgingly threw himself back across the chasm, this time without ending up on his stomach.

"What's up?" he said, arriving next to Finn again.

Finn hung his head, refusing to meet Tom's gaze.

"I… I… don't know how to jump…" he managed.

"What? You're kidding me right?" Tom laughed. "How can you not know how? Did you not jump fences and puddles back down on Earth?"

Finn looked up at Tom, defeat etched on his face.

"Well… no… I didn't… I… I… ok look…here it is… I was in a damned wheelchair my whole life ok!"

Tom's mouth hung open, unable to muster a reply.

"I've been in a damned wheelchair since I was five years old. When I told you that I hit my head in a skiing accident, that wasn't exactly true. I mean, I was at a skiing resort in France an' all but I wasn't skiing. I've never done that. I hit my head when my chair crashed down some stairs at the lodge."

"Oh…" Tom managed. Unable to think of anything more to say.

"I would have told you, but when I woke up here - I mean when I died an' all, I could stand. I could walk for the first time ever. I felt normal, not just some stupid cripple in a damned chair. I've never leapt fences or jumped puddles and if I try to jump that gap, I'm not gonna make it. I know it! I'll fall and be sliced to pieces on the rocks. You'll be carrying me back in Tupperware!"

"You climbed up this mountain didn't you?" Tom said encouragingly.

"Well… yeah… eh… I guess, but that was different. I mean that was just walking, I can do that…"

"Some of that climbing was a lot more than walking," Tom pushed. "You're practically an amateur mountaineer now. I bet if you just went for it, you'd make that jump easily."

Finn didn't seem to be listening. He had turned to

stare at the screaming men, stones on their backs, bent over in agony.

"I should be down there with them," he said. "All my life I rejected being disabled. I would look down on other people in chairs as if I weren't one of 'em. I was better than them, in my own head anyway. That's why I should be down there heaving them stones, too damn proud to admit that I used to be in a wheelchair. I'd understand if you didn't want to hang out anymore. I mean, I wouldn't want to be friends with me either…"

"Don't be stupid," Tom fired back.

Mastema was beside them in an instant - they'd never even seen her jump back across.

"Alas you have repented and turned from your sin my dear," she said, gripping the sleeve of her robe with a mangled hand and wiping the bloody 'P' from his forehead. "Now please do hurry up, we have much more wonderful climbing to do before our day is done!"

"After you then mate," Tom said turning back to him.

Still looking broken but seeming partially rejuvenated at least, Finn grabbed the hems of his robe.

"Screw it," he said finally.

He ran at the chasm, eyes unblinking and focused. Reaching the edge, he jumped. For a second Tom didn't think he was going to make it. Mary screamed from the far side. His front foot landed on the far ledge but his second didn't make the gap. He fell backwards, toppling over the side, grabbing the edge with his hands at the last second. He hung there, dangling - a red scourge on the mountain.

Tom ran towards the gap, shouting on instinct for Finn to "hang on!" But before he could do so, Mastema grabbed the hood of his robe, stopping him dead and nearly decapitating him in the process.

"He must do it himself!" she cried pointedly at both Tom and Mary.

Finn hung there, fingers bent in agony as they held the weight of his body, slowly losing grip and slipping closer and closer to the edge.

"Pull yourself up Finn!" Mary screamed at him, standing over the ledge, wanting to reach for him but feeling Mastema's glare from across the gap imploring her not to. She gasped. Finn's left hand slipped completely. He was now hanging on by the last few fingers on his right hand alone. He cried in agony and then with an almighty howl swung his left leg onto the ledge. This took some of the weight from his right hand. Roaring with a determination that shocked all of them, he pulled himself over the ledge then in one agonised motion he collapsed - sprawled on the side, gasping for breath.

"Well done Finn!" Mary squealed, throwing herself onto him.

"What the hell? Geerrof me!" Finn chocked through laboured breaths. "Thanks for the hand," he continued mulishly, pulling himself to his feet.

Mastema was beside them in an instant. "There are no helping hands on Mount Purgatorio my dear! It is forbidden!"

"Well it shouldn't be," Finn spat back, brushing the rock dust off his robes. "Why's it forbidden anyway?"

"This mountain is watched by many. There are laws. Those cloaks can't hide you from the gaze of some." She warned ominously. "Break one of these laws and it won't be St Michael's you'll be going back to, oh no my dear, it will be somewhere much worse. A place beyond your comprehension. You won't be counting the days, or the months, or the years, but the eternities in a place with no doors."

69

Tom swallowed back a dry painful gulp, and so, he sensed, did Finn.

Chapter Eleven
A Room of One's Own

The journey to the second terrace was another back-breaking two-hour climb. The air getting hotter and harder to breathe with each laboured step towards the top. Tom was quickly learning that feelings like exhaustion and muscle cramps weren't merely troubles of the living, oh no, the sensations were just as crisp in the afterlife. Mary, on the other hand, seemed positively sprightly. The brush with Finn a few hours back had been swiftly forgotten and she was now leading the group and in exceptionally good spirits; in fact, she'd even begun humming a tune to herself as they walked.

"Will you give it a rest?" Finn moaned from the rear.

"No, I shan't," she gleamed back at him, increasing the volume another notch.

Tom wondered how she did it. Her woollen tights alone (which flashed from under her robe with each purposeful stride forward), in this awful heat must have been cooking her legs like boiled lobsters.

"So, what exactly do these robes hide us from anyway?" Finn panted.

"Oh, most low-level demons I would think," Mastema replied.

"And what about the robe that Cato guy wore? The yellow one. What does that do?" Finn pushed through laboured pants.

71

"Cato's robe signifies his neutrality and his lack of angelic heritage my dear," she replied. "It identifies him simply as a servant of the mountain and he can't be touched by either side while he wears it."

"Where did the robes come from?" enquired Tom abruptly from Mastema's other side.

"The robes were a gift," she exclaimed matter-of-factly. "Each angel in heaven received a red robe, woven by Saint Patrick – who once made this very same journey. Before the time of the robes, the mountain was a constant battlefield. Those were the days my dears."

"And what about these robes?" Tom continued, motioning to his own. "Who do these belong to?"

"There have been many fallen angels my dear," Mastema simpered, letting her gaze drift off and lapse into old forgotten memories.

That was a sobering thought. If angels fell routinely on this mountain then what chance did he have? Not much, Tom surmised glumly. He pushed ahead to walk alongside Mary who had detracted herself from the conversation. Maybe *she* could lift his spirits.

"Wait up!" he called ahead to her.

She turned dutifully and waited for him to catch her.

"So," he said panting. "I wanted to ask you something…"

"Yes?" she replied quizzically.

"How long have you been at Saint Michael's?" he panted.

She stared at him with narrowed eyes.

"I forget how long," she replied passively. "A long time I guess. Maybe thirty years? Or longer? Wow that's quick! Don't they go in a blink! What year is it now?"

"Twenty-nineteen," Tom replied, stunned.

"Well thirty-three years then I guess. I died in

nineteen-eighty-six. Around the time that whole Chernobyl thing was on the news. What ever happened with that anyway?" she puzzled.

"Oh, not much, just a few radiation deaths and the odd case of thyroid cancer," he quipped sardonically.

"You must have learned a lot in thirty-three years," he guessed.

"Oh yes," she replied matter-of-factly. "I've learned loads of useful things. I gained all the merits I needed years ago. Apparently, it's not enough to get to that next place though," she said with the slightest twinge of resentment in her voice. "There's still that final exam. For some people it hardly takes any time at all. Then for others it's not so easy. I guess I fall into the latter category."

Tom could see the thought had upset her, but she was hiding it well.

"Do you want to go '*On*'?" he asked.

"Of course. Everyone wants to go '*On*'. Why wouldn't they? Who'd want to be stuck at a school for eternity?"

"I guess..." he replied thoughtfully.

"Don't worry, you'll be one of the quick ones. I can always tell," she said, barely concealing the jealousy in her tone.

Tom wasn't so sure. He still couldn't figure why he was accepted at the school. Didn't Uriel say something about a lineage he'd been born into? He couldn't fathom what that might mean. He'd lived a relatively uneventful life. The only thing of note to have happened to him was when his brother had died. That had been four years ago. His older brother Scott had been in the army. He'd been stationed down at the barracks at Foxden in Norfolk. It was awful what happened. He shuddered at the memory, swallowing back those feelings of grief that had taken him

73

so long to get over. Maybe you never really get over them completely. He hadn't thought about Scott in a long time. It had been a huge deal back then. National news coverage of the whole thing. Everywhere he turned it was there. He couldn't escape it. His body was found in the woods not far from his abandoned guard post. Four bullet wounds to his chest. They never found who did it. No culprit was ever officially identified or charged. Tom's dad being a lawyer, had participated in extensive legal action to have the circumstances around the death publicly re-examined. But despite his dad's best efforts, despite all the time and all the money and all the anguish and heartbreak it had caused his parents, the verdict remained open and the death officially went down as unexplained. In the end Tom had been left bitter and angry at the lack of answers his family had gotten. He had only been eleven at the time, but he felt it had aged him, he'd felt the lamentable loss of the innocence of youth.

The only good thing to come out of the whole ordeal had been his dad's job. His work on the case had been well publicised and the next year he was made partner at his firm 'Dean, Whitney and Campbell'. Despite the promotion, Tom secretly knew that all the fight had gone out of his dad after that last verdict. He would make fatherly gestures and go through fatherly motions, but motions and gestures were all that they were. His eyes seemed perpetually narrowed like he struggled to keep them open, like he hadn't slept a single night since Scott had died. He would come home in the evening and eat his dinner at the table as normal and then he would retire to the living-room and make his way through a bottle of Laphroaig in his chair in front of the golf channel, exactly as he'd always done. He would even laugh occasionally or share an amusing anecdote while they watched an old rerun of *Friends* for the three-hundredth time, but it was never the same. The look of pain was set firmly over his eyes like the paint on an old garage door – impossible to chip away.

That had been four years ago. He guessed his parents would have to go through the whole thing again now that he'd gone and died too. Guilt washed over him like a freezing wet blanket. He hadn't thought about his parents again since arriving at St Michael's. He'd been too distracted with all the bizarre things that had happened to him since. Suddenly he had another thought. *What if Scott was at St Michael's?*

"Mary," he said eagerly, attempting in vain to contain his excitement. "Do you know a boy named Scott Woolberson at Saint Michael's?"

"Relative of yours?" she guessed.

"Yeah, he was my brother," Tom replied, feeling his heart start to race in anticipation.

"I'm afraid I've never heard of him…" Mary said, looking at him tentatively. "But that doesn't mean he's not there. There's thousands of kids at that school and I hardly know any of them. All the friends I had moved on and left me. I'm glad I've got you now though."

The smile seemed to return to her face at that thought. Just then, Finn came running from the back to catch them.

"What you lot whispering about?" he croaked.

"Oh, nothing," Mary said quickly and started whistling the tune she'd been humming earlier.

"That's another eighties nut right there," Finn whispered to Tom from the side of his mouth. "Been at St Michael's that long the place has addled her mind."

"I heard that!" she piped, momentarily interrupting her whistling.

"What about you?" Tom asked Finn once Mary had

stalked off ahead. "Have you heard of a Scott Woolberson?"

"Nah, sorry mate," he said, looking carefully at him. "Never had the pleasure. But who knows he could be around? He's not in my House anyway. Even if he's not you're gonna see him again eventually. We're all going to the same place in the end. Unless he was a proper nutjob of course."

Tom considered this and resolved to ask around when they got back to the school.

Mastema had caught them up now. The physical toll of the treacherous hike up the mountain seemed to have totally unphased her, despite the frailty of her physique - her mood was as sickeningly sweet as ever.

"Behold my dears!" she shrilled. "The second terrace!"

She pointed at the cliff edge looming above them. There was no high-pitched screaming from this terrace Tom noticed. The place was eerily quiet, silent in fact. They climbed the last thirty or so feet, rounding the last bend onto the second terrace. There were no statues at the gates of this one. It seemed totally deserted. An empty plateau. Barren as a desert. Like an abandoned gas station on a long stretch of road that was no longer used. Then he saw them. They were huddled against the side of the mountain. They blended in so well that you almost missed them. They were completely camouflaged, grouped together like beggars, all along the side of a steep wall. The sheets they wore seemed to be identical in colour to the orangey sandstone of the mountain. All of their eyes were closed shut, were they sleeping? They're weren't moving or screaming in agony like the residents of the first terrace. Their stillness was eerie, like the whole terrace was being haunted by them.

"Behold, the envious souls of the second terrace!" Mastema declared gleefully. "Eyes sewn shut with wires to prevent them from seeing and envying the good fortunes of others!"

They stood just to the right of Mastema, quietly assessing the group huddled against the rock. Tom shuddered at the thought of having his own eyes sewn shut with wire (he did a quick double blink just to make absolutely sure that they weren't already).

"Do they talk? Or just sit there?" Finn asked.

"What do they have to talk about my dear?" Mastema replied. "The envious lives they've each lived? I'd imagine they are all too ashamed to mutter even the smallest of words to another."

She turned now to Mary, eyes gleaming and smiling widely. Mary had been quiet since they entered the terrace. She seemed to have drifted into a distant reverie, not listening to Mastema and the others, but simply staring, unblinking, at the beggars huddled against the wall.

"You would know about that wouldn't you my dear?" she asked curiously.

"Me?" Mary replied, returning from her distant trance and looking momentarily awkward. "I'm not sure what you're talking about."

"Oh, really?" Mastema continued. "So, you didn't spend long summer afternoons watching out of your bedroom window? Hoping and praying that one of the children would trip and fall or break an ankle? Or even wishing your own sickness on them - maybe then they'd get to experience the sedentary life of a shut-away."

Mary fell silent again. She was looking at her feet now. A crimson blush seemed to steal across her face, starting at the cheeks, then working its way gradually up past the eyes and to her forehead.

"Yes, that *was* me. How did you know that?" she said finally, still looking down at her feet.

"Come now my dear, the guilty cannot hide on this mountain. They stick out like gravestones in a wheat field."

Mary blushed harder and crushed her hands into tiny red fists.

"You don't know what it was like!" she blurted, rounding on Mastema suddenly. "I couldn't run, I couldn't spend the afternoon laughing and playing in Waterlow Park with everyone else, I couldn't go roller-skating or cycling or skateboarding. I couldn't even walk too quickly without gasping for my breath."

She broke down into breathless sobs. Tom was watching her nervously, not quite sure how to react.

"Too many hospital visits, too many nights spent in the emergency room with my mum telling me I had to go at my own pace, too many coughing fits brought on by taking the stairs too quickly. Can you imagine that?" She sobbed, wiping her puffed cheeks with the crimson sleeve of her robe.

"I just eventually stopped trying. I just stayed inside. In my room alone. I gave up. I moved the little people around the rooms of my McKinley dollhouse that my grandmother had left me when she died, and I fantasised about living a life free of the constant torment. Being able to go outside with my friends and go out to the movies at the weekend and maybe I'd meet a boy and we'd go on a date and do things that teenagers are *supposed* to be able to do! I was envious, madly so... I burned with it."

She collapsed to the ground and buried her face into her knees – gasping and wheezing (the old symptoms starting to come back).

Mastema rounded on her - swinging her head around

crookedly to stare at Mary's crumpled form. Mary raised her head slowly. Tears were brimmed heavy in her eyes and Tom watched one fat swollen bead escape down her cheek.

"You see the error in your ways now, my dear?"

Mary nodded at her weakly which let another flurry of tears escape down her cheeks.

Mastema gripped her sleeve with one mangled grey hand and wiped the bloodied 'P' from Mary's forehead.

*

"You know I was in a wheelchair for God's sake," Finn muttered to Tom under his breath. "Talk about an overreaction."

But Tom wasn't listening. He was looking at Mary and seeing her in a way he never had before, the way she must have been when she was alive – fragile, scared, lonely, in need of a friend. He wanted to comfort her, put his arm around her and tell her that everything was better now. He was starting to feel real affection for her. He wasn't sure whether that was platonic, or something else entirely. Something new he hadn't experienced before. He held out his hand and slowly helped her to her feet again. With his other hand, he brushed some of the dust off her robe then smiled at her comfortingly.

Once they were all back on their feet and the storm was over, Mastema rounded the three of them together, grouping them to the far side of the terrace away from the huddled beggars beside the rockface.

"Up to the next terrace then?" Finn said glumly.

"No, I think that will do us for today my dears," she said looking resigned.

"About time!" Finn cried triumphantly. "Let's get out of here!"

79

Tom did not relish the prospect of descending all the way back down the jagged face of the mountain. They were so high now they could hardly see the lake anymore. The yellow speck that was Cato's robe had long since disappeared. It had taken them hours to climb to where they were now. No doubt it would take the same time again climbing down, except significantly more dangerous now the cliffs were below them. One misplaced foot and they'd go tumbling over the edge, sure to be impaled on some perilously sharp rocks that waited patiently below for some fresh meat to slice into. He groaned internally at what lay ahead and began walking back towards the entrance to the second terrace.

"Not that way my dear!" Mastema chimed.

Tom stopped, turning his head to stare back at her enquiringly over his shoulder.

"But that's the way back down isn't it?" he protested.

"Not today it isn't," she replied mysteriously.

"What do you mean?" Mary whispered, wiping away the last of her tears.

"I think today we shall enlist the help of an old colleague of mine," she replied, with a hideous wink at Mary, screwing up the features of her already mangled visage.

"Who's that then?" Finn griped from behind her, picking up a loose stone and flinging it off the edge of the mountain.

"He is the angel of Zeal my dear, and if you don't watch your tone, I'll arrange it with him to leave you behind."

Finn skulked away from the edge and fell back into line obediently.

"Where is this angel?" Tom asked politely, careful not to exact the same reprimand as Finn.

"He's supposed to be on the fourth terrace, though being a mite over-zealous he is prone to patrolling the whole mountain, and, I may be mistaken, but I do believe he's been following our progress since our arrival on the mountain."

"Really?" Mary asked. "Where is he then?"

"He is above us my dear! Can you not hear him?"

"I can't hear anything," Finn piped, ducking his head behind Tom's quickly to avoid Mastema's testing glare.

"That's because you're not listening," Mastema replied coolly.

She motioned for quiet with one bent finger toward her black lips and they fell silent. Tom forced his ears to hear but it was deathly silent still. He imagined he could hear the drop of a pin if one of them were to spill one from their pocket. He looked at Finn who shrugged at him, clearly unable to hear whatever it was they were meant to be hearing. Mary had closed her eyes, she seemed deep in concentration, struggling to hear anything within earshot. Tom closed his own eyes and pushed as hard as he could. Somewhere between the silence, he could hear the faint sound of the shore from the lake below. The waves gently washing onto the sand, then retreating again to repeat the process; and he could hear the faint crackle of flames coming from the mountain's peak, like the fireplace in your neighbour's living-room that you could almost hear from outside their window; and he could hear the very faint flapping of wings or talons or... hang on a minute.

"What's that sound?!" he blurted.

"What sound?" Finn complained. "I can't hear anything."

"It sounds like wings!" Tom replied, scanning the air above him.

"Yes my dear!" Mastema beamed, delighted. She

81

clapped her grizzled hands together, unable to contain her glee.

Finn and Mary scanned the air above them, still unable to hear the wings that Mastema spoke of.

"Can't hear nothing," Finn puffed, resigned.

Mastema wasn't paying attention. Her gaze had drifted up and her eyes now focused on something that was just out of their field of vision. She smiled.

"Salathial is that you dear?" she whispered.

There was a sudden gust of wind so strong that it blew Tom off his feet. He looked to his side and saw Finn and Mary had also been blown over and were sprawled on the floor to his right. The wind battered them like the reverse thrusters of a Boeing 747 coming in to land.

"What's going on!?" Finn shouted over the chaos.

As quickly as it started, the wind stopped. Violently and abruptly, which seemed to disorientate Tom even more than it had from starting in the first place. A man stood staring down at them. His wings spread gloriously wide, fresh from his recent landing. His long blonde mane fell tangled onto his bare chest that was marked heavily with thick white scars. In fact, his entire body seemed to be covered in scars, like he'd fallen into a bathtub full of razorblades as a child or wrestled bare-chested with a lion and lived to tell the tale. Under the scars his body was lean and toned, and his skin was burned a dark olive brown. His piercing eyes were a cerulean blue and right now they were burning fiercely into the three of them on the ground.

"Hello," he said calmly, despite the threatening look in his eyes.

"Eh… hi," Tom stuttered back timidly.

"So, you are the visitors I've been hearing so much

about," he stated matter-of-factly.

"Eh… yeah that's us," Tom replied.

Mastema shuffled awkwardly to where the rest of them stood and clapped a grizzled hand to Salathial's shoulder.

"My dear Salathial! Thank you so much for joining us."

"Hello Mastema," he said, turning to face her. For the briefest of seconds, a look of total disgust played on his face, before quickly disappearing and shifting to a look of patient welcome. Mastema didn't seem to notice.

"Salathial, would you be so kind as to escort us off this mountain?" she asked casually, as if the task were something that could be accomplished in seconds.

"Of course," he replied coolly.

Mastema turned back to Tom, Finn and Mary who were hastily pulling themselves back to their feet. "It seems we have managed to hitch a lift my dears!"

"Hang on a second!" barked Finn. "What about that 'P' on his head?" He said pointing at Tom. "Doesn't he have to purge his sins as well? Seems only fair, since we now all know I spent every day in a wheelchair like a pathetic cripple."

Tom, who had forgotten all about the bloodied letter stamped on his forehead, stared back at him blankly.

"I do believe," Mastema began, "that since it is his first day with us, we shall grant him a pass."

Tom grinned back at her widely. He wasn't sure what sin it was that he'd need to be purged of but he was glad he didn't have to do it all the same. Finn started to protest but was quickly quilled by Mastema's heady glare. She grabbed the hems of her thick robe and quickly wiped the residue of Cato's blood from Tom's brow.

Salathial had moved to the cliff that encircled the second terrace and was staring back at them calmly.

Mastema ushered them all towards him and to Tom's disgust, she took her mangled clammy hand and grasped his own hand within it. She then instructed the rest to join hands, so they stood in a makeshift daisy-chain behind Salathial who held out his hand and (with the briefest look of disgust) took Mastema's hand within his own.

"Hold on tight," he said turning back to them.

"Wait a minute…" Finn began. "You're not thinking of jumping off that cliff are-"

Before he could finish, the sounds of their combined screams had drowned him out completely. Salathial had batted his wings with one hard swoop and they were lifted into the air immediately. Hanging beneath him, joined by the hands, like a cable of ants that had taken a tumble off the side of a leaf. The force of the take-off nearly ripped Tom's arm from its socket, but Mastema's vicelike grip clenched around his hand so hard he felt his knuckles might shoot out of his skin like tiny ping-pong balls. With his other hand he held on to Mary, who's shrill screams echoed into the cool night air as they climbed higher. Finn hung at the bottom of the chain, bellowing profanities as he clung for dear life to Mary's tiny hand with both of his own. Mastema cackled with exhilaration as Salathial flew them off the mountain and out towards the lake thousands of feet below.

The flight off the mountain was surprisingly short, or at least that was what Tom had thought as they landed hard on the sand five minutes later, coughing and spluttering and nursing their crumpled hands. Finn, who had finally cut-off from his stream of profanities, was now cradling his arm and squealing.

"My hand! My hand, it's broken!" he cried, as he lay curled on a heap in the sand.

"Oh, be quiet Finley!" Mary fired at him. "I wasn't

holding it that hard!" She stood brushing the sand off her robes and threw Tom a tiresome look as he brushed the sand off his own. Tom smiled back at her and they shared a silent giggle as Finn slowly returned to his feet.

"Salathial my dear, you have been most kind," Mastema crooned to their escort.

He waved off her kowtowing indifferently. "My pleasure," he said calmly, "but there is one thing you can do for me." He reached into the simple loincloth at his waist and retrieved a folded piece of parchment which he then handed to her. "See that Gabriel receives this immediately and tell her that she has been forewarned."

"Of course, my dear!" Mastema gleamed back at him. "And thanks again for the lift!"

Chapter Twelve
The Beautiful and Damned

The journey back to St Michael's seemed mercifully short. It was no time at all before the boat broke ground back on the tiny shore that rimmed the bedrock of the tower, and in it the doors of the service elevator. Mastema collected back the robes, now sodden with water and sand, and stashed them in the brown buckled case that she carried off the boat with her. Arriving back in the dungeons forty-five minutes later, she bid them a brief farewell then hobbled back hurriedly through the slimy cells that lined the narrow corridor, as if her mind had turned to other more pressing business.

Tom, Mary, and Finn dragged themselves into the polished wooden elevator and wearily hit the button for the Revelation Floor, sinking back against the railings and collapsing into the corners. Soon after, they were sat comfortably in plush leather armchairs back in the common room, stretching out their stiff muscles and yawning drowsily.

"I'm beat," Tom said to no one in particular.

They'd spent the entire night down in Purgatory and now the day was breaking outside – rays of sunlight were peaking in through the long narrow turret-like windows and spraying technicolour light across the room through their intricate stained-glass designs. Tom watched the rainbow of colour move over the grand marble fountain at the centre of the room. The light sparkled and danced as it hit the water, like emeralds and rubies pitched through the surface in exchange for wishes.

"Why don't you use the restrooms?" Mary asked casually.

"I don't need…" said Tom, puzzled by the suggestion.

Mary burst into fits of giggles. "No, we don't do *that* anymore!" she managed through her hands. "Why don't you introduce Tom to the restrooms?" she said, looking over at Finn who was crumpled into a leather chesterfield armchair.

"Fine," he grumbled, not bothering to open his eyes.

Finn groggily led a highly confused Tom out of the common room and back into the dark hallway.

"They're just over there," he said stifling a yawn.

They walked the short distance then stopped outside the quintessential male logo set in tile on the thick wooden door.

"After you," he mumbled.

Tom pushed through the door and instead of being greeted by the usual line of urinals, cubicles and sinks that accompanied a standard gentleman's lavatory, there were, what appeared to be, tiny rudimentary apartments lined against the wall. They reminded him of the first-class cubicles that'd been on the Qantas flight to Melbourne when they'd visited his Uncle Sam. Tom's dad had spent the extra penny and booked them the upgrade not long after Scott had died. Despite the opulence, it was one of the most miserable flights he can remember being on.

"What are they?" he asked, confused.

"Open one," Finn replied.

Tom walked over to the first one, which happened to be occupied, so went to the next and pushed open the door. Inside was like a miniaturised one-bedroom studio apartment, that you might expect to find on Airbnb - if it had existed in the nineteen-thirties. Instead of flat screen tv's and pothole airplane windows, this compartment held a miniature four-poster bed with rich crimson bed sheets tucked tightly at the corners and gleaming at him invitingly. To the side of the bed, heavy vintage-style curtains were pulled over what must have been a window at the rear of the restroom. There was a dressing table with a long mirror and a little bedside table propped beside the bed on which sat three sand-filled hourglasses. One small, one medium and one large.

"I'll leave you to it," Finn said, closing the door behind him and leaving Tom alone in the little room. Needing no further invitation, he quickly removed his clothes down to his underwear and pulled back the crimson sheets on the bed, slipping himself under them. The room was lit by a single candle that hung from a pewter hook attached to a polished wooden board on the wall. Without feeling the need to blow it out, Tom closed his eyes and sank slowly into the warm comfortable bed, letting out a long and contented sigh of gratitude.

What he achieved wasn't exactly what he would call sleep, but he found he was able to disconnect and 'switch off' in a way that was completely new to him. Like turning his old iPhone to flight-mode, all incoming thoughts were directed elsewhere and there was a 'Closed for Business' sign hung in the shop window of his subconscious. It wasn't until the sun had gone down again and night had fallen once more that Tom finally stirred and opened his eyes peacefully, seeing the candle still burning on the wall beside him. Feeling rejuvenated, he pulled back on his old jeans and t-shirt and quickly made the bed as best he could behind him – the result wasn't very neat, but he left it anyway.

He exited the cubicle and washed his face quickly in one of the washbasins outside the cubicles. Staring himself in the mirror he saw the same boy he'd known all his life. Nothing seemed to have changed about him now the life had gone out of him. His skin was porcelain white but that was more a side-effect of being British rather than an indicator of his mortality. His eyes once piercing blue had gradually turned grey as he'd gotten older, like the freckles that had once been scattered abundantly across his face, had now been replaced by the clear inflectionless skin he saw in the mirror. His thick brown hair was currently plastered scrappily against his forehead, so he wet his hands under the faucet and used his wet fingers to drag the hair back and place it into something loosely resembling his usual style.

Just then, the door of the cubicle next to his own was pulled open and Finn ambled out, stretching his back, one arm over his mouth, stifling a yawn.

"Evening," he said from behind the fist that was clenched over his mouth. "Thought I might as well take a kip as well since I was here. How was yours?"

"It was really good, actually. I'm feeling much better now."

"Me too," Finn replied.

"Do you do that every day then?" Tom asked.

"No, don't be silly," Finn guffawed. "Only when the mood strikes really. We don't need sleep like we did back on Earth. You're still new here so your mind is still working the way it used to with all the old routines an' all – telling you that you need to sleep when in actual fact you don't need any sleep at all. I'll come here a few times a week usually, just to get away from everything. It's nice to get some peace."

The clock on the wall behind them said the time was a quarter to nine.

"We better get to class, I suppose," Finn said, quickly fixing his long bangs in the mirror. "Then after that we'll get you some new clothes. We don't want everyone thinking you're some kind of dirty hippy that wears the same shirt all the time."

"That would be great," said Tom, looking down at the sweaty t-shirt he'd worn yesterday that was still slightly sticky from lake water and sand. He pulled his crumpled timetable out of his jeans pocket and looked at what his first class was.

Heavenly Art 9-10pm – Room 1A 342nd Floor – Professor Santi

"What've you got first?" Finn asked.

"Art I think," Tom replied.

"Lucky you!" he laughed. "Who with?"

"Professor Santi? He any good?"

"No idea," Finn replied. "I get Professor Simoni. Guess you're on your own with this one."

Finn left Tom outside the Revelation common room and headed off down the corridor. Time was short before first period started but Tom wanted to quickly check if Mary was still around to see if she had the same class. Stepping inside, he saw the common room was mostly empty, aside from a small group of popped-collar eighties boys sat on the edge of the fountain, most likely intent on skipping class. There was no sign of Mary. With a brief sigh, Tom left and headed off in the direction of the elevators.

Arriving outside Room 1A a few minutes later, he pushed through the heavy wooden door and entered the classroom alone. As he was quickly becoming accustomed to, he was greeted by no ordinary classroom. This room was stunning. He even thought that he recognised it from a family trip they'd taken to Rome back when Scott was still alive. It was a perfect replica of The Stanze – or the Raphael Rooms as they're more commonly known – which are housed within the Vatican Museums. It struck him that Professor Santi must in fact be the celebrated Italian Renaissance painter and architect, 'Raphael Santi'.

The room was split into four connecting chambers, each displaying its own array of spectacular frescoes on the walls - painted by Professor Santi himself and then by his apprentices who continued his efforts once he'd died. The most noticeable difference for Tom was that instead of being full to the brim of jostling students, haughty tour guides and overly keen tourists like he remembered, it was empty except for the scattering of chairs and paint stands that were placed sporadically around the series of connecting rooms.

Professor Santi himself stood at the front of the first chamber they entered. Tom felt a twinge of guilt knowing that he'd visited his tomb personally back on Earth, which was on display to the public in the Pantheon in Rome. Regrettably, he hadn't been as respectful as he now wished he had (he remembered taking a selfie with his brother in front of the grim alter and possibly throwing a peace sign or something similar at the camera). He quickly shook off the painful memory.

The rest of the students filed into the chambers behind Tom and he was pleasantly surprised to see that Alice and one of her giggling friends were among the group. Tom took his place at the paint stand, which was furthest from the front, wanting to hide in the corner as much as he could. The rest of the free stands were quickly taken too. Tom recognised a few of the kids from his Ancient History (Revisited) lecture he'd had first period the night before. He tried to focus on admiring the paintings that lined the walls like the other students were doing, but from the corner of his eye, he watched the progress of Alice and her friend and secretly prayed that she would take the free stand next to his. No such luck – the stand was taken swiftly by the tall blonde-haired kid with the tan flares he recognised from yesterday. He grimaced at Tom as he took his seat behind the wooden paint stand and Tom quickly looked away, realising that he may have been ogling the boy as he sat down. Alice found herself a free stand a few places in front of Tom, in the first chamber of the connecting rooms.

As Professor Santi began, there was immediate jostling as everyone collected their paints and brushes from the store at the front of the room. Tom, who had no idea what he was doing, tried to look inconspicuous and not as if he were simply copying every movement of the boy with the tan flares. In the store, the good brushes disappeared quickly and by the time Tom got himself to the cupboard there were only two brushes left. Both of which were heavily frayed and seriously lacking in bristles. He grumbled and picked the one he considered the least mangled.

"Here take this one," said a voice from behind him.

Tom turned and nearly dropped his tray of paints when he saw that the voice had come from none other than Alice herself.

"Oh… err… thanks," he muttered, dropping the old brush on the floor and immediately reaching for the brush she held out to him. She laughed and bent to the floor to retrieve the fallen brush.

"You're new here right?" she guessed.

"Yeah - second night," Tom replied.

"I'm Alice," she smiled at him. Tom could feel his heartbeat accelerate in his chest as if it'd just been injected with a syringe full of adrenalin.

"I'm Tom," he replied quickly, trying his hardest to seem casual. She smiled again, revealing a row of perfect white teeth and Tom looked away quickly realising again that he'd been staring for a little longer than is polite. She turned and left him alone in the store cupboard holding his shiny new brush that she'd just given him. Tom looked down at it briefly – it was just as perfect as she was. The smooth bristles even seemed to resemble her perfect mane of sleek blonde hair. He gripped it tightly, as if it were now the single most valuable item he owned. He stepped back out into the classroom, realising that Professor Santi had already started the lesson and received a few muffled guffaws as he hurriedly returned to his paint stand, dropping his palette of paints in the process. The class had been tasked with emulating one of Professor Santi's own frescos of Adam and Eve which was on the ceiling of the chamber adjacent to theirs. The students huddled below the ceiling, craning their necks upwards to get a glimpse of the painting in question. Thinking he had a rough idea of what to do, Tom returned to his stand and began drawing a pencil outline of the scene from memory.

The painting included the figure of a fully exposed Eve which Tom felt mildly embarrassed about sketching. Thankfully, Adam's 'member' was concealed by a leaf so at least he didn't have to contemplate that aspect of the painting. He was always rather fond of art back on Earth, so this class, he found quite enjoyable. He also had a good view from where he stood of Alice's progress on her own painting which, he noticed, was taking shape rather nicely. The only part of the class he found slightly annoying was having to repeatedly return to the adjacent chamber to get another look at the painting they were meant to be imitating. On one such trip, he happened upon Alice, who herself had returned for another look.

"Incredible isn't it," she said, craning her neck to take in the full painting.

"Yeah, it's pretty amazing," Tom replied genuinely. "I saw your painting - you're really talented."

"Thanks," she blushed. "I've been taking this class for nearly twenty years, so I was bound to improve eventually."

Tom fell silent, momentarily speechless at her brazen revelation.

"You're from the nineties then?" he asked hesitantly, after quickly doing the math in his head.

"Nineteen-ninety-nine," she smiled back at him. "Missed the millennium by three months. Apparently, it was quite a party."

Tom didn't know, having not been born himself until two-thousand and four. He felt strangely sad as he realised they'd never been on Earth together at the same time. She'd died long before he was even born.

"I take it you're a noughties kid then?" she asked.

"Oh, eh yeah I am," Tom replied. "Born in two-thousand and four."

"That would make us the same age then," she smiled back at him.

"Oh… cool," Tom replied, quietly elated by this fact. "You're American, right?" he guessed, judging by the accent.

"Carmel, Indiana," she replied, matter-of-factly. "We're ten a penny in this place. You don't meet many Brits."

Tom begged to differ knowing the first two people he'd met had both been English, but he held his tongue. "I guess," he replied softly.

"Anyway, better be getting back to my masterpiece."

She smiled at him again and left him beneath the fresco of Adam and Eve alone.

Chapter Thirteen
The House of Deuteronomy

Next period was back with Professor Suetonius and Tom was relieved to see Finn waiting for him outside the classroom.

"How was art?" he asked.

"Oh, not too bad," Tom replied absent-mindedly. His thoughts were still lolling lazily on his brief encounter with Alice.

"You must have something wrong with you," Finn muttered as they pushed through the door and took their familiar seats in the same spot as yesterday.

The class bustled to a quiet as Professor Suetonius wrapped his chalk duster against his desk, booming in his haughty accented voice for people to take their seats. Just as he was about to commence with the lesson, the door opened again. The creaking hinge echoing loudly across the classroom and distracted heads turned enquiringly to see who'd dared make the intrusion. It was a boy.

He stepped through the threshold slowly and turned to stare at the classroom, which had momentarily frozen in place. He seemed to stand there assessing the room for an awkwardly long period of time. There was complete silence as the room's occupants waited with bated breath for the next move. Eventually the silence was broken by a loud cough from the seats nearest to the front and everyone returned to normal again. Tom, however, couldn't draw his gaze from the boy who'd made the intrusion, who was now politely asking Professor Suetonius to excuse his lateness. He seemed like any ordinary kid, except there was something not quite right about him and Tom couldn't put his finger on what it was. It wasn't his crooked nose or his ungainly tuft of near pitch-black hair. Nor was it his eyes which had remained perfectly still and calm despite the fact that half of the class were still staring as he took his seat in the same row as Tom and Finn. It wasn't the fact that he wore clothes that were from an era that he couldn't place, and it wasn't the smile that had crept knowingly across his ghostly white lips the moment he had taken his seat and the lesson had resumed. It was none of those things. There was something else about him. Something intangible. Something innately wrong that was clear the moment you first set eyes on him.

There was a feeling about him. Something like the feeling you might get when your mind wakes up in the middle of the night but your body is still asleep, and you just lie there trapped in your own skin, unable to move or coax your mind back to the land of sleep where you lay blissfully ignorant of your own paralysis. It was a paralysing feeling. That's how he would describe it. That's how he felt when he looked at this boy, like his mind was awake but his body was paralysed.

Finn elbowed him hard in the ribs. He hadn't noticed but his gaze had remained fixed on the new boy and Professor Suetonius had paused the lesson to glare at Tom who clearly wasn't paying attention. Leaving the class forty-five minutes later, the new boy let them pass at the end of the marble aisle. Tom felt his gaze on his back as he shuffled by him. It may have been his imagination, but he felt suddenly cold while close to this boy and he could feel his arms break out in a frantic rash of goosepimples that prickled his skin like tiny insect eggs.

Back in the hallway, Finn decided that he would take Tom for a visit to the Deuteronomy common room for free period. The floor designated to the House of Deuteronomy was located quite low in the tower, on the eleventh floor, only a few floors below the dungeons.

"I'm telling you, it sucks," Finn said, as they exited the elevator.

One thing he noticed immediately about this floor were the paintings on the walls. In Revelation, the walls were lined with triumphant frescos of Michael and various other angels relishing their victory over evil. The paintings all depicted winged angels brandishing flaming swords or bows with quivers of arrows or harps and all looking beautiful and glorious in equal measure as they smited their foes. The paintings down here however were darker. There were no triumphant angels, no harps or winged cherubs. Instead the frames contained a litany of the most disturbing artwork Tom had ever seen. The first painting contained a horned beast with the body of a man and the head of a goat clutched hold of a new born baby that suckled at his manly teat affectionately.

The next painting, Tom would later be told, was by Peter Paul Reubens and was called *Saturn Devouring his Son*. It was the original (the painting on display in Madrid was a fake). To say the painting caused him some distress as he walked by it would have been putting it lightly. He couldn't take his eyes away from it. The sheer horror of what was depicted in the painting drew him in like a mosquito to a bug zapper. It was a thing of nightmares; like that scene in Stephen King's '*IT*' that was deemed too appalling for the film adaptation.

The next painting was called *The Torment of Saint Anthony* by Michelangelo (again it was the original). Saint

Anthony was depicted aloft in the air, carried by a scandalous band of demons that were intent on ripping him limb from limb. Apparently, it was Michelangelo's first painting and quite different from his other forays into religious art. Why the walls were lined with such distressing images was troubling him as they pushed through the heavy door into the Deuteronomy common room.

"What was that all about?" he asked Finn, as he quickly signed him into the guest book.

"You mean the paintings?"

"Yeah," Tom said, the crack in his voice revealing just how shaken he actually was.

"Pretty nasty aren't they. You get used to them after a while. I think Raphael has a woody for dark artwork. He's one twisted individual if you ask me."

The Deuteronomy common room was markedly different from his own. There were no windows and the room was lit only by the waning candles on the tables. It had the same feel as the dungeons except without the cells lining the walls. There were couches and armchairs but no marble statues or fountain at the centre of the room. Instead there were cabinets and bookshelves scattered haphazardly among the chairs. As they walked through the seats, Tom got a good look in one of the cabinets. On the top shelf was a large stone, slightly stained on one side with what could have been blood (although it was brown instead of red).

"What's this rock?" he asked, pointing through the glass.

"A bit of a grim history that thing," Finn replied. "Apparently that was the rock that Cain bashed his brother Abel over the head with."

"Oh," said Tom, now feeling slightly sickened by it. "I guess that is blood then after all."

99

He crouched on his knees and examined the bottom shelf of the cabinet. What he saw made him fall back hard onto this backside, hands bent awkwardly beneath him. There was a severed head propped on the shelf staring back at him.

"What the hell is that?" he cried, pointing at the cabinet.

"Oh, ha! That's the head of Medusa," Finn laughed, watching Tom edge slowly away from the glass. "I'd watch out for those things," he said, gesturing to the cabinet. "They're called '*Curiosity Cabinets*' - the room is full of 'em. They've all got weird and wonderful artefacts in 'em that Raphael has collected over the years, and some of 'em you definitely don't want to get too close to."

"Weird and wonderful?" Tom asked dubiously, not quite sure he'd use that exact phrasing. "More like weird and disgusting."

"Yeah they are a bit disgusting aren't they," Finn agreed, plopping himself into a blood-red leather armchair. Tom stared at the severed head, resisting the urge to vomit. It was a hideous sight, wrinkled to the point that its facial features were indistinguishable from the folds of its leathery skin. Sunken eye sockets like empty pits stared out at him. The same sockets that'd once held the eyes that could turn a man to stone, according to the Greek legend. The hair was the worst part as you might expect. Dried snake scales hung limply from the desiccated scalp where its hair should have been. He looked away again revolted, wondering why someone would want to keep something like that on a shelf.

"You should see our book collection too," Finn piped, pulling one of the volumes from the bookcase behind his chair and throwing it onto the coffee table in front of him with a loud smack. Tom picked the book up and examined the cover.

Malleus Maleficarum

"It's Latin?" He said puzzledly.

"It's the *Hammer of Witches*," Finn stated. "First edition."

Tom flicked open the book and stared at the first page. There was a drawing of some clergyman, his name was '*Henricus Institoris*' according to the text underneath.

"Caused quite a stir back in the day that book apparently, we had a whole lesson on it in our Notable Literature class," Finn continued. "Thousands of women were burned at the stake because of that book alone. They say it tells you how to recognise a witch and how to kill one."

Tom flicked through the dusty pages dismayed to see that the entire book was in Latin.

"So how *do* you kill a witch then?" he asked curiously.

"Hell if I know, I wasn't listening," Finn replied casually. "If I had to guess, I'd say the best way to kill a witch is to force them to sit through an hour's lecture on that book. It nearly killed me."

Tom snickered and pushed the book back to him. Finn replaced the book in the cabinet and pulled out another, again chucking it onto the table between them with another loud smack.

"More witches?" Tom guessed, picking up the second book.

"Nah, that one's angels this time," Finn replied coolly.

Tom stared at the dusted cover. It was so old he felt

he should be using tweezers to turn the pages. He imagined himself surrounded by snooping historians with magnifying glasses, yelling at him to '*be gentle!*' and '*don't breathe on it!*' as they observed him handle it amateurishly. Oddly, he noticed, there was no name on the cover.

"What's this then?" he asked curiously.

"That's the '*Book of Soyga*'," Finn replied. "Although I think it's meant to be read backwards so that would make it the 'Book of Agyos' I guess. It's one of only two existing copies though, I know that."

"Why backwards?" Tom asked puzzledly.

"Not sure. Something to do with hiding its true meaning. It was owned by some crazy occultist guy who used it to try and contact Uriel and Michael."

"Bet they liked that!" Tom scoffed.

"Exactly. Imagine it pissed Michael off pretty badly. No idea why someone would want to contact those prudes anyway. Can you imagine trying to have a phone conversation with Uriel?"

Tom, who'd only met Uriel once the day before, pictured the strange angel dressed head to toe in green clothes and brandishing her strange magnifying glass that could see into the past.

"She's quite bossy, isn't she?" he offered.

"That's one word for it," replied Finn. "But I can think of another B-word I'd rather use instead."

They both sniggered and Tom placed the book back on the table.

"So, did they manage to contact her then?" he asked.

"Oh yeah, I bet she talked his ear off. Probably couldn't get her to shut up after a while. Don't think he got through to Michael though. Makes sense. Why would Michael want to speak to some crazy occultist when he's got demons to be slayin' n'all."

102

Tom nodded his agreement. Finn hopped out of his seat again and walked to another bookshelf close by and extracted yet another book from the shelf.

"Now, this one's a real page turner," he said, chucking it onto the table.

"What is it?"

"*The Keys to the Kingdom of Fire*'. Last remaining copy. They don't want us knowing about this one. I only know what my mate George told me about it. Apparently, the author of this book adapted it from one written by the Devil himself, not something they're going to teach us about in Notable Literature anyway that's for sure. I'm not sure it's even meant to be down here. Someone must have left it 'cos it's been here for ages."

Tom picked it up hesitantly and examined the cover. There was a small engraving in the bottom right hand corner – 'LCR'.

"It wasn't me who told you this right, but they say that book there, contains the means to summon the Devil."

He let the words hang ominously while Tom put the book back on the table quickly as if it had burnt his fingers.

"Is it true?" he asked.

"Who knows?" Finn shrugged. "Looks pretty authentic to me, did you see the engraving in the corner?"

"Yeah – 'LCR'," Tom replied. "You think that's short for Lucifer?"

"Must be…"

"Let's put it back," Tom urged, starting to feel a tad uncomfortable being so close to the book.

Finn grabbed it and stashed it back in the bookcase across the room.

"What's that over there?" Tom said suddenly,

pointing to a large cabinet at the back of the room that was made completely of glass. He pulled himself from his seat curiously and made his way over to the glass cabinet, ignoring the stares of the boys sat nearest to it. It was dark so he had to press his nose to the glass to see inside. It was a feather, an admittedly large feather, about two feet in length. It hung suspended in the centre of the glass cabinet as if dangled on a string, although Tom could see no such attachments on it. It was simply hanging there in mid-air, floating on its own accord, as if being levitated by some unseen magician or wizard brandishing their wand at it.

"*That* belonged to Lucifer, or so they say," Finn said quietly. Tom jumped at the voice, unaware that Finn had followed him over. There was a large smudge on the glass through the circle of condensation where his nose had been.

"Fell from his wing during some great battle," he continued. "Raphael must have swiped it and kept it in here all these years. A souvenir I guess."

"He's got a bit of a fascination with the devil this guy doesn't he," Tom said flatly, pressing his nose up to the glass again.

"Well, funny you should say that..." Finn replied mysteriously. "Apparently Raphael and Lucifer were quite close before that whole war started; thick as thieves, or so I heard it. He was even close to switching sides and joining up with him. I think it was Gabriel in the end who persuaded him otherwise. Still though... Makes you wonder."

So, Raphael and Lucifer had been friends? Tom thought curiously. He wasn't sure how he felt about that. He knew Raphael was certainly a shady character based on what he'd seen thus far of the Deuteronomy common room, but was he evil? Surely not. *Michael and Gabriel must trust him anyway to let him teach here at this School surrounded by all these kids.*

"I told you he was one twisted individual," Finn sniggered over his shoulder. "If I was Michael, I'd get rid of him, just for good measure, be on the safe side you know, in case he ever changes his mind and joins up with the dark side. Like Obi-Wan taking out Anakin with a blaster rife before he ever learned to use a lightsabre."

"You think he'd do that?" Tom said, wonderingly.

"Who knows?" Finn replied. "He's sick enough to keep a severed head in a cabinet, that's proof enough for me. Anyway, we better get going; that's just about third period."

Chapter Fourteen
The Garden of Eden

Before he knew it, Tom's first month at St Michael's had come to an end. He was gradually falling into the steady routine of classes, free time spent relaxing with Finn and Mary and infrequent naps in the restrooms whenever he felt the need to escape from the hustle and bustle of the school.

There was plenty for them to do during the day when classes had finished. The tower itself had over five-hundred floors which would take years to explore completely, and on top of that his friends had shown him most of the hotspots where pupils liked to hang-out during the day. There was the Otium which contained a swimming pool that was like something out of a holiday brochure from the nineteen twenties. Everyone was required to wear old-fashioned bathing suits that looked like pyjamas and the girls had to wear white rubber swim caps that had chinstraps attached to keep them in place. Also on offer at the Otium were several pistes for fencing; indoor archery for budding toxophiles; and an archaic form of golf where you hit rocks out of the tower into the emptiness (Tom and Finn had visited this medieval driving range one morning and realised quite quickly that they were both entirely useless at golf, neither had managed to hit a ball more than twenty yards away from the tower). Finn tended to shy away from anything involving too much physical activity, still harbouring an innate diffidence around his ability to do anything too athletic. Tom kept telling him that he was entirely able-bodied now and could do exactly the same level of activity as everyone else, but he stubbornly refused to accept that fact. Mary on the other hand had taken to life after illness as naturally as a fish unleashed into the open ocean. Her sprightly vitality was infectious to be around, and she often accompanied Tom to the Otium for fencing - a pastime she took quite seriously, although her favourite place was still the library.

Next to Madam Bertin's tailor shop and Ambrosia's convenience store, there was a dusty old cinema screen that showed reruns of old movies dating back to the silent film era of the nineteen-thirties, and there was a restaurant called Soyer's that was run by a Frenchmen called Alexis Soyer who'd been one of the most celebrated chefs in Victorian England. Reading the chalkboard propped outside it one day, Tom had noticed that dining there was reservation only and needed to be booked months in advance. It was said to boast some of the best chefs to have lived in its kitchen, so if you wanted to dine there you could expect to part with more than a few coffers full of shekels. Unsurprisingly, the restaurant was mainly frequented by the faculty and the Heads of House as none of the students could afford it.

Despite still feeling the regular urge to eat, which had of course become a learned behaviour during his time on Earth, it was now no longer a necessary part of his day, as the sustenance food provided was of course no longer needed. Thus, there were no mealtimes at St Michael's, which had taken some getting used to, but that didn't mean the students didn't occasionally eat for pleasure or simply to reminisce about the sensation it had given them while back on Earth.

Therefore, as well as Soyer's restaurant, there were snacks sold at the minimart like establishment called '*Ambrosia's*', next to the tailors on the seventy-sixth floor. Tom had visited with Mary during the previous week to purchase some barbeque flavoured crisps with the allotment of Shekels he'd been given by Uriel. They'd taken them to the library and shared them on a sofa in a quiet corner while discussing what foods they'd enjoyed while on Earth. There was also, on very special occasions, grand banquets that were held in the library to celebrate significant events, or if Michael, the school's patriarch, defeated some unspeakable evil that was threatening the school's safety and the Heads declared a time to rejoice. During these events, the school would often gather in the library to celebrate with a lavish feast and enjoy entertainment that was put on by the staff and various special guests. These events were, however, so infrequent that Finn said he'd never had one during his time at St Michael's, and Mary, who had been at the school much longer, had only experienced one such banquet and it had been in her first week. She had been very disappointed to find that they weren't a regular occurrence.

Excursions from the school were thankfully more common than the banquets. They had to be booked months in advance so the necessary safety precautions could be taken, and suitable escorts could be arranged. These escorts were usually in the form of warrior angels that occasionally helped out the school with security and chaperon duties. The last excursion Mary had been on was during the previous year when they had visited the Elysian Fields with Professor Appleseed and his Celestial Botany class. It'd taken them four days to get there, but it was apparently well worth seeing once they did finally make it. The worst part, as always, had been mushing

through the squishy terrain that surrounded St Michael's.
The perpetually water-logged marshes that spanned as far
as the eye could see. Apparently, it rained three-hundred
and sixty-two days of the year around St Michael's and
the ground was so saturated that if you stood still for long
enough, you could completely disappear into the mud.
Once you finally got past the squelching marshes (which
in itself was nearly a day's walk), the remaining four-day
trek had been quite pleasant - through fields and forests,
over hillsides, across rivers and along the shores of great
lakes. The weather was always perfect as, once you got
away from the flat plane of marshes around St Michael's,
the terrain rose above the rain clouds and the sun was
that little bit closer which made for a warm pleasing
temperature that wasn't as stiflingly oppressive as you
might imagine. When Tom had asked Mary what the
Elysian Fields had been like, she'd replied – *"It was
beautiful, apart from all the naked people."*

There were six classes a day at St Michael's, which
were broken up by the hour's free period that they were
allowed after their second class, and the second free
period was after the fourth class. Most of Tom's classes
were a mixture of students from the Houses of
Revelation and Deuteronomy but there was the
occasional student from Numbers who was usually
someone who'd elected to continue with the class long
after they'd finished the required five-year syllabus. After
the mandatory five-year course, you were required to sit
an exam on the subject which counted towards your
merits for graduating from the school. There were
preliminary exams at the end of every school year, but
these were more to give the staff a measure of your
progress on the subject, rather than counting towards
your tally of merits. As Tom understood it, once you'd
collected the required number of merits, you could

graduate and move on to wherever the pupils went to after they'd advanced from the school.

One night, after classes had finished, the three of them had retreated to the Revelation common room and had started discussing their lives back on Earth. Finn, as it turned out, was from Chorley in Lancashire and was a roaring Red Devil's fan. He'd had season tickets to the disabled section at Old Trafford and he'd never missed a game while he was alive. He said that one of the only good things he could say about being in a wheelchair was the fact that the disabled section at football grounds provided for infinitely better viewing than the normal seats, as they were often located only feet away from the pitch. He'd said he could smell the freshly cut grass he was that close, and he still thought about that smell while napping in the restrooms sometimes. Growing up he'd been an only child, which was just as well he said, as there was no way in hell he was sharing his dad's time with some girl who needed driving to dance lessons, girl scouts or anything else that he considered a complete waste of his dad's time in the evenings.

Mary on the other hand was from London – a little street called Picket Post Close directly opposite Highgate Cemetery. She'd watch kids running through the gravestones from her bedroom window when the sun was out and occasionally, on her good days, her mother would take her across to the cemetery and they'd sit on the grass and have a picnic by the grave of Karl Marx, and she would read her books and eat the jam sandwiches that her mum had made them. She'd loved reading while she was alive, and after she died she was ecstatic to find the huge collection of books available in the library here at St Michael's. She often spent her free time down there, curled up in a corner with a large book, while Tom and

Finn hung out in the common room or tried their hands at golf.

Although they'd only visited the Deuteronomy common room that one time, Tom was keen to go back and explore the rest of the Curiosity Cabinets that they had down there. Finn had mentioned that the one Tom did have the displeasure to look inside must have been the tamest one of the lot, as he'd thrown up all down his front after seeing what was hiding in the curiosity cupboard in the far corner of the room (which he recommends viewing by the way).

Mary, who thought Finn was "morally simplistic and narcissistic," hadn't gotten on with him since their first meeting a few years back. According to Mary, Finn had been quite rude to her about her clothes for no good reason at all. She had just been minding her own business one night on her way to Heavenly Art when he'd sneered something completely inappropriate about her shoes to her from outside the elevator and she'd ended up in tears. Finn, who couldn't remember the incident in question, refused to apologise when it was brought up one night in the common room. Fortunately, after thirty minutes of back and forth arguing, with Tom acting as an unwilling mediator, they had reached an uneasy parlay on the subject and it wasn't mentioned again.

On Thursday, Finn had taken Tom up to the tailors to order some new clothes, which according to him he '*desperately needed, or everyone would stop talking to him.*' The tailor was a French woman called Madame Bertin. Apparently, she had been the official couturière (or dress maker) for Marie Antoinette during her time married to Louis XVI of France. At that time her dresses had been the talk of Paris (and indeed, across most of Europe), and she had delighted in telling them both about her time working for the Queen in the Palace at Versailles and how she had brought 'haute couture' to the forefront of popular culture.

When she was finally done, she handed Tom an order form and told him to take a seat in the waiting room and fill it out. The form seemed simple enough, it asked for the specific style you wanted, the era the clothes you required were from, what materials they were made from as well as the size and fit etcetera; then below that there was a large box where you were required to sketch the outfit you wanted. This puzzled Tom, as although he was quite fond of art and of drawing, he wouldn't exactly consider himself a fashion designer. He turned to Finn.

"How closely to this drawing is she going to make my clothes?"

"Don't worry, it's just meant to be a rough sketch," he replied.

"Oh, good, because if she does do it exactly as I draw it, I'm going to look pretty ridiculous wearing it."

Satisfied with his sketch, he handed the form back to Madame Bertin. He'd decided to keep it simple since it was his first time. So a standard pair of navy jeans and a plain black t-shirt was his safest bet he imagined. The order came to six shekels, leaving Tom fifty-four shekels and a few agora in his coin purse. Madame Bertin stashed the order in her drawer and told him the clothes would be ready tomorrow evening at eight.

He was beginning to worry about what he would do when he ran out of shekels, he vaguely recalled Uriel mentioning that there were ways to make money at the school, but he couldn't recall exactly what those ways were.

"What do you do for more shekels around here?" he asked Finn as they made their way back down to the Revelation common room.

"I'll tell you if you promise not to laugh," he said firmly.

"I promise," Tom prompted.

"Well... I help with the gardening."

"That's not so bad," Tom said, nonplussed. "I didn't even know there was a garden."

"Yeah there's a garden terrace way up top. I'll take you up if you want?"

"Yeah sure," Tom replied, quite excited by the prospect of some greenery for a change.

They waited until the elevator pinged open on the Revelation floor then Finn hit the button for '*Gardens*' (which were on 480). The doors opened out into a lush greenhouse garden, brimming with life and colour. Tom sighed audibly as he stepped out into this secret Utopia he'd yet to be shown.

"This is fantastic!" he trilled, breathing in the strong scent of begonias that hung in baskets outside the elevator door.

"Yeah, it's not bad," Finn replied blankly. "Reminds me of work though so I don't come up here other than to put in the odd shift."

"How do I get a job here?" Tom quizzed, eagerly.

"Calm down, it's only flowers. You're not going soft on me are you?"

Tom wasn't paying attention. He was stroking the trunk of a large palm tree that hung over the path.

"I'll put in a word for you – see what I can do," Finn conceded.

"Thanks mate."

"There's plenty of girls work here y'know," Finn said encouragingly. "Maybe you'll meet Alice?"

"Does she work here?" Tom asked, trying to sound nonchalant.

"She does the occasional shift I think..." Finn

speculated, flicking a butterfly from his shoulder that had intrusively taken residence there.

"I've kind of spoken to her already…"

"You did? You sly dog!" Finn said, rapping him on the back.

"Yeah back in Heavenly Art with Professor Santi - she's fifteen like us."

"Figures. Most kids here are around that age," Finn replied.

"And American…" Tom continued.

"No accounting for taste."

"Anyway, I was gonna tell you. I saw her with Professor Newton after class finished. He handed her a note of some kind. It seemed pretty shady to me – like they didn't want to get caught or something."

"Really? Wow… Bet he's doing her. What a paedo. Though, I guess in his time most guys married their thirteen-year-old cousins and no one blinked an eye."

"Nah, surely she's not like that?"

"How would you know? You've only spoken to her once," Finn jibed.

"I just don't get that feeling from her, that's all." Tom replied, musingly.

The path wound meanderingly through the garden terrace which was domed under a large glass habisphere, like Professor Newton's astronomy classroom. The air was humid and thick, and clouds of water vapour hung in hazy swirls in the air – like Tom's bathroom once did after one of his exceedingly lengthy showers. It was like a little private, cultivated rainforest that was completely isolated from the bustling crowds of the school. There were birds chirping and singing in the branches of the palm trees and Tom spotted a family of technicolour parrots swooping carefree above them.

"This is a good time to come up here," Finn said ponderingly. "Gets busy first thing in the morning when class gets out. I think we might be the only ones here, except for Professor Appleseed of course, who'll be hiding around here somewhere. Better not let him catch me up here or he'll have me watering the banana plants."

Mary, as it turned out, worked in the library. As Finn put it, "Where else would she work? She spends so much time down there anyway, she might as well be getting paid for it."

Tom was fond of the library and its impressive gold-plated ladders that slid elegantly along the bookshelves, but he thought if he had the choice, he'd rather work on the garden terrace. Who knows, as Finn said, he could always be presented with another opportunity to speak to Alice if they ever had a shift together. Even if that wasn't to be the case, he still considered it a nice place to be spending his hours out of class to get some extra pocket money for books and snacks from Ambrosia's or maybe even some more audacious looking clothes from Madame Bertin's tailor shop, if he was feeling brave.

After they left the garden terrace, Tom told Finn he was going to use the restrooms for a while, as he felt in need of some time to unwind. One aspect of the restrooms he'd found pleasantly surprising was the changing décor, which was drastically different depending on which floor of the tower you were on. He'd found his favourite ones so far were on the Astronomy floor, near Professor Newton's classroom - as these restrooms, as well as having exceptionally comfy beds and planetary themed curtains and wallpaper, also contained fancy telescopes that pointed through individual windows in each cubicle. Tom had spent hours during the previous week staring at the heavens before class started. The planets seemed so much closer from this vantage point.

He could easily see the surface of Mars and had spent time examining the canyons and mountain ranges of the red planet, imagining himself walking on the surface and wondering whether mankind would ever make it that far. Then he'd turned the telescope slightly to the right and was greeted with a perfect view of Jupiter and the swirling storm clouds that gave it its distinct appearance.

He'd been fascinated to learn while at school on Earth that, unlike Earth and Mars, Jupiter had no surface (at least not in the sense that we're familiar with). In fact, the entire planet is made out of gas of varying viscosity – starting in the outer atmosphere where the gas is very light, it gradually gets heavier as you make your way towards the centre, until the gas is eventually turned into a liquid ocean. This ocean then gets gradually thicker as you keep descending, until the thick, sludgy liquid gas near the bottom finally turns solid. So, there is no surface to be walked on – only gradually solidifying gas. And the same was true for the other gas giants – Saturn, Uranus and Neptune.

Tonight however, Tom wasn't in the mood for stargazing. He found himself an empty cubicle and reclined on the bed, resting his arms behind his head and stared at the slowly spinning antique globe that was placed on the night stand by the hourglass timers.

He'd come to the restroom with the intention of finding some time to think about his brother, Scott, who had been lurking on the fringes of his conscience for the first time in what felt like years. The realisation that Scott had been at (or was currently attending) St Michael's had initially filled him with excitement, but now the prospect had inherited another feeling that gave him cause for concern: that feeling was guilt. He knew he shouldn't feel it, but he felt it regardless. It was that voice inside his head - the one he couldn't ignore no matter how hard he tried, the one with the accusatory tone, the one with the voice that sounded so much like Scott's own voice , that told him it was his fault Scott had died, as after all, wasn't he the reason Scott had joined the military in the first place?

Scott, while he was alive, had been many things - a good brother, a good listener, a fantastic footballer, but a good role model he was not. He'd been in trouble with the police on more than one occasion and one night their father had taken Scott aside with the intention of a heartfelt man-to-man discussion regarding his behaviour and there had been a colossal falling out. His father had insisted that Scott was setting a bad example for Tom and he would prefer if Scott moved out of the family home and found a flat of his own, so Tom could avoid going down the same avenues as he had. Scott had been furious but was determined to do what was right by his younger brother, so he resolved to join the army so he could stay out of trouble. Six months later, he was dead. Tom was distraught and couldn't help but ask himself - if he weren't around then would Scott have had to join the army in the first place? These feelings of guilt had been a lot to process at that time being so young and they manifested in flashes of violence at school and at home. Numerous fights, broken noses, hurt feelings and broken friendships had culminated in him being suspended from school for two weeks which had left his parent's (who were already struggling with their own grief) all the more distraught. It had been ironic that the main intention of sending Scott away was to stop Tom from following him down those roads that led to all the trouble, but in the end, Tom had found himself going down them anyway and ultimately, they'd led him to the same place Scott had ended up. They'd led him to his own untimely demise.

Despite the unfortunate irony in both of their passing's, Tom still felt that were he to see Scott again in this new and unexpected plane of existence, he would owe him a heartfelt apology for the part he'd played in his death, no matter how tertiary that part had been. His own death, as he understood it, had been entirely unavoidable. That plane had had his number on it since the day it started it's manufacture in the Boeing or Airbus assembly building, from its maiden flight all the way to its doomed one, it had been destined to end Tom's life while he lay on his bed, wholly oblivious to the eighty-eight tonnes of aluminium hurtling towards his exact position, destined to remove him from this life and send him to the next in a thousand pieces.

He wondered morbidly what state his body had been found in, or if it was even found at all. He knew that when the plane from the Lockerby bombing had crashed into those houses in that small town in Scotland a few days before Christmas, the sleeping residents remains were never found. They simply disappeared. Maybe there was nothing left to find in those situations. Maybe when a plane hits you you're smashed into pieces so small that you're collected with a dustpan and stored in a jam jar of black dust. The remnants of what was once a living breathing person, now proportionate in size to a jar of strawberry preserve.

He hoped that if he were found, they'd buried him by the sea in the grave plot next to his brother, overlooking the Yorkshire Coast where they'd walked together as boys, so full of life and so ignorant to what would befall them. He could only imagine the toll having to bury both children would have taken on his parents. His father already a shell of his former self after Scott's death, and his mother so dumbfounded by her grief that she seemed to exist in a glass ball of absolute calm, most likely a result of the copious amounts of antidepressants and anxiety medications she now ran on daily.

Lying there on the bed in the restrooms on the Astronomy floor, he felt an increasing sense of helplessness that slowly started to consume him. For the first time in longer than he could remember, he held his head in his hands and let the flood of emotion overwhelm him completely. Tears welling in his eyes then streaming down his cheeks in burgeoning torrents.

Chapter Fifteen
This Side of Paradise

He wasn't sure how long he had lain there and let his emotions get the better of him. Two hours, maybe three? Once the tears had finally subsided, he got up and assessed his face in the mirror. His eyes were bloodshot and red, and his cheeks were burned crimson from where he'd been rubbing them. He straightened himself out then gave himself a quick slap on the face and said, "*get a hold of yourself Tom.*" He was used to burying his emotions and he felt weak and embarrassed at letting them overcome him like that. He bustled out of the cubicle and splashed his face in the sink, letting the cold-water cleanse him and cool his skin. Thankfully, he appeared to be the only one using these restrooms at that time and he quietly thanked God that no one had heard him crying. Using a hand towel to dry his face, he pushed out of the restrooms and back into the hallway.

He could see the door for Professor Newton's classroom a short distance down the hall. He was about to continue in the other direction towards the elevators when he heard something strange, muffled voices coming from Professor Newton's classroom. One of the voices was Raphael, the grim sulking tone was unmistakable. He recognised it from when they'd been caught red-handed on the five-hundredth floor, then been escorted swiftly to the dungeons for their first visit to Mastema and what would become their (very memorable) first 'school trip' together. Tom paused at the exit to the restrooms and strained his ears to see if he could identify the second voice. It sounded female, he could tell that much. The voices grew louder, the female voice now scolding Raphael in sharp punctuated tones.

It was risky, but (for some inexplicable reason known only to his subconscious) he simply needed to find out who that second voice belonged to. He crept silently towards the classroom door, which was ever so slightly ajar, and stopped a few feet away from the entrance. Pressing himself against the wall, like a cartoon portrayal of a cat burglar, he listened.

"The note was quite clear!" snapped the female voice.

"What would you have me do exactly?" Raphael replied.

"Remove him!"

"I can't just do that, it would be too noticeable!"

The female voice went quiet, taking its time to consider its response.

"What became of the woman? Is she dead?" she asked finally.

"Dead by her own hand," Raphael replied.

"And the boy?"

"She killed him of course, when she suspected what he was."

"Michael must not know of this," the female voice commanded firmly. "He must be kept in the dark. Do you understand? He must not know!"

There was movement, then the door started to open from the inside. Tom froze. His heart was beating so fast he could no longer distinguish the separate thuds. It simply thrummed like the wings of a humming bird, one continuous high-pitched note within his chest cavity. The door swung open fully and Gabriel backed out.

"See that it is done. The trouble that boy could bring, I cannot imagine. It could be the end of us!" she said anxiously through the open door.

Tom reacted on instinct. He spun himself in place and bolted for the next door down, opening it and launching himself inside in one swift motion. Thundering footsteps erupted from back down the hall. They were going in the opposite direction, she hadn't seen him. He collapsed against the door, breathing in heavy floods of air as he sank to the floor. *That was close... Too close,* he thought to himself.

The classroom that he'd entered was dark and empty. There was no domed roof or spectacular display of the heavens in this classroom. It looked like it hadn't been used in centuries, more of a store cupboard than a place of learning. He waited until he heard Raphael's footsteps leaving the adjacent classroom, then pulled himself to his feet. Quietly, he opened the door and peered out into the hallway. It was deserted.

*

Tom's thoughts were racing as he made his way swiftly back to the common room. '*What boy were they talking about?*' '*What woman?*' '*Why would they cause so much trouble?*'. He burst into the common room and found Mary seated merrily in her usual armchair at the very back.

"Hi!" she said, noticing his approach and marking her page in the large book she was reading with what looked like an old sock. "You don't look so well Tom, What's the matter?"

Tom quickly explained to Mary the conversation he'd overheard on the Astronomy floor.

"So?" he said, too impatient to wait for her response. "That's weird right?"

"Definitely," she said, still mulling over Tom's voracious recanting of the events. "You know, you really shouldn't be eaves dropping on the Heads of House, Tom. You could get in so much trouble."

"Never mind that," he said impatiently. "Who do you think they were talking about?"

"I don't have the slightest idea," she replied, frankly. "What kind of wicked woman would kill her own son?"

"Yeah but Raphael said she only did it because she 'suspected what he was.' What do you suppose that means?"

"Maybe it means he was evil?" Mary offered.

"I think we can agree on that much," Tom said without satisfaction. "They're at this school with us whoever they are, anyone come to mind?"

"You mean apart from Finley?" she grinned. "No, I can't think of anyone fitting that description."

They left the common room shortly after and headed for their next class. Tom's mind was still buzzing with questions about what he had heard earlier. *An evil boy at the school guarded by angels? Guarded by Michael himself? The highest-ranking archangel who had cast Lucifer down into the abyss and defeated countless other demons since that time. It didn't seem plausible how someone could get in here and be walking around amongst everyone else, completely unnoticed. The place had Death for a doorman for Christ's sake!*

Next period was music (or Pleasing Music through the Ages to give it it's full name listed on Tom's timetable). He didn't mind this class, especially since he'd heard that one of the teachers at the school at the moment was none other than John Lennon. Apparently, the music teachers, like the teachers from a lot of the other departments, were highly rotational and only a select few stayed on as staff in a permanent capacity.

For now, the teacher they'd gotten hadn't been an ex-Beatle, but he had turned out to be quite an entertainer none-the-less. Mr Holly was his name (though he'd told them to call him 'Buddy' from the outset). Apparently, he was famous for a few years in the fifties when rock 'n' roll was just getting up and started, then he died at just twenty-two years old. Like Tom, he was a member of that exclusive club whose members could claim to have died as victims of a plane crash. Only this guy Buddy had actually been on the plane when it crashed into a field in pastoral Iowa one cold night back in February nineteen-fifty-nine. There'd been other musicians on that plane too, or so Buddy had told them, but Tom hadn't heard of any.

"They called it '*the day the music died*'," Buddy told them proudly.

He had some energy about him, that was for sure. A gangly, bespectacled, bow-tied young man with a well-mannered yet mischievous nature, the kind of presentable young man parents preferred to see taking their daughters to proms and high school dances, Tom imagined. During their first class with him, which had been a few weeks ago now, he had pulled out his Fender Stratocaster and played them one of his hits that'd gone to number three on the '*Billboard Top 100 chart*' back in fifty-seven. It was called '*Peggy Sue*'. Tom couldn't help beaming as he watched Buddy jive away on the makeshift stage at the front of the classroom. Mary, sat next to him, clapping along as the young teacher crooned and tapped his foot to the beat, eyes gleaming at them through his thick horn-rimmed frames. When the class ended, Tom felt like he'd been at a rock show rather than a music class.

The classroom had been set up to Buddy's specifications. It resembled a town hall, lined with foldable chairs all facing a wooden stage at the front where he stood. Later on, Tom had had a fantastic time asking Mary about all the music teachers she'd gotten over the years. There had been Beethoven, Mozart, Handel and Bach from the classical period; and then there had been this medieval Italian guy called Guido who had claimed to be the 'inventor of western music', or something like that; then there had been Miles Davis and Robert Johnson (who apparently had made a deal with the Devil to gain mastery of the guitar in exchange for his soul – but it can't have been true, otherwise he would've went straight to hell without collecting two-hundred pounds and not teaching music to a bunch of kids at St Michael's); and more recently they'd had a few teachers who'd been a huge hit with the kids still around from the late seventies and early eighties. Mr Bolan who'd been in a band called T-Rex and Mr Morrison from The Doors had both sent the girls wild (apparently one girl named Amanda-Jayne Belnik had fainted and had to be propped in a chair and slapped repeatedly in the face until she came round again). Tom was eagerly looking forward to seeing what teachers he'd get during his time at St Michael's.

He'd almost forgotten the conversation he'd overheard on the Astronomy floor until it came crashing back to him the next morning when classes had ended. Finn had met them outside the common room and they'd signed him in as usual.

"Why don't you spend some time at your own house for a change?" The lanky youth behind the desk had said.

"Shut it four-eyes before I sock ya," Finn spat back.

Tom had poked fun at Finn for the Americanism

which had rolled off his tongue so naturally he hadn't even noticed it.

"You've been spending too much time with these yanks mate. Since when do people from Chorley say 'sock ya'?" he'd laughed at him.

Finn had gotten all shy and muttered something about 'socking' Tom too if he wasn't careful. It was when he'd mentioned that they should spend more time down in the Deuteronomy common room that Tom had suddenly remembered the conversation that'd been worrying him from the previous evening. He quickly regaled Finn with the troubling tale.

"I bet it's that creepy kid that sat next to us in Ancient History," he offered.

Tom, who'd forgotten all about the boy who'd made his arm break out in a field of goose pimples, pictured his pale ashen face and was suddenly convinced Finn was right.

"I've got another class with him too – *Immortal Moralities* with Professor Kant. I overheard some girls saying they saw him talking with Raphael in the garden terrace last night," Finn continued.

"It has to be him then, I'm sure of it," Tom said, now all but convinced. "They said his mother had killed him once she suspected what he was. What d'you think that means?"

"Maybe he's some kind of part frog part rabbit demon?" Finn offered.

"I'm serious, Gabriel sounded really worried about him. Like she thought he was the antichrist or something…"

"More like she thought he needed some antiperspirant. Did you smell him? He stank!"

Tom fell silent and Mary moved beside him on the

couch.

"I wouldn't worry about it too much, Tom. Whatever it is, Raphael and Gabriel will take care of it," she said placing her hand on his shoulder comfortingly.

Tom appreciated her warm touch. It'd been a while since he'd felt the reassuring hand of another person. He was growing increasingly fond of Mary and he wasn't sure what that meant exactly. He'd never had a female friend back on Earth. He'd had acquaintances of course but nothing that came close to what he would describe as a friendship. This lack of female companionship meant he didn't know where the line was drawn between friendship and romance or if there even was a line to be drawn in the first place. The way Mary sat hip-to-hip with him on the couch just now made him think that she was perhaps harbouring similar feelings, yet neither of them knew exactly what they were or what to do with them. His inexperience with girls and romantic relationships in general left him confused about how to proceed with the matter. He still daydreamed about Alice and could picture the way she whipped her long blonde hair like a rope lassoing his attention to her every time she entered a room, but he was beginning to wonder if dreams were all that would ever be. He would rather something real and maybe that was what was growing just now between Mary and him. Unlike Finn, he didn't mind that her choice in clothing was slightly out of the ordinary and drew mocking glances wherever she went; he found it appealing. He even thought it lent her a certain charm and originality that made her different from everyone else, but in a good way, and Tom was finding himself increasingly taken with it. He almost felt privileged in a way that he could recognise this about her. It was like he alone could see past the material surfaces that made everyone else sneer at her and see what was underneath that baggy blue jumper with the holes and those knitted polka-dot tights that looked so itchy. When Tom looked at her, he saw her for what she was: an incredibly kind and beautiful young woman.

Chapter Sixteen
A History of St Michael's

Tom sat by himself at a small desk on the second floor of the library, staring at the cover of the large book that Mary had left for him. Her shift had started later that day and Tom had offered to take her down and keep her company while she catalogued records, checked indexes and returned books to their homes. The book she'd left was called *'A History of St Michael's'*. She'd said that everything he wanted to know about St Michaels was in this book, which made sense judging by the size of it. Tom flipped it open and read the brief introduction.

> *St Michaels was founded approximately twelve hundred years before the birth of Jesus of Nazareth by three of God's most trusted Angels; Michael, Gabriel and Raphael. The purpose of the institution is to transfer the knowledge held by the Watcher Angels to the souls of mortals so that one day they may join their order and ascend to the Realm of the Watcher.*

Tom remembered as much from Gabriel's speech to the new students at the orientation he'd attended in this hall on his first day. He flipped to the page of contents and quickly skimmed the list. The second chapter caught his eye – *Topography of St Michael's – pages 50 - 65.* He

129

flicked to page fifty and read the first few paragraphs.

St Michaels School for Watchers is located in the Fields of Vilon, also known as The First Heaven, situated between the realm of Purgatory and the Second Heaven. The tower is so big that it stretches beyond the First Heaven and ends approximately five-hundred cubits into the Second Heaven. The First Heaven is under the administration of Gabriel, and thus, is home to water; the element to which she ascribes. The landscape is characterised by dark clouds heavy with moisture, vast swamp lands and by great rivers and lakes that punctuate the land there. During the rainy season, these bodies flood their banks and the entirety of The First Heaven becomes one great ocean. It was from this ocean that God sent the great flood that washed away all of mankind (save for Noah and his Ark.)

Since St Michaels has so many floors, only the first five hundred reside within the First Heaven. The remaining floors are in Rakia (known as the Second Heaven), which falls under Jurisdiction of the Archangel Raphael. It is forbidden for any uninitiated student at St Michaels to enter the Second Heaven, since it is home to John the Baptist and to Jesus of Nazareth. The lands there are characterised by pearly beaches and crystal shores and by great forests.

Tom flipped back to the table of contents and

scanned the list again, turning this time to *The Faculty at St Michaels – pages 240 - 257.*

The faculty at St Michaels is selected by the three Heads of House. Each Head selects the persons they wish to teach the students under his or her own House. The faculty members are selected based on the criterion each Head holds most vital for that subject. The pool of ex-mortals from which the faculty are selected reside within the Third Heaven, which is home to the Gardens of Eden.

Each faculty member serves on average six months to a year as staff at St Michael's, before returning to the Third Heaven (which they are all, without exception, eager to return to). On returning, they are often accompanied by the archangel Azrael, who holds dominion over the Third Heaven, and collects a store of the fruit known as 'manna' (which is the primary food source of the angels) to take back to St Michaels.

During their stay at the school, the classrooms of each faculty member are modified to the individual specifications for their 'ideal learning environment'. Then, when they leave, the classrooms are reverted back to their original state. Michelangelo famously had his art room at the school converted into an exact replica of the Sistine Chapel, which he said, 'was as good, if not better than his original'.

Tom flipped back to the contents again, this time turning to *Graduation from St Michaels – pages 2,345 – 2,371.*

Upon successful graduation from St Michaels, the student will have successfully acquired knowledge sufficient to join the ranks of the Watchers as a Trainee. They will be taken by their Head of House to the five-hundredth floor of the tower, then from there they will ascend to the Second Heaven through the upper levels of the tower and then onwards through the Third, Fourth, Fifth and Sixth Heavens, until they are eligible for entry to the Seventh Heaven, which is the Realm of the Watcher and of the Lord God Almighty. At this stage, they will be given the suffix 'el' to their name which denotes a heavenly being.

Mary (who had been fifteen feet up a ladder propped against a bookshelf across the room, when he last looked) was suddenly by his side again.

"Find the answers you were looking for?" she said, peering at his current page over his shoulder.

"Eh, yeah, sort of," Tom replied. "It's so big it'd take me years to read it all."

"I haven't read it all yet and I've been here for thirty years," she admitted, bashfully, "but it's great for reference though. Have you found the chapter about the lineage yet?"

Tom had forgotten all about the lineage. He remembered Gabriel mentioning something about it during orientation but had completely forgotten to follow up on it.

"Oh yeah!" he cried. "What is that all about?"

"Why don't you turn to the chapter and see?" she smiled.

Tom flipped the heavy book back to the start and found the chapter on lineage – *The Angelic Bloodline - pages 80 – 91.*

"That's the one," Mary said, peering over his shoulder again.

The chapter began with a small quote.

And there shall come forth a shoot from the stump of Jesse, and a branch shall grow out of his roots, and from this branch the descendants of Michael shall come forth.

"What does that mean?" he asked, perplexed.

"Why don't you keep reading," she proudly prompted.

Tom turned back to the book and read on.

Three thousand years ago, The Lord instructed Michael, his most trusted angel, to start a bloodline on Earth. A bloodline from which would arise a league of Watchers to serve The Lord in Heaven and protect the realms of God from the advances of Satan. Michael was given the name Jesse (or Yishai in Hebrew, which means 'God's Gift'), when he was born the son of Obed, and grandson of Ruth and Boaz. He lived a simple life in Bethlehem, in Judah, with his wife who bore him seven sons and two daughters. He worked as a sheepherder where he could spend the majority of his time in commune with The Lord.

One day, the prophet Samuel was sent by The Lord to visit Michael in Bethlehem and anoint the next King of Israel as one of his seven sons. With God's guidance, Samuel would choose to anoint David, the youngest of Michael's sons, as the next King of Israel. The royal lineage of King David would eventually give birth to Jesus of Nazareth, the son of the Lord God Almighty and descendent of the Archangel Michael, nearly one thousand years later. When Michael finally died, at the age of one hundred and three, he would return to Heaven and be remembered as one of the four ancient Israelites who died without sin.

Every student admitted into St Michael's School for Watchers is from the angelic bloodline that Michael began over three thousand years ago. However, not all of Michael's descendants are eligible for enrolment; those who have surpassed the age of eighteen are beyond the age of requirement and are no longer sufficiently malleable to become a Watcher. This is principally because the years spent on Earth shape the minds of man to the extent that they are no longer open to the true learnings of the divine. The mind of the adult has grown past the age of enlightenment; the age in which a young Watcher's mind can be expanded to the extent that it can accommodate the knowledge *passed down from the angels. An adult faced with such knowledge would simply regard it as incomprehensible and gobbledygook, whereas the young Watcher can see the knowledge for its true form and its true purpose.*

Tom hesitated while he processed what he had just read, *descendent of Michael? Me? Are they serious?*

"Is this true?" he said, staring up at Mary in disbelief.

"Afraid so," she grinned.

"So, everyone here is…" he began.

"Yup," she confirmed. "Every last student is a descendent of Michael."

"Does Finn know about this?" he blurted, unable to wrap his mind around the sheer scale of this astounding revelation.

"I doubt it," Mary sneered. "He probably wouldn't care anyway if someone had told him."

"This is definitely something they should tell you from the start." he said, slightly annoyed that he was only finding out about this now.

"Well, maybe they'd prefer students to find it out for themselves?" she shrugged.

"Does this mean we're descendants of Jesus too?" Tom asked, willing to believe anything now.

"Well no. Remember Michael (or Jesse as he was called back then) had seven sons and two daughters who each had their own lineage. So the chances of being descended from Jesus are extremely slim. It is possible I guess, as you'll learn in *Ancient History Revisited,* he did father two children, but it's very unlikely. You are however one hundred percent a descendent of Michael, and so am I," she smiled. "Isn't it strange how all of our family trees meet at the same place three thousand years ago? It's like we're one big extended family."

"Yeah, I guess you're right," Tom replied, unsure of
how he felt about this – especially since he had his eyes
on one particular member of that extended family who he
definitely would rather he wasn't related to.

"Anyway, did you find the chapter about The
Headmaster?" Mary asked.

Tom didn't know how much more of this he could
take, but he flipped back to the table of contents
obediently and found the chapter he was looking for near
the centre of the list. *The Headmaster -pages 457 – 465.*

*The position of Headmaster at St Michael's is
presently filled by the archangel Azrael (formerly
known as 'the Angel of Death'). He has held the
position at the school since retiring from his previous
role in the year 1147 AD. Azrael is the second longest
serving headmaster at the school after Raziel; who
served since the school's creation in 1196 BC. Azrael
does however hold the title of the longest serving
Angel of Death; he has escorted the souls of Jesus of
Nazareth, John the Baptist and Peter the Apostle to
the Afterlife, amongst others of note. As Angel of
Death, Azrael's touch was deadly to any living soul
who came into contact with it. However, if you have
already departed from the land of the living, there is
still good reason to fear Azrael's touch: a single prod
from his finger is known to cause excruciating agony
to souls in the Afterlife.*

Headmaster's Duties

The main duties of the headmaster at the school include: transporting those students who fail to graduate before the Indelible Deadline back to the Gates of St Peter to await judgement; transporting faculty members to and from The Third Heaven; and…

"Hang on a minute," Tom said, turning to Mary in confusion. "There's a deadline?"

"Yes," she said solemnly.

"How long is it exactly?"

"Fifty years. Look, there's a whole chapter on it, if you flip back to the contents."

Tom quickly did the math in his head.

"That means you've only got… seventeen years left!" he said incredulously, his voice cutting through the sacramental silence of the library.

Mary nodded. He could tell she was trying to look like this fact didn't bother her, but he knew that it did. He flipped back to the contents and found the required chapter – *The Indelible Deadline – pages 117 - 123*. He read through the first page of the chapter quickly.

The Indelible Deadline was put in place at St Michaels by the Archangel Gabriel, after centuries of having students languorously neglect their time at the school. Now each new student has a total of fifty years in which to graduate. Failure to do so will result in excommunication from the school and deportation back to The Gates of St Peter to await judgement. Upon arrival at The Gates of St Peter, they will not receive any special treatment from the guards and will be sent to the back of the queue, to wait the several months it will likely take before it is their turn for Judgement.

"Wow…" Tom said looking back up at Mary. "That doesn't sound good. I'm sure there's nothing to worry about though; you'll be out of here long before Finn or me."

"I'm not so sure…" she replied, feebly. "I'm great at all the academic stuff and I ace all the written exams. It's just the physical exam I always seem to fail."

"Physical exam?" Tom replied, curiously. "What physical exam?"

"Oh, Tom it's so awful!" she cried suddenly.

"What is? What is it?" he urged.

"It's the mirror!"

"The mirror? What mirror?" A mirror didn't sound so bad. Tom was proficient in mirrors. He'd been styling his hair in them since he was six years old.

"The mirror they use for the final exam. It's like a window. It sits in a room up on the five-hundredth floor. They walk you up there one by one like you're being led to your own execution!" she said, voice starting to tremble.

"What's in this mirror? Where is it a window to?" Tom urged.

"Hell!" she cried, collapsing onto his shoulder and clutching her arms around his neck.

"You only get three attempts and I've already had two…" she sobbed.

"Three attempts to do what exactly?"

"Destroy it!" she cried.

"Destroy what?" he asked, struggling to hold her steady and comprehend what he was hearing at the same time.

"You know, one of *them*," she whispered. "A *demon*…"

Tom struggled to process what he'd just heard. *Destroy a demon? Surely they wouldn't expect a student to be able to do that?*

"I'm not sure I understand," he said quietly. "This mirror is a window to hell?"

"Yes," she said, lifting her head and wiping a heavy tear from her eye. "They keep it covered, but when they pull the cover away and leave you in the room alone, you can see it. It looks like a city, with big buildings and streets and cars. Except it isn't a city at all, not one like on Earth anyway. The buildings are on fire and there's a constant storm that blows through the streets and everything is covered in layers of orange dust. The sky is all black and scorched and the heat looks unbearable and the noise… Tom the noise… the noise is deafening. I can't do it! I don't want to. Not again! I've only got one attempt left then I'll be deported!"

She was crying into his shoulder again. He didn't know how to react. The prospect was terrifying, a door to hell in the tower! A door to hell that you had to stand in front of and wait to face something that he couldn't even wrap his head around – a demon. He stroked the back of her head and waited for the sobs to subside, until eventually she pulled away. Tom felt the wet pool of tears she'd left on his shoulder as he helped her right herself.

"I don't want to do it again," she mumbled, raising her eyes to meet his.

"Is it that bad?" he asked, already knowing the answer.

"Yes. It really is. Last time Gabriel had to rush in and save me."

Tom grimaced.

"It spoke to me," she revealed. "It told me I was worthless. Told me that stupid little girls belong in the dirt with the worms. Especially sickly and weak ones like me. It told me it was surprised that my mother had kept me alive for as long as she did and that if she'd had any sense, she would have drowned me in the bathtub, and it said she was so much happier now that I'm dead."

Tom knew this was hard for her to say. He even suspected that it might be the first time this information had left her lips. She was confiding in him something shamefully secret that she'd held on to on her own for such a long time. Something that had been building inside of her to the point of bursting, and now finally the moment of release had arrived, and she'd chosen Tom to confide in. He hated to see her this scared, but he was helpless, he knew that if she wanted to graduate from here one day and avoid being abandoned at The Gates of St Peter, then she would have to face that mirror again, and she would have to do it alone.

Chapter Seventeen
The Un-Timely Murder of Alice Albright

That evening, Tom had his first Celestial Botany class with Professor Appleseed. The class was held in the garden terrace and Tom was pleased to find himself back there. He felt his worries dwindle as he pushed through the hanging canopy and into the beautiful gardens. The strong smell of begonias filling his nostrils as he stood at the entrance and surveyed the lush Garden of Eden.

The actual Garden of Eden (he now knew thanks to *A History of St Michael's*) resided in the 'Third Heaven' – a place called '*Shehakim*' - that was where all the teachers at St Michael's went back to after their tenure at the school had ended. He wondered if it looked anything like the place where he stood now. It must have been infinitely bigger than the relatively modest gardens they had here at the school, but he found it hard to imagine how it could be any more beautiful.

The book had also described how the actual Garden of Eden contained both the *Tree of the Knowledge of Good and Evil* (from which Eve had picked the apple that led to her and Adam's banishment from the Garden), and the *Tree of Life* (which sat at the very centre of the Garden and which everything else revolved around). It was guarded at all times by two Cherubim angels that kept anyone from

141

stealing the fruit from the tree (a fruit said to be so powerful that it granted those who ate it *eternal life*). The notion had confused Tom. He assumed that since the Garden of Eden was in Heaven, then surely you had to be dead to get to it, meaning eternal life would already be a redundant concept.

The class had gathered near the back of the terrace next to the large samanea tree. The starlight bounced from their faces as it shone luminously through the large glass habisphere. Professor Appleseed had issued each of them with a small trowel and thick leather gloves. There was only ten or twelve of them in the class, as the groups had to be kept relatively small to avoid disturbing the fauna in the garden.

Neither Mary nor Finn had this class with him, but there was one familiar face that he certainly didn't mind seeing again: it was Alice. She smiled at him, as she watched him approach the group that was gathered under the tree.

"Hello again," she said, as Tom took his place with the rest of the class.

He noticed that she wasn't accompanied by the usual cohort of giggling deputies that seemed to constantly be at her side. He liked her much better on her own. In his experience, girls like her always found it easier to be themselves when they didn't have to maintain the perpetual façade of 'cool' around their followers.

"Hi!" Tom said, trying to sound casual but failing miserably.

Professor Appleseed instructed the class to find a partner that they would be working with for the day.

"Do you want to pair up?" Alice asked him, catching him off guard.

"Sure, that would be great," he replied, dropping his

trowel to the floor and feeling his cheeks turn a bright shade of pink. He always seemed to lose motor control in his hands whenever Alice spoke to him.

The class was tasked with collecting three different species of edible fruits from the garden, then meeting back under the tree after an hour to discuss what they'd found. Tom, who had attended two weeks of Scouts before throwing in the towel, knew nothing about foraging or any kind of survival in the wild for that matter. He considered himself as useless as a chocolate teapot in any kind of survival situation and suspected that he would have lasted no longer than a few hours back on Earth if, say, he'd found himself locked out of the house one day. They'd probably have found him curled in a ball at the back of the garden, frozen to death or poisoned from sampling his parents potted plants in a desperate attempt to satiate his hunger. The daydream amused him, but it was pretty much entirely accurate.

Alice led him away from the rest of the group and deep into the undergrowth. Tom followed obediently, letting her take the reins on this Robinson Crusoe like expedition. They walked half blinded by the foliage around them, pushing large leaves and branches aside as they carefully stepped through the plant life. Tom suddenly had a thought which distracted him from everything else around him.

"There aren't any spiders in here, are there?" he asked, conversationally.

She laughed. "Are you afraid of them?"

"Well as a matter of fact, yes," Tom replied, batting a large flying insect from his shoulder.

"Don't worry, I don't think there are any poisonous ones," she said, still laughing at him.

Great, Tom thought to himself. *As long as they're not poisonous. God forbid they be poisonous. But what about all the*

143

ones that aren't poisonous? He suddenly envisioned a large bird-eating spider, remembering that they weren't poisonous and felt a shiver run down his spine.

Alice had gotten quite a bit ahead of him now and he hurried to catch up with her. When he found her, she was stood under a particularly colourful looking tree that had sprouted some kind of yellowish fruit that Tom had never seen before.

"What are these?" he asked, reaching up and picking some of the fruit from the branch nearest to him.

"They're called Soapberries," she replied.

Tom put it to his nose and sniffed it. It didn't smell particularly soapy to him.

"Excellent if you're looking to make soap or hair dye, but not so great for eating I'm afraid. Unless you want crippling stomach cramps."

"Oh," Tom replied, remembering his daydream and dropping the fruit to the ground. "I'll pass on the soapberries then, I think."

"I'm pretty sure that if we keep heading in this direction for another five minutes or so, we should come across a pitaya tree," she said, pointing in the direction behind her.

"Excellent. Lead the way," Tom replied, cheerfully, having absolutely no idea what a pitaya tree was.

They trampled on through the undergrowth, Alice leading the way, and Tom slowly bringing up the rear. He watched her expertly navigate herself around a prickly looking bush, and before long he found himself unable to look away from her. She moved with an ethereal fluidity. She took to this environment so naturally. He imagined she must have been spawned from some heavenly garden like this, instead of midwestern America, like she'd told him in Professor Santi's art class.

"What's it like where you're from?" he asked, as she held back a branch to stop it from slapping him in the face.

"Oh, it's ok," she replied casually. "There's a lot of rich people with big houses and fancy cars. I wish I'd gotten to see more of the world though. I never really left Indiana while I was alive. I never even got to go to my senior prom…"

She turned suddenly melancholy, as she examined the old memories from her life, then brushed the feeling off just as fast as it'd come on.

"What about you? You're from England aren't you?" she asked.

"Yorkshire," Tom said proudly. "Home to Sheffield United Football Club and the Arctic Monkeys."

"The who?" she asked, puzzledly.

"Never mind," Tom replied, forgetting that particular band wouldn't have existed while she was alive.

He wanted to ask her what awful thing had cut her beautiful life so short, but he was beginning to think it might be rude to ask (akin to an inmate asking another inmate what awful crime they'd committed to be banged up in prison for so long). Thankfully, he didn't have to ponder that thought for long.

"So how did you die?" she asked offhandedly, as if she were merely commenting on the weather, rather than posing a deeply personal question.

Tom was unsure how to phrase the bizarre means by which he'd met his end. He remembered the looks on Finn and Mary's faces when he'd told them and didn't want to relive that disaster again. So, for both of their sakes, he decided he would tell a little white lie to avert the dumbfounded response that would surely come after the revelation.

"Motorcycle accident," he said quickly, unsure of

145

where that particular answer had sprung from.

"Hmm," she said, seeming to consider this. "You're not one of those idiots that thinks they're Evel Knievel are you?"

"Who?" Tom asked, genuinely puzzled.

"Oh yeah, I keep forgetting we're from different times," she chuckled. "Still, you don't seem like the motorcycle type to me."

"Ok, that was a lie," Tom said, before he could help himself. "I just didn't want to get the same reaction I got the last time I told someone how it happened. I'm sorry…"

She frowned at him, then after a moment's consideration she said, "okay, I forgive you. But no more lies."

Tom breathed a quick sigh of relief. For a second, he thought he might have ruined things with Alice for good.

"It was a plane crash," he said abruptly, catching her off guard again.

"Honestly, this time?" she said, raising her eyebrows at him doubtfully.

"Cross my heart, hope to die."

"In case you hadn't noticed that promise doesn't mean much anymore," she replied, and they both laughed.

"I'm serious though, I did die in a plane crash. Well I wasn't on the plane you see, it was more like I died when a plane crashed into *me.*"

She stared at him incredulous. Eyes as wide as two large soapberries. "Really? You're kidding me, right?" she gaped at him.

"Afraid not," he replied, solemnly.

"How does that happen? Were you hanging around on the runway at the airport or something?"

"No, I was just in my bedroom playing Xbox."

"Playing what?"

"Never mind," he said quickly. "Basically, a plane crashed into my house. I was the only one home thankfully, but yeah, that's how I died."

"Wow. You definitely deserve some kind of award for that one, most action-packed way to die?"

Tom smiled. He found he was comfortable talking about this around her. Although the topic of conversation wasn't exactly the most romantic, he suspected they were starting to get on quite well together regardless.

"So how about you?" he asked, attempting to keep the momentum of the conversation flowing.

"I drove a train off a bridge," she said quickly, managing to keep a straight face.

Tom burst out laughing. "Very funny," he said. "But seriously, how did it happen?"

They'd walked out into a little clearing around a small pond that was hidden in the midst of the wildlife. She sat on the grass beside the water and looked up at him. "Haven't you heard?" She said feigning surprise. "I was the Green River Killer's last victim."

Tom sat on the grass beside her and stared out at the pond. There were yellow tropical looking fish swimming lazily through the shallow waters.

"They're banana fish," she said, noticing him watching. "Aren't they lovely?"

Tom wasn't sure how to respond. "Who's the Green River Killer?" he said, finally.

"Gary Ridgeway," she said, staring at the banana fish intently.

Tom fell silent. Then, to his surprise, she ejaculated the whole story like it'd been desperate to escape her lips.

"We were visiting my grandparents in Seattle. That's where I met him. He said his name was Gary. He was

147

nice. He showed me a picture of his son and asked if I needed a ride home. I got in his truck and it had all these kids' toys scattered around on the back seat. I remember thinking '*this guy must really love his kids*.' He was really chatty. Asked me what I was doing out here on my own. He drove me to a little cabin at the edge of the wood, not far from the highway. Said he needed to grab something real quick and I should just wait in the car, and he'd be right back."

Tom was stunned at the rate this was rolling off her tongue. The fact she could even speak about this was impressive, let alone recant the whole sordid tale for the god-knows how many'th time. She spoke about it with an easy calm that was almost unnatural. In fact, it was downright spooky.

"You don't have to... if it's too hard," he offered, while she paused for air.

"No, it's ok," she said, firmly. "I want you to know." She gritted her teeth and picked up where she'd left off. "When he came back, he was acting really strange. He wouldn't look at me. I asked him if he was going to start the truck and he said he didn't need to."

Tom was feeling uncomfortable. He wasn't sure he wanted to hear this. Their pleasant walk through the gardens had quickly turned quite sinister.

"Alice, seriously," he said quietly. "You don't have to do this."

She continued regardless.

"He swung something at me. It was a crowbar or something. I didn't even know he was holding it. It hit me in the face right under my eye and my head whipped back and hit the glass. Then he hit me again, and that's when I blacked out. Uriel showed me the rest. It was horrible what he did."

"That's awful," Tom said, appalled by what he'd heard. "I'm so sorry Alice." His pained expression reflected the agony he felt hearing her recant her story.

"You've nothing to be sorry for," she replied, facing him now. There was pain in her eyes, but it wasn't as clear as he expected it would be - like it'd been diluted over the years since it happened. Perhaps each time she relived it, the experience left her a little bit at a time, an exorcism of sorts. Maybe that's what she was doing now; recanting the tale to exorcise the pain. Like ripping off a band aid repeatedly until it no longer hurt.

"What were you doing wandering the streets at night in a city you didn't know?" Tom blurted, before he could help himself, then immediately regretting the question.

"It wasn't at night," she said, defensively, eyes furrowing. "It was early morning... Real early. Sometime before seven I think. I was out running along Pacific Highway not far from my nana's farm. He stopped when he saw me. He was so friendly I just assumed he worked for my grandpa or something and was on his way down to the farm. It wasn't until years later that they found me, down by the Green River behind the Tacoma Airport. By that time, there wasn't much left of me. They had to use DNA samples to identify my body. They found a match with my mother and that's how they knew it was me."

"Uriel showed you all this?" Tom asked, disturbed yet curious.

Alice nodded. "In that magnifying glass she keeps in her office. She thought I'd want to know, when they found my body n'all, so she sent for me. I got called out of class and taken down to her office and she told me they'd found me. I was buried in the woods, with six other girls. She'd known this for years, of course, but she thought I'd want to know that they'd found me. I asked if I could see, and she refused but when I insisted, she finally took out her goldfish bowl thing and we watched it together. We watched the police dogs, and my parents crying, and we watched them give me a proper burial. I liked that part. It's so long ago now, I'm mostly over it, I guess. It still hurts thinking about it sometimes, but not as much as it used to."

She brushed two fingers under her right eye then lifted herself off the grass and walked around the edge of the pond. "Look there it is!" she smiled back at him, pointing off into the underbrush.

Tom got up and followed her as she led the way through a short crop of bushes to the tree that was hidden near the far edge of the pond.

"So, this is a pitaya tree?" he asked, arriving beneath it. It was an odd-looking thing. Sort of like a cross between a cactus and a palm tree, but with strange purple fruit growing from its branches.

"Thank you for telling me all that," he said, eyeing her carefully as she reached up and picked a large purple bulb from the closest branch. "You really didn't have to relive that for me. You should've just told me you were in a motorcycle accident or something."

"It's ok," she said, reassuringly, as she handed the strange fruit over to him. "Everyone knows anyway. It was the talk of the school back when it happened. Gabriel even had to issue a bulletin announcement to tell everyone to stop discussing it in the corridors."

Tom felt uncomfortable. He didn't like the fact that some vile, murdering coward had had his slimy hands all over her. He didn't like the fact that she'd been left in the woods to rot with the corpses of six other girls who'd also fallen victim to this monster's charm. He felt like he'd gotten off easy compared to the way in which she'd met her end. He couldn't imagine anything more horrible than what she'd described.

When he looked up, Alice was staring at him. "You're not going to treat me any differently now you know what's happened to me, are you?" she asked, timidly.

"Of course not," Tom assured her.

"Good," she said, smiling at him. "Because we've still got two more edible fruits to find!"

Tom beamed back at her. How quickly she'd switched back to her jovial light-hearted self was astonishing – *what an extraordinary girl*, he thought as he followed her back into the bush.

Chapter Eighteen
The House of Numbers (Babylon Revisited)

After class had finished, they had a free period to spend as they pleased. Despite what he'd told her in the gardens, Tom was seeing Alice in a completely different light now, but this new light shone even brighter than the one before. There were layers beneath the surface and he'd started to peel them away and discover the intricacies of who she really was, the nuances of her person. Much more than a pretty face it seemed.

He felt ashamed for judging her that way; like he expected her looks to be the sole attribute defining her character. As they left the terrace, Tom went to say goodbye, but she cut him off before he could start.

"You're in Revelation, aren't you?" she asked abruptly as she brushed aside the hanging canopy concealing the exit.

"Yes. How come?" Tom replied.

"I'm guessing you've never seen the Numbers common room before, have you?" she continued.

"I haven't, actually."

"Well," she said, almost afraid now. "Would you like me to show you?"

Tom barely needed a millisecond to consider before agreeing to the offer. As was becoming habit, he let her

lead the way as they filed out into the corridor.
Incidentally, the Numbers common room was only one
floor down from the garden terrace, so for the first time
since arriving at the school, he found there was no need
to take the elevator.

The staircase spiralled around an unfathomably large
drop in the centre. Tom peered over the edge
precariously, seeing no bottom. It spiralled down so far
that the floors at the furthest reaches of his sight became
blurred and dark, merging into the darkness. It was like
staring over the edge of the Earth into oblivion. He
wondered, if he were to jump, just how long it would take
for him to hit the bottom. Long enough to tire from
screaming, he suspected. Would he simply fall in silence
for the majority of the descent? Like a skydiver without a
parachute, hitting terminal velocity, then plummeting at
the same continual speed until impact.

He wondered what it must've been like for the
people on the airplane that had so rudely plunged straight
into his bedroom. Were they unconscious at the moment
of impact? Or were they awake and fully aware of what
was happening? Strapped to their seats. Oxygen masks to
their faces. Quietly bracing. Utterly helpless to avert their
impending doom.

He wondered if the pilots had made the conscious
decision to direct the plane into his row of houses. Maybe
it had been to avoid the more densely populated area at
the heart of Bridlington? Maybe the co-pilot had locked
himself inside the cockpit, disengaged the autopilot then
trimmed the plane nose-down, launching a one-man
vendetta against mankind and steering the aircraft directly
into the ground, like that nutjob from Germanwings.
Taking his own tortured loneliness out on hundreds of
unsuspecting passengers.

He guessed that Uriel must know more about the

exact circumstances surrounding the crash. She had, after all, known all the details of Alice's murder at the hands of that deranged serial killer in Seattle. Maybe she knew everything about every student at the school and all the gory details about how each of them had died. She'd probably watched each of their deaths in her little magnifying glass while reclining at her desk in the Enrolment Office and sipping a milkshake from Ambrosia's.

Alice seemed to have noticed that Tom had broken away into his own quiet reverie. She hadn't felt the need to break the silence, as she led them noiselessly down the stairs to the House of Numbers. The only sound the slapping of their feet on the cold stone steps as they descended.

The floor designated to the House of Numbers spread before them as Alice pushed through the heavy wooden doors. It was entirely as Tom had expected it to be. Pristine. Immaculate. Opulent. Beautiful. Like the palaces of middle eastern princes or the penthouse at Trump Towers. Everything was illuminated with gold and crystal. A fountain flowed next to the doorway, right there in the corridor, splashing water into a shallow pool filled with pearls.

"Wow…" Tom uttered. Rendered nearly speechless by the magnality of it.

"Pretty cool, yeah?" Alice said, throwing Tom a seductive wink. "Wait until you see the common room."

She led them through the golden halls, staying patiently quiet while Tom absorbed his surroundings until at last, they arrived at the door to the Numbers common room.

"Ready?" she said.

He didn't know what to expect. Probably some

ridiculously grand suite to match the opulence of the corridors. As the heavy doors swung open, Tom was immediately struck with the sounds of trickling water that was audible among the chatter from the students. The room was so bright that he had to shield his eyes at first, while Alice quickly signed him in, until they adjusted to the light fully. Starlight flooded the room.

Since the House of Numbers was happily located in the upper reaches of the tower, it sat enviously above cloud level, so no constant rain battered the windows like the levels below. The light was clearly an integral part of the architectural design of the common room. It bounced off the gold surfaces and ubiquitous mirrors, illuminating every last corner of the room.

Among the gold furnishings and intricately designed mirrors were fountains. Dozens of them. The rhythmic splashing punctuated the air. Each fountain rang in its own unique key created by its own precise flow of water. The effect was such that, when placed on top of each other, each sound complimented the others like sections in an orchestra, creating a sweet musical tapping that was exceptionally pleasing to the ear.

Next to each fountain was a neatly situated coupling of couches and armchairs that were occupied by small groups of students who were chattering quietly or engrossed in their books. At the centre of the room was a large circular garden with trees shading those tables beneath them. Alice perched herself into a delicate looking lounger close to this garden and Tom sat down next to her.

"So. Was it better than you expected?"

"Definitely," Tom replied. Still marvelling at the room.

"I'm used to it now," she said. "It'll be twenty years for me in a few months since, you know, the whole

Seattle thing. Twenty years since starting at St Michaels. You know Gabriel told me I'm tipped for prefect selection if I wanted it. It's tempting. It means I would get a pass from the final exams and get an extension on the deadline. But you have to have been here for twenty-five years before you're eligible, so I'd have to wait another five."

"That's not so long," Tom replied. He'd never asked himself *how* the prefects here had gotten to be prefects in the first place. He guessed that explained why most of them looked like they'd been around for well over fifty years: they didn't have that *indelible deadline* thing forcing them to take the final exams and graduate.

Alice was frowning now, she didn't seem overly thrilled about the concept of her twentieth anniversary quickly approaching. Tom changed the subject. "So, tell me more about Indiana. I've never been to the States before…"

"What do you wanna know?" she asked, smiling again.

"Where did you go to school?" he asked randomly.

"Carmel High. I was head cheerleader."

"Of course you were," Tom sighed, rolling his eyes.

"What does *that* mean?" she said, frowning at him.

"You just look like the type, that's all. I didn't mean anything bad by it," he offered, apologetically.

"Well anyway…" she continued, brushing off Tom's rude interruption. "Like I was saying, I was head cheerleader. Youngest in the school's history as a matter of fact - which annoyed plenty of the senior girls. But they didn't dare mention it as my father was on the school board and he controlled the budget for all the other extracurriculars at Carmel. Anyway, I ran practice every Tuesday night, then every Friday we travelled with the team. 'The Carmel Greyhounds' – bit of an ironic name considering we had just about the slowest team in the state. We had our own customised Greyhound bus with our logo on the side instead of the usual Greyhound badge, and every Friday we would attach streamers to the bus and make sure everyone was feeling the school spirit."

She was enjoying herself now, Tom could tell. The old memories of her life down on Earth before the murder had perked her up to the point of frenzy. Tom nodded along encouragingly while he listened to the cymbals song of her voice and when she would pause for input, he would say things like *'that's great!'* and *'wow! Really?'* until she almost tired herself out with talking.

"And for my birthdays, my parents would take me to Indiana Beach and I would ride the Hoosier Hurricane over and over until I threw up!" she said excitedly. "Then for my sweet sixteen, my parents were planning this enormous pool party at our house and they even said they would get speakers and a stage set up so one of the local bands from Carmel called *The Big Casinos* could play live, and then…"

She broke off abruptly, lost in her thoughts again. "…And then, the snow started to fall," she whispered almost to herself.

"That's one way to ruin a pool party," Tom tried, jokingly.

"Yeah," she whispered. "I forgot about the snow…"

"So, it snowed?" he asked.

"It snowed really heavy that year," she whispered. "It was only September, but the snow came down like it was the middle of January, deeper than it had been in years. They said it was the worst snow Indiana had seen since the fifties. Fall of ninety-nine. My farewell fall…"

She looked almost troubled now as the memories

came flooding back to her.

"It got so cold the pipes all burst, and the heating wouldn't work. We almost froze to death those first few nights. The snow was so bad my dad and brother had to dig us out of the back door. They said it was going to keep falling like this for at least another week. So, so… my mom wanted to get us out of town. She suggested visiting her folks out in SeaTac… in Washington."

Tom suddenly realised where this was headed. How had he been so slow on the uptake? He cursed himself and tried a desperate attempt to change the subject before it was too late.

"I've been meaning to ask you," he broke her off.

She looked up surprised by the sudden interruption. "Meaning to ask me what?" she said hesitantly.

"Professor Newton…" Tom began, not sure where he was headed with this. "I saw him hand you something after class last month, I was just wondering what that was? That was all."

"Oh…" she said, seeming suddenly embarrassed. "Oh right… that…"

She hesitated ever so slightly as she considered how to word her reply. Tom desperately tried to hide the fact that he was now petrified. His palms had started to sweat. He'd never seriously considered the idea that Finn had been right and Alice and Newton were having some kind of sordid affair and he'd caught them exchanging love notes or something equally as repulsive, but now he was positive that those were the words that were about to roll from her tongue, breaking his fragile teenage heart in one fell swing of the hammer. Or maybe she would lie. Maybe she would try and cover it up and invent some elaborate excuse for the secret note exchanging between her and the handsome yet much older astronomy professor. He braced himself for what was about to come, Alice hadn't noticed but he'd clutched the fabric of the lounger so tightly in his hands that they'd turned an angry shade of red beside him.

"Well, I guess there's no harm in telling you," she said slowly. This was it, Tom's heart was about to shatter into a million pieces inside his chest. It was milliseconds away, and he could feel it pounding furiously against his ribcage.

"Professor Newton was, handing me an invitation," she said, finally.

An invitation? Tom thought frantically. *An invitation for what?! What does this sick pervert have planned for her?! An invitation to a romantic dinner for two, I'll bet! Or even worse an invitation to his bedroom!*

"What invitation?" he asked timidly, ignoring the ceaseless pounding in his chest that was now accompanied by a painful ringing in his ears.

"An invitation to Bricktop's," she said cautiously.

Bricktop's?? What the hell is Bricktop's?

"Oh right, what's that then?" he asked, trying his best to sound only mildly interested.

She looked around before answering. There was a group of girls not far away that had been watching their conversation closely but now seemed to be staring off in random directions, as if they'd just very nearly been caught in the act of eaves dropping.

Alice moved in closer and lowered her voice to the faintest whisper. "It's like a secret club… a nightclub, or 'day club' I guess you'd call it here."

"A nightclub?" Tom asked, unable to hide his fervent curiosity now. The girls at the seats closest to them turned to stare again at his words.

"Ssshhhh!" Alice whispered. "Yes, a nightclub. But it's invitation only. It opens once a month and membership is extremely limited. In fact, I'm not sure if I'm going to get in trouble now I've told you about it."

A secret nightclub at St Michaels? Tom was intrigued by the prospect. He'd never been old enough to go to nightclubs back in England. The closest he'd gotten were the rather dismal school dances they'd held at Bridlington High at the end of every term. Sometimes some of the kids from fifth and sixth form would sneak in whiskey or vodka in hip flasks they kept in secret pockets they'd cut into the lining of their jackets. The teachers were none the wiser. Or if they did see they just didn't care. Tom could never tell which.

"Why's it called Bricktop's?" he asked curiously.

"She owns it," she smiled. "Ada Bricktop. She's a dancer and she sings. She used to own *Chez Bricktop* in Paris and other clubs in Rome and South Carolina too. Now she runs Bricktop's at St Michael's and the only admittance is by invitation only."

"So, Newton was inviting you to this nightclub then?" he asked, not yet completely unconcerned that there might still be something untoward in his intentions.

"Yes, he invites all his favourite students," she said proudly.

"Oh… Are all his favourite students attractive females by any chance?"

"No, of course not," she said reproached. "He invites a few boys as well."

"So, who else goes to Bricktops then? Apart from Newton and his preferiti," he asked.

"Well, maybe you should come and see?" she said, smiling wryly.

"You can invite me?" Tom blurted, causing the girls nearby to stare again.

"I'm not sure, maybe I can. I'll check with Newton

later. I've got him last period tonight."

Tom couldn't hold back the sheepish grin as it crept slowly across his face. *Invited to an exclusive nightclub by the prettiest girl in school. You're doing pretty well for yourself these days, old sport.* His mind swam with fantasies of potential outcomes for this date. *Was it a date?* he wondered. He wasn't sure. Besides, it wasn't even set in stone yet, Newton might refuse his invitation (*probably to fend off any unwanted competition, the old perv – keep your filthy hands off Alice, she's mine!*)

"When is it?" he asked, careful to keep his voice as low as possible now.

"Tomorrow at noon, 12pm 'til late. I've got to go now – Philosophy with Cicero."

She led them back out into the grand Numbers hallway and then back out onto the dark flagstone floors beside the elevators.

"I'll let you know as soon as I know," she said, outside the elevators.

"Sure," Tom replied. "But how will you -"

Before he could finish, the elevator doors pinged open and a rabble of students spilled out. Alice shrugged at him as she pushed her way inside the elevator, and they pinged closed before Tom could finish his sentence. *How will you let me know though?* he thought, as he watched her disappear behind the cold steel doors.

Chapter Nineteen
The Love that Dare Not Speak its Name

Tom pulled out his timetable, unsure of what he had next. He had known the entire plan for his night earlier that evening, but upon the news that he may be attending a secret nightclub at the invitation of Alice Albright, his mind had gone totally blank.

Notable Literature 12-1am – Room 33C, 46th Floor – Professor Wilde

Tom had had three prior classes with Professor Wilde over the past month. Mary would be there, which was good, but no Finn – his thoughts broke off - Mary! He'd completely forgotten about Mary! Ever since he'd been swept away in conversation with Alice at the start of Celestial Botany, he'd forgotten all about Mary! Wasn't he just thinking to himself earlier that day that he could potentially be falling in love with Mary? Was that him? Was that the same person? So much had changed since then, he wasn't sure how he felt now. Was it possible to be falling in love with two different people at the same time? He didn't know. He didn't have any experience with this sort of thing. He was a total novice when it came to romance and relationships. He'd never even had a proper girlfriend before. There'd been this one girl back in Bridlington that'd paid for his Home Economics supplies one day with a fifty-pence piece, as he'd forgotten his, and later that day someone had whispered to him that she fancied him, but that was it. That was the single line on the single page of the single book in the series called *Tom Woolberson's Guide to Relationships*. And it wasn't exactly a best seller.

Conflicted and lost in thought, he found himself down on the forty-sixth floor. He had no memory of getting in the elevator and consciously pressing the button to take him down, but he supposed he must have done since he found himself there anyway. He walked the long corridor and found room 33C. Mary was waiting for him outside with a delighted grin spread across her face.

"Hi Tom!" she beamed, as he approached.

"Hey!" he smiled back at her.

"How was Celestial Botany? Did Professor Appleseed show you the Dragon's Blood tree they've got up there? Apparently, it's the sole ancestor of all the Dragon's Blood trees they've got down in Yemen. You know its sap is red? That's why it's called Dragon's Blood: because it looks like its bleeding!"

Tom nodded in mock fascination and felt a wave of guilt wash over him like a cold blanket. He felt guilty. He actually felt guilty. Surely there was nothing to feel guilty about? He was a free man after all. There was no ring on his finger. He was free to talk to as many girls as he wanted, but still, there was a niggling at the back of his mind that told him it was right that he felt guilty. It was right that he owed Mary more than what he was currently letting on. It was like his brain was split into two. Jekyll and Hyde. Lennon and McCartney. Zuckerberg and Saverin. The two hemispheres of his brain were duelling like dragons locked in a fiery battle, breathing swathes of flames and slicing scales with razor-sharp talons. One side wanted to try his luck with Alice – the glitz, the glamour, the potential for endless notoriety among his peers and celebrity status amongst the boys at St Michael's. Then the other side saw Mary as the safer bet – the warm, comforting, gentle niceties that accompanied a stable relationship built on the strong foundations of friendship. He wanted all of these things. He wanted Alice *and* Mary and for them all to live happily under one roof, although he knew that could never happen. He didn't know how, but somehow, he'd led himself down a path of no return. At the end of this path someone was going to get hurt. He sensed its inevitability. *That's why you feel guilty, old sport*, he thought to himself.

Mary led them inside the bright classroom and grabbed their seats near the back. Although it was midnight and the sky outside was dark and speckled with stars, this classroom was illuminated with daylight. The windows looked out onto a lush green meadow which seemed just out of reach, although Tom knew it was impossible as they were forty-six floors up in the tower and God knows how many floors above the Earth. Somehow, the windows had been enchanted to show this lush scenery just outside the building. An 'angel's trick' Mary had called it when he'd asked her about it. The classroom had been modelled after one of Professor Wilde's favourite classrooms at Magdalen College in Oxford, and the large nineteenth century sash and case windows looked out onto a view of Addison's Walk and the Meadow that sat just across the river from the campus.

Although the room was beautiful and bright, Mary had also told him about the dark past that had befell their teacher back on Earth. Professor Wilde had been a popular poet and playwright back in London in the late nineteenth century. He was celebrated for his characteristic wit and dazzling conversational skill and had been a colourful 'agent provocateur' in Victorian Society, until he was unceremoniously detained and imprisoned for 'gross indecency' ("Which basically meant he had sex with men," Mary had told him).

With his reputation in tatters after lengthy and very public court proceedings, he was outcast from the high society in which he'd revelled. While imprisoned, he endured long hours of the hard labour to which he'd been sentenced. Hours of walking a treadmill and picking the knots out of old navy ropes which left his health and mental state in flagrant disregard. He collapsed while in prison due to hunger and exhaustion and ruptured his eardrum when his head hit the floor. A few years later, after his release, this injury would prove to be a contributing factor in his contracting of meningitis - from which he would ultimately succumb, in a dingy hotel room in Paris in the year nineteen hundred.

Tom enjoyed Professor Wilde's lectures and found him quite entertaining, his reputation for lightning-quick wit was surely well deserved. Right from the start of their first lecture (which had been on The Divine Comedy by Dante Alighieri) the man's charming flippancy had been impossible to resist. At one point, while talking about Dante's accusal and eventual banishment from Florence for corruption, he'd mentioned his own experience with exile.

"Alas, it was my own yearning for a life of concealment that led me to escape the shores of England to Paris. It seems the world has grown suspicious of anything that looks like a happily married life. Lest I can no longer trust myself to live amongst the brutes and illiterates, whose views on love and art are incalculably

165

stupid. Life is never fair and perhaps it is a good thing for most of us that it is not. My ordeal had filled my soul with the fruit of experience, however bitter it tasted at the time. If nothing else, I took refuge in knowing that everyone is born a king, and most people die in exile."

As was the feeling in many of the classrooms at St Michaels, the immersion was so complete that when it was time to leave he almost completely forgot where he was. He'd walk out the door at the end of class, expecting to emerge into the bright sunlit corridors of Oxford University, and would be shocked to find himself face-to-face with the hard-stone halls of St Michaels.

The remainder of the classes that night were laden with distraction. Tom couldn't concentrate. He was feeling anxious and also excited to find out if Newton would grant his invitation to the clandestine club that Alice had described. A place where the crème de la crème of society at the school would sneak off to once a month and mingle. He wanted badly to be accepted there, even if it was just to spend more time with Alice and fend off advances from any unwanted suitors.

More than that though, he found himself just wanting to fit in and to be accepted by the masses here at St Michaels. He'd always been a bit of a loner back at Bridlington High, from his first awkward few years through to his later ones, the one or two friends he'd had weren't the kind that got invited to all the parties.

Ever since Scott had died, he'd felt himself slowly drifting into isolation. He'd felt alone even when he was around people. No one except for him could understand what he was going through. The feelings of loss and guilt weighing on his soul like steel shackles, depriving him of the ability to connect with others and be light-hearted and jovial like teenagers were meant to be. He'd carried this weight for as long as he could remember. So long now that it had become a part of him.

When classes that night finally ended, Mary had noticed that something wasn't right with him.

"Everything okay, Tom?" she asked, as they were leaving their Immortal Moralities class with Professor Hume.

"Of course," he said cheerily, sounding a lot more assertive than he felt.

"You've been pretty quiet all day. I may not know you *that* well, but I think I know you well enough to tell when something's on your mind."

He'd been worried this might happen. He didn't want to lie to Mary. He respected her and knew from experience that once you started a lie, you often had to add a dozen more lies to it just to get yourself out of the situation. Then, like a house of cards, once one lie was revealed, the rest of them came tumbling down after. Laying the rickety foundations of a house of lies was the last thing he wanted to do with Mary, so he decided to at least tell her the partial truth, if only to save himself from further embarrassment later.

"I might be going to a party later," he said, as they made their way back out into the dark hallway.

"Oh, that sounds fun," she said, hesitantly. "Whose party is it?"

"I'm not sure exactly. A friend invited me," he said, trying to carefully avoid revealing too much information.

"I didn't know you had friends," she said jokingly. "I mean, other than myself and that dope Finley of course."

"Yeah, well, we just met actually. I would invite you but…"

"No, don't worry about that!" she said, reassuringly. "You go and have fun and you can tell me all about it after, if you want."

"Sure," he said, smiling at her now. That went better than he thought it would. He hadn't let on more than he needed to, and Mary seemed fine with it, though he did sense the slightest tinge of suspicion in her voice at the end there, but that was to be expected, he supposed. Besides, he wasn't even invited yet. Alice had said she'd let him know as soon as she knew, and she still hadn't let him know yet. In fact, he hadn't seen her all night. She was missing from their Heavenly Art class earlier and Tom had been actively looking out for her at every opportunity; in the halls and in the library and up at Ambrosia's, but there had been no sign of her. As far as he knew she'd disappeared into the ether, back to the heavenly garden from where she came. Like a rare exotic bird, there one minute and gone the next, never to be seen again.

Mary walked Tom back to the common room, where they'd agreed to meet Finn, once classes were out that morning. As they rounded the last corner of the Revelation hallway, they saw her standing there. She was reclined against the wall waiting for him, looking as lovely as ever; blonde hair falling casually over the shoulder of her denim jacket. Mary seemed to stiffen at the sight of her, like a cat bracing at the sight of an approaching fox.

"Hi," Alice said, smiling at him, then eyeing Mary warily.

"Oh hi, Alice," he said awkwardly, turning to Mary just as she'd opened the door to the common room.

"I'll see you later, Tom," Mary said briskly, disappearing through the door.

Alice raised her eyebrows at him as if to say, '*what's her problem?*', and Tom's cheeks flushed crimson, feeling immediately guilty for what had just transpired in the hallway.

"So…" Alice said, coolly. "I've got something for you." She pulled a folded slip of yellowed parchment from her jeans pocket and handed it to him. He unfolded the note carefully and quickly read the elegantly printed message that was inscribed on it.

I, Professor Isaac Theodore Newton (PRS), formally request the company of Master Thomas Woolberson for drinks and gossip at Bricktop's Private Members Club at noon this morn.
Very truly yours,
Isaac.

"Well?" Alice said, grinning widely at him.

"You did it!" he grinned back at her. "That's brilliant!"

"I have my ways," she said, mysteriously.

Tom wasn't sure what that meant, but he sure didn't like the sound of it.

"So, what are you going to wear?" she asked, eyeing his rather plain looking attire. Tom had been alternating between the plain black t-shirt he'd bought from Madame Bertin's last week, and the top he'd been wearing upon his arrival at St Michael's, which was also black but had a small picture of Pennywise the clown printed on the front.

"Eh… I'm not sure," he said, looking down at his crumpled t-shirt and feeling more than a little underdressed.

"Come on, we're going to Madame Bertin's," she said, heading off down the corridor.

"But, I haven't got time to put in a new order!" Tom yelled after her.

"Don't worry, she has off-the-rack!" she shouted over her shoulder.

Tom hurried after her, feeling both excited and terrified. He didn't want to wear some hilarious eighteenth-century garb that had frills and bows and those buckled shoes that Newton wore. Maybe Alice would even want him to wear a powdered wig? This was going to be a nightmare. He hadn't signed up for some fancy-dress party. Maybe that was the plan all along? Invite Tom and dress him up like a clown so he can be paraded around the party and have tomatoes thrown at him while he performed tricks and juggled for them. The court jester. *Well not on my watch!* he thought to himself. He hands down refused to wear anything that would make other people laugh at him.

He liked the clothes he was wearing now. The black allowed him to fade into the background and become an anonymous blender-inner among the rabble. Perfect for staying incognito and flying below the radar and avoiding the laugh riots that were directed at other unfortunate souls wearing much more conspicuous clothing, like Mary. Poor Mary. Was she mad at him? She didn't look happy to see Alice waiting there for him and she'd escaped into the common room before he could even say goodbye. Maybe he should just forget about this party and go back and hang out with her and Finn today? He quickly shook off the idea. No, he couldn't do that, he was committed now. And apparently, he was also committed to dressing like a royal pansy.

Alice hustled them into the elevator and hit the button for the seventy-sixth floor.

"What does she have 'off-the-rack' exactly?" Tom asked, when he'd finally gotten his breath back from running after her.

"A good selection," she said confidently. "Don't worry, you're going to look great - I'll help you pick!"

Tom wished he felt as confident as she did. He'd never had a good experience with a woman picking out the clothes he wore. When he was little, his mother used to dress him and his brother in matching green and orange dungarees and cut their hair into matching mullets; a hairstyle commonly associated with the Beastie Boys and the nineteen-eighties or with redneck truck drivers. Not with English kids from the mid-noughties. He didn't know whether she was intentionally trying to dress them like Oompa-Loompas or if it was just a happy coincidence, but once he'd grown old enough to care about the clothes he wore, he'd outright refused to let his mother pick anymore outfits for him, no matter how many jumpers she bought him for Christmas.

The doors pinged open to the mini mall like establishment on the seventy-sixth floor. They passed Ambrosia's and headed directly for Madame Bertin's. Thankfully, she was quiet. As they pushed through her door, the bell rang a pleasant jingle to alert her to their presence. She bustled out of the back with her arms full of long materials and a needle and thread bitten between her teeth.

"Bonjour mes chers!" she said, dropping the needle into the large pile between her arms.

"Hello, Madame Bertin," Alice said, pulling up to the counter.

"What can aye do for you today, my dears?" she said, in her heavily accented voice.

"My friend Tom here would like to see your off-the-rack collection please."

"Of course! Of course! If you would follow me please."

She led them into the back room, past endless racks of partially made dresses and jeans.

"What ees the occasion may I ask?" she said over her

171

shoulder as they walked.

"It's a sort of party, I guess," Tom fumbled, as he stepped over a large roll of material.

"Oh wonderful! I love a part-ee! Such part-ees we would have at the palace! The food, and the music and the champagne. Such grandeur, you wouldn't' believe!"

Tom trailed quietly behind her. He was anxiously anticipating the elaborate garments he was about to be strung up in. Alice had followed them into the back, and she was grinning widely, clearly amused by the look of panicked apprehension on his face.

"You look scared," she whispered.

"A bit," Tom replied.

"Don't worry, everything will be fine. You trust me, don't you?"

"I do," Tom said, and for some reason he meant it.

Madame Bertin had taken them into a small room at the end of the long hallway. "This is where I keep my private collection," she said, in a low seductive voice. She reached into a cupboard at the back of the room and pulled out several hangers with long suit covers on them. Tom held his breath as she handed him one of the hangers.

"I think this should be about your size," she said. "Why don't you take eet to the changing room across thee hall and try eet on, my dear?"

Tom eyed the hangar warily and did as he was told. Closing the door behind him, he hung the suit cover on the hook and began to quickly get undressed. He unzipped the black bag and underneath was a rather dashing looking maroon suit. He held it up against his chest and assessed himself in the mirror.

Not as bad as he'd expected. Not bad at all actually. It looked expensive. It was unbranded, of course, but it certainly wouldn't have looked out of place draped on a mannequin in the window of a Gucci or Armani store. There was a plain white shirt under the suit jacket, and he pulled that on first before pulling on the trousers, slipping into the jacket and fastening the two buttons in the middle. It was a little tight but over all a pretty good fit, considering it hadn't been made for him. The shirt was just loose enough that it wasn't too tight around his broad shoulders, which were often a nuisance when it came to fitted clothes. He didn't have shoes, but he reckoned he still looked pretty decent. Alice had been right. He could trust her after all. What a relief that she hadn't been secretly planning to dress him up as a clown and parade him around the party like a performing monkey. Even if it turned out that he was wrong to trust her so freely, the best way to find out if you can trust somebody is to trust them.

"Ow aar you getting on, my dear?" Madame Bertin called from the hallway.

"Good thanks!" Tom called back. He gave himself one last look in the mirror then decided he was satisfied enough to be seen in public. He pushed open the door of the changing room and emerged slowly out into the hall. He hated this part: the grand unveiling. He was too self-conscious to be breezy about it. He walked woodenly, legs stiff and back straight, like a cross between Robocop and Frankenstein.

"Don't you look handsome," Alice teased.

"Oh, shut it," Tom replied, bashfully.

"Aye think we have found aar prince charming! A perfect fit!" Madame Bertin squealed, enthusiastically. "Aar you 'appy?"

"Sure, I'll take it," Tom said.

"Excellent!" she replied. "One night's rental is fifty shekels."

173

Tom grimaced. He didn't expect it to be that expensive. That would almost be his entire allotment of shekels gone in one go. He looked at Alice who nodded encouragingly and flashed him a thumbs up. Groaning, he stepped back into the changing room and retrieved the small coin purse Uriel had given him from the back pocket of his jeans.

"Come with me my dear and aye will ring you up," Madame Bertin said, leading the way back down the long corridor.

Chapter Twenty
Horns of Plenty

Alice waved him a quick goodbye outside Madame Bertin's and promised to meet him at the top of the stairs outside the House of Numbers at noon (she hadn't revealed the location of where Bricktop's actually was yet). There were plenty of floors Tom hadn't visited. Well, hundreds in fact, but he would think something as ostentatious as a nightclub would be hard to hide.

Tom looked down at his hand which was carrying the large black suit bag containing his purchase for the day. He'd only worn a suit once before in his life and it'd been to his brother's funeral. The thought didn't exactly put him in the mood for merriment. He supposed this suit was maroon as opposed to black, and it fitted him a lot better than his funeral suit, which had been so large that he kept on tripping over the trouser legs whenever he walked.

He stood there outside the elevator for a few seconds considering his options. He could go back to the Revelation common room and see Mary and Finn, but then he'd have to explain why he'd rented the suit and likely have to dodge numerous questions regarding the party and its host. He didn't know how much trouble he'd get into for revealing the fact that there was a secret soiree held in the tower at the end of every month to his friends, but he thought it best to bite his tongue on the matter. The last thing he wanted to do was get himself or Alice into any trouble. She might never speak to him again and that was a thought too painful to consider seriously. Instead he decided he would take some time to himself. Maybe he would go for a wander in the garden terrace and stretch his legs a bit. He had been sitting down all day after all.

He slapped the elevator call button and waited the three seconds or so that it took to arrive (*these elevators really were remarkable*). Stepping inside, he hit the button for the garden terrace and waited patiently for the doors to close. Just as the two metal ends were about to meet, a hand reached out and stopped the doors dead in their tracks. It was that boy again. The one with the black hair and the crooked nose and the eerily calm expression that seemed to be eternally painted on his face.

He stood staring at Tom as the elevator doors retracted, then walked calmly into the elevator without saying a word to him. Tom could feel the hairs on the back of his neck stand on end as the boy approached him. The way he'd looked at Tom as he stood outside the elevator had been deeply unsettling. His eyes seemed to bore holes into him, and he'd looked him up and down as if measuring his proportions, so he knew how much butter to buy for cooking him later.

Tom had stepped aside and allowed the boy the space nearest the buttons. It just registered that he'd been holding his breath since first seeing the boy. He let out a long silent exhale into his chest and looked away quickly as he caught the boy's eye to his right. He felt the goosepimples start to break out on his arms again, as the elevator doors finally started to close.

What was it with this kid that made him so creepy? He watched the boy evaluate the wall of buttons and noticed that he hadn't added his own destination on top of his own. Was he going to the garden terrace too? Now he thought about it, he vaguely remembered Finn telling him that some girls had overheard Raphael and the boy locked in heated discussion somewhere in the gardens. Was he going there to meet Raphael again? Tom needed to know. He wasn't sure why but this was something he felt superseded all his other plans.

He had been planning on taking a detour to one of the lockers in the restrooms to stash his rented suit for an hour, but now he thought better of it. He wanted to follow this kid and see what he was up to. Something about him was just so unsavoury that it was obvious when you looked at him. He just looked so out of place, like the body he was in was more of a rented suit than something he was born into.

Tom flashed again on the conversation he'd overheard in Professor Newton's classroom. Gabriel had seemed almost scared at the time, which was a frightening concept in itself. She'd said something about a note… Hold on *a second… Hadn't that angel who gave them a lift down from Mount Purgatorio handed Mastema a note to give to Gabriel? He had!* Tom was instantly furious that he hadn't made this connection earlier. It was so obvious now he thought about it. This was the note they were talking about. Salathial had been his name (if he remembered correctly). What *did* an angel that guarded a mountain in Purgatory want to inform Gabriel about so urgently? It must have been a warning. A warning about this kid standing inches from Tom at this very second. Those goose bumps on his arms didn't lie, there was something wrong with this kid and he was going to find out what.

The doors pinged open at level four-hundred and eighty. Tom looked at the boy expectantly, but he didn't move a muscle; he merely stood there gazing serenely back at him. The goose bumps on his arms were now so big they resembled thousands of individual nipples standing erect in the cold. He motioned with his arm as if to say, *'after you'*, but the boy didn't move. He now had no other option but to leave the lift first before the doors pinged closed again and he was trapped in that steel cage forever.

He stepped over the threshold quickly and the boy followed. He was now forced to slowly lead the way towards the entrance to the gardens with the boy at his rear. He was unsure of who exactly was doing the following here - was he the one being followed? This wasn't the way he'd played it out in his head. He brushed aside the hanging canopy and turned to see the boy reach up and grab it too, just as he was letting go.

The gardens were surprisingly empty considering classes had finished not that long ago. He swung to the left and took the path that led sharply in that direction, hoping beyond hope that the boy wouldn't follow him. He didn't. He continued straight into the centre of the gardens and Tom felt a flood of relief wash over him. Having that boy so close behind him, drilling holes in the back of his head with his beady black eyes, had been tantamount to torture. The urge to turn around and face him had been almost unbearable. There's this feeling you get around certain people where you just instinctually know that this was someone you should never turn your back on, and this boy radiated that feeling in spades.

Tom considered his next move. He really hadn't planned this far ahead, and he was still holding onto his rented suit, which was annoying him. He could continue to walk leisurely around the gardens hoping that by chance he may happen upon Raphael and the boy deep in huddled discussion, and he'd get just close enough to hear some of it; or he could find a nice looking tree and sit down and take a nap, like Rip Van Winkle, and hope that by some divine deliverance, they came to him. He decided on the former option. Chances were that this creepy looking kid had come here again to rendezvous with that duplicitous snake, Raphael, and one way or another Tom was going to find out what all the fuss was about.

The path he'd chosen to swerve down was narrow and deserted, the trees bent over the path which ran straight forming an almost Kubrick-esque, one-point perspective tunnel of vision. Of all the paths he could have chosen to walk down, this one was by far the most menacing.

Tom was now realising just how much this part of the gardens resembled the giant maze from The Shining - not somewhere you wanted to get lost if you wished to avoid being beaten to death with a roque mallet. Pushing those particularly disturbing thoughts from his head, he continued down the seemingly deserted rabbit hole; his eyes and ears primed for the slightest sign of movement, other than his own.

As the trees that arched above grew denser, the path grew darker. It wasn't long before Tom was wishing he'd thought better of this daring reconnaissance mission and had just gone to the restrooms for a few hours instead. As the path grew darker still, it started to wind and then forked into two adjoining paths. *Left or Right?* he thought to himself as he approached the unexpected intersection in the road. He hadn't realised that the garden terrace was this hard to navigate. Whenever he'd been in it before he'd always had Alice or Finn to lead the way and now he was alone he was starting to wish he'd brought a pouch of breadcrumbs to fashion a trail behind him. He decided on the path to the left - if he could stay towards the outer walls of the garden then maybe he could follow it around

179

and end up back at the entrance once he'd gone full circle.

Shortly after the fork, the path started to grow lighter again as the dense overgrowth dispersed. He could see the sky once more through the glass dome above and his growing unease started to dissipate slightly. The path ahead wound meanderingly through the tropical plant life and the only sounds were the rhythmic chirping of insects and the loud squawking from the birds. Now the sun was visible again overhead, it was starting to grow hot and humid and he could feel the sweat brimming on his forehead.

He wondered if anyone had ever gotten completely lost in here and collapsed from heat exhaustion due to extended exposure. Maybe he would be the first one stupid enough to accomplish that feat. He knew it got pretty cold in here at night and he kept a wary eye on good places to shelter just in case his casual stroll through the gardens turned into a Bear Grylls style survival situation. Not that he could die of cold now he was already dead... At least he thought he couldn't. He hadn't been made aware of the particulars that governed the biology behind his current state of being. He felt the same as he had before except without the need to eat or sleep or urinate and he still felt temperature change, which gave him reason enough to fear spending the night freezing under some bush in the garden.

A loud squawk directly above him broke his train of thought and made him duck and throw his arms to his face, as if he were under attack from dive bombing fighter planes. The offending parrot swooped from a branch just overhead and flew off into the lofty heights of the glass dome. Tom cursed it under his breath as he looked around to make sure no one had seen his exaggerated display of cowardice.

The path had started to wind to the right in the direction away from the outer wall and he felt his unease return at the prospect of becoming irrevocably lost. The path had forked twice more since the first time and each time he'd taken the left option in order to stay closer to the outer wall, but now the path was slowly making its way inwards and he worried that his earlier plan was now redundant. He was being taken inwards, into the belly of the beast, where the paths likely spiralled and twisted together like a giant bowl of spaghetti, and his chances of finding the exit again would be virtually non-existent. He'd become the minotaur of the garden terrace, endlessly walking the spiralling labyrinth, becoming feral and wild until his clothes and hair were completely unrecognisable.

Mary or Alice would stumble upon him years from now deep within the jungle and would scream in terror at the savage beast he'd become. By that time, he would have forgotten how to converse with other people so he would simply grunt at them and wave his club that he'd brandished from a felled tree, until they ran from him, arms flailing, cries for help sending parrots and paraquats flying like doves to the sounds of gunfire.

He followed a sharp bend in the path that was so tight it almost caused him to double back on himself. The twist was such that it allowed him a brief glimpse of the path he'd just walked on, through the sparse foliage in the in-between. He squinted through the amorphous trees lazily, having lost all desire to navigate himself. He was now a slave to the whims of the never-ending pathway, letting the garden be his guide, wherever it may take him. It was almost liberating in a way knowing that he now had no control over his destination.

He let his eyes wash over the colourful bushes and hanging branches between the paths when he saw movement there - it was quick but there was definitely movement there. Something had moved on the path before the curve had rounded it back on itself. Normally he wouldn't have paid it any mind, assuming it was simply a bird or an insect or some swinging marsupial of the jungle, but the shape he'd seen had been distinctly humanoid. A black faceless shadow had ducked quickly behind a tree as his eyes had swept past it. There was someone following him...

Tom froze in place, his heartbeat accelerating to fever pitch in his chest. His mouth had gone as dry as a seashell left in the wind. His eyes traced back over the section of undergrowth where he'd seen the black figure move, scanning intensely for any more signs of movement. He tried to swallow and almost choked as the dry husks of his throat clasped together around a dry pasty chalk of saliva. He barked loudly, releasing his airways and there was another rustle in the bushes as the rasping sound left his lips.

"Hello?" he said tentatively. Not really expecting a reply. "Is anybody there?"

The bushes were still for what felt like a full minute after the oscillations of his voice had settled. There was no echo, but it'd felt like his voice had echoed back at him repeatedly, reverberating in his head for what felt like an eternity after he'd spoken (*Hello? Hello? Hello? Hello? Hello? Is Anybody there? There? There? There? There?*). The silent echoes of his mind were taunting him. He'd been walking around the garden terrace for about thirty minutes and he'd already succumbed to madness. *Well done old sport*, he thought scathingly. *Next thing you know you'll be having full conversations with yourself as well. Why not find a nice volleyball with a handprint face on it and call it Wilson while you're at it?*

Suddenly, there was another rustle in the

undergrowth between the paths. This time, louder. Tom watched as the branch of the tree closest to him moved a full foot to the side, revealing the thick trunk beneath it. From behind the trunk came a voice.

"Hello Tom," it said in a calm nondescript manner.

Tom felt like the floor had been pulled from beneath him. A cold stone weight dropped down his throat, through his stomach and settled in the twists of his intestines, freezing his insides. He could no longer feel the thrumming of his heart in his chest. By all accounts it had stopped at the sound of that voice. Dead. Silent. Waiting. He was frozen to the ground, unable to move a muscle while the voice threatened to break the silence again.

"Hello?" Tom managed through trembling lips.

The branch nearest to him pulled aside again, revealing the trunk once more and this time a dark figure stepped out from behind it. It stood in the shadow under the branches, face obscured by leaves from the tree. Tom's heart had started to thud again in his chest. Slowly at first, then accelerating at lightning speed to an inhumanly rapid pace. The figure stared at him through the branches and he could see its feet partially revealed beneath the underbrush. It was wearing trainers. Reasonably trendy trainers now he thought about it. How strange...

"Who's there?" Tom said, barely hearing his own words over the demon pounding of his heart.

The branches rustled again as the black figure took a step closer. "Don't you recognise my voice?" it asked, serenely.

Recognise? Why would I recognise? Tom thought to himself disorientated. He stepped back, finding his legs could move again, the terror that had engulfed him relinquishing slightly. The bushes shook again as the figure stepped through them, this time moving the

branches completely away from its face. Tom stood there
dumbfounded. The figure had emerged onto the path
beneath the overhanging branches of the tree. It was still
dark, but Tom could see its face. It was a person. A
person Tom knew very well. A person Tom had loved
more than anyone on the face of the Earth. A person
taken from him when he was only eleven years old.

It was his brother. It was Scott.

*

"Scott..." Tom breathed, voice shaking, eyes widening
slowly as they gradually began to well with tears, emotion
flooding into every fibre of his being. Sweet, pure joy the
likes of which he'd never felt before, began to etch itself
slowly across his crumpled visage. Scott smiled as he
watched the emotion overwhelm his younger brother.
Tears were streaming down Tom's face. Heavenly, divine,
untainted, sweet welcome tears of absolute beautiful
happiness. He ran into Scott's outstretched arms and he
let out a slight gasp as their bodies collided. Scott held
him in his long powerful arms while Tom sobbed tenderly
into his shoulder.

"It's you," he choked between breathless sobs. "You
came back..."

They stood locked in each other's arms for what felt
like an eternity. An eternity of God-given happiness that
Tom had longed for, for longer than he could remember.
His wish *had* come true. Scott was here again. Scott had
come back to him and they were together again. The tears
wouldn't subside, and Scott gripped him tighter in his
arms.

"Ssshhh," he whispered gently. "It's alright... I'm
here now. I'm not going anywhere, ok?"

"You promise?" Tom managed, as the sobbing gently subsided.

"Yes, I promise," Scott said comfortingly. "Besides, you came to me... I've been here waiting all this time."

"You've been here?" Tom asked, wiping his puffed-up eyes with the flat of his wrist. "At St Michael's?"

"At St Michael's," Scott confirmed.

"But why?" Tom asked confused now. "Why has it taken this long? I've been here for weeks. Where've you been, Scott?"

"I've been waiting," he said patiently. "I've known since the day it happened. Since the day that plane crashed into your bedroom. Uriel told me of course. She called me out of class and told me everything. Told me you'd be coming here to St Michael's. I wanted to see you right away, but she wouldn't allow it. Said it was a bad idea. Said it was best I let you settle in by yourself for a while. Said you had friends to meet and if I was in the picture you wouldn't meet them in the same way. She knows everything that Uriel does. I think she can see into the future too you know, though she'd never admit to it. So, I've been waiting in the wings. Watching from the side-lines. I watched you go into Madame Bertin's earlier with that pretty blonde girl then watched you leave and head towards the lifts. I guessed where you were going. You love the gardens as much as I do. I've spent so much time here over the years. I've been walking around these paths looking for you. I spotted you a few minutes back and I followed you. I didn't want to scare you. You looked so nervous walking by yourself without that greasy kid you're always with or that red-haired girl who follows you everywhere."

"They're my friends..." Tom said tenderly, smiling up at him now.

"I heard you got sent to Mastema on your first day.

185

When I heard that I said, 'that *has* to be my little brother, no doubt about it now.' You've grown so much since I last saw you. You're almost bigger than me now."

He punched him on the shoulder affectionately and Tom beamed at him.

"I've missed you so much," Tom said, fighting back the tears again.

"How's mum and dad? Are they ok?" Scott asked.

"No, not really…" Tom replied glumly. "They were never the same after you died. None of us were. I wanted to shut out the world and curl up and die."

"Don't think about that now," Scott urged. "We're together. That's all that matters."

Then all at once, Tom was overwhelmed with a sudden need for answers.

"What happened to you, Scott? What happened down at those barracks? Who shot you?"

Scott's brow furrowed as he looked off into the distance. He could see his eyes playing back the events that took place that fateful day. That horrible wet day when Tom's world had been shattered. When the phone had rang while they'd been sat in the living room watching the television and all of their lives had been changed forever. Irrevocably broken. Smashed beyond repair. There was pain there in his brother's eyes. Desperate, furious pain. Pain that hadn't been diluted over the years like Alice's had. Perhaps it hadn't been long enough for him. Perhaps it took decades for the raw agony to subside.

"Now's not the time." he said at last.

"What do you mean?" Tom pushed.

"I mean this isn't the time for that, Tom. I'll tell you everything, one day, I promise I will. But for now, let's just be happy to see each other again, after all these

186

years."

He hugged Tom again and ruffled his hair affectionately.

"Hey! Stop that!" Tom laughed, finding himself falling back easily into the old routines they'd used to share.

"It might've been my imagination, but when I spotted you earlier, it seemed like you might've been a bit lost?" Scott observed.

"You noticed huh?" Tom replied. "Well, it wasn't your imagination. I'm completely lost. I had no idea the garden terrace was this big."

"Yeah, it can be a bit of a maze if you don't know where you're going. Don't worry I know exactly where we are," he smiled down at him.

It was so strange seeing him again. His brain almost refused to believe the signals being sent from his eyes, like it was an exceptionally realistic daydream he was having, and he'd snap out of it at any second. Or maybe those echoes he was hearing in his head earlier had spiralled into a fully blown case of insanity and he was simply imagining himself talking to his brother. Perhaps some passer-by would happen upon him standing alone conversing with a somewhat oblivious tree trunk. Neither scenario bothered him. He didn't care. Scott was here with him and that's all he'd ever wanted since he was eleven years old. It didn't matter if it turned out that Scott was only a figment of his imagination. It didn't matter because everything that had happened to him since he'd arrived at St Michael's seemed too inconceivable to be real - what was one more hallucination added to the long list of hallucinations he was probably already having? That's why nothing could change the unimaginable elation he was feeling at this moment.

Scott watched him with an inquisitive expression. He

looked the same as he had the last time Tom had seen him. Perhaps a little leaner and worn-out maybe. His shaggy brown hair was windswept and dishevelled, the opposite of Tom's own hair which he'd always kept neatly styled. Their facial features were more or less the same but there was stubble on Scott's chin, which had just started to grow less patchy in the year before he died. Now he supposed it was fixed permanently at that length.

He was taller than Tom by at least four inches. Scott had always been tall, so tall in fact that the high school basketball coach had begged him to join up, but he'd declined, having his heart set on joining the football team instead. And what a football player he had been. Top goal scorer three seasons in a row for Bridlington Football Club. His dad still had the trophies on the mantlepiece at home. He refused to take them down and Tom still caught him polishing them occasionally when he thought no one was looking. At least he used to catch him doing it while he was still alive, he'd forgotten that was no longer the case.

It was hard to believe he'd never see his parents again, but then again maybe he would? What was it Finn had told him? *Everyone goes to the same place eventually?* he wasn't sure what that meant, but it gave him a warm feeling knowing that one day he might see his mum and dad again, and they could be together as a family, like it always should've been.

"Come on then. Follow me and I'll get us out of here," Scott said, leading the way along the path. "What were you doing in here getting yourself so lost in the first place?"

"I followed someone in," Tom replied, thinking he might as well be honest about it. "Maybe you saw him? Creepy looking kid with a crooked nose and black hair?"

"No, I didn't see him. You were by yourself when I saw you heading for the elevator. What were you following him for anyway?"

"Because he's up to something," Tom replied, feeling slightly disheartened now he realised he'd likely missed his chance of doing any eaves dropping on the kid.

"Oh really? What d'you think he's up to?" Scott snickered, amused by his brother's mindless mission.

"I'm not sure, but he's definitely up to something."

He quickly told his brother about the conversation he'd overheard on the astronomy floor between Gabriel and Raphael, and how he suspected that this kid he'd followed into the gardens was most likely the subject of said discussion.

"I wouldn't read too much into it," Scott said after a moment's silence. "That Gabriel has always had a stick up her butt about something . She sent me to the dungeons for a whole week in my first year at St Michael's."

Tom looked at him, incredulous. "A week? What did you do?!"

"Oh, it was nothing that bad," Scott said shrugging it off. "I just gave Professor Wollstonecraft a bit of a fright with a grass snake I'd found in the gardens."

Tom snorted loudly then burst out laughing. That was quintessential Scott. He hadn't changed a bit. He was always doing stupid stuff like that back on Earth and getting himself in trouble with the teachers at school. Unfortunately, his exploits hadn't stopped at the edge of the school grounds. He'd found himself in trouble with the police on more than one occasion. Tom remembered vividly the time that Scott and his friend Dale set the old farm house at the edge of the village on fire, and the whole place had gone up in a towering inferno. It'd taken three fire engines a whole day to put the fire out completely, and all that was left of it after the flames had finally died down, was smouldering rubble where a house had once been. Scott was arrested the next day. The police had shown up at their door around lunchtime after receiving a tip from a local busybody in the village. They'd taken him down to the station and questioned him for six hours. He was only sixteen at the time so they couldn't slap him with the full felony arson charge, but he did get done with destruction of property and was extremely lucky not to have been sent to the young offender's institute over in Wetherby. In the end they'd slapped him with a two thousand pound fine that their dad had to pay off.

That summer Scott had been grounded for four straight months. Tom had to pass him meals through the door of his bedroom as he was on full lockdown and sentenced to solitary confinement in his room with no tv or visitors. Tom had snuck in almost every night and they'd watched movies on their mum's laptop together. It was hard to believe but that had been one of the best summers of his life, huddled around that laptop each night on Scott's bed, sharing the crisps and sweets he'd smuggled in for him. He even suspected his dad knew that Tom had been creeping in to visit Scott, but he'd never pulled him up about it. Maybe it was because his dad had a brother too and knew all about the secret bond that existed between brothers. Uncle Sam was in Australia now, so they hardly ever saw him. He'd emigrated out there when Tom was six and they only saw him once every two years at best.

"It's this way," Scott said when they reached another fork in the road, leading them down the path to the right. "Speaking of snakes, I meant to ask you, which house did you get put in?"

"I'm in Revelation," Tom replied. "How about you?"

"Well that explains how I've managed to successfully evade you for this long. I'm in Numbers."

"I've been to your common room. It's incredible! So much better than the other ones."

"Yeah that Gabriel is a bit of a show-off, I think. Likes to keep her own House looking the grandest. I've no idea why I ended up going for that bucket of water in the end. I initially went to grab for the torch then something changed my mind and before I knew it, I was waterboarding that poor snake with the full bucket."

Tom flashed back to his own experience with the snake in the tepee like tent they set up in the library during orientation; he'd reached for the torch on pure instinct, maybe because it was the only thing within arm's reach. He knew he had to do something as he was milliseconds away from being snake food. He wondered if the Heads had ever let the snake actually bite anyone. *Probably* he thought reproachfully. They'd probably stand there not moving a muscle with those calm expressionless faces they'd worn during his turn with the snake while it ate some poor sod whole. That was probably the first hurdle you had to get over on the path to becoming a Watcher – 'avoid death by snake' and you get your tick in the box. Then the next hurdle was 'avoid murdering obnoxious eighties prefect and make it successfully to the elevators with your record still intact'. *Two boxes ticked within hours of arriving at the school. Job well done!*

"What is that thing you're carrying around anyway?" Scott asked, motioning to the black suit bag under Tom's arm.

"Oh, it's a suit for later," he replied suddenly embarrassed.

"A suit? You got lunch with the Queen today or something is that it?" Scott laughed.

"No nothing like that," Tom assured him. "It's just

some party I've been invited too."

"A party? Really? Look at you Mister Popular! Been here all of four weeks and you're already dominating the social scene! You must take after your big brother," he smirked.

"Yeah well you know me…"

"Apparently I don't!" he replied.

Tom felt guilty for giving his brother the wrong impression. It was true he had made friends surprisingly quickly when he'd arrived at St Michael's, and he had somehow managed to strike a brief acquaintance with one of the prettiest girls he'd ever laid eyes on, but that hadn't been the case during the awkward few teenage years he'd endured back on Earth after his brother's death. Maybe things were different now and he'd finally start taking after his big brother who'd been one of the most popular kids at school.

It wasn't long before Scott managed to weave them out of the tangle of paths that compacted deep within the extensive gardens and out into the clearing next to the main exit. He didn't want to leave his brother, but he knew he'd agreed to meet Alice at noon, and he suspected that appointment was soon approaching. As they walked closer to the hanging drapery concealing the exit, Tom looked up and the large skeletal clock that hung against the clear glass of the dome confirmed that it was indeed fifteen minutes to twelve.

"I've got to go…" Tom said turning to face his brother. He wanted to stay here with him in the garden terrace forever. They had so much to catch up on, his brother and him. So many memories to reminisce about and so many gaps to fill in the glaring space that existed between this moment and the time that they'd last seen each other. "But I don't want to…" he added solemnly.

"Don't worry…" Scott said fondly. "There's going to be plenty of time to catch up. I'd say we've got at least forty-six years together at this school unless they chuck one of us out before then."

Tom snickered, but he still felt miserable to be leaving. Scott grabbed him by the shoulder and pulled him in for a quick hug that turned into a brief headlock before they broke apart laughing. This was what he'd been missing. This was everything that had been stolen from him. He left Scott standing under the skeleton clock, pulled aside the canopy and headed for the restrooms. He only had ten minutes, but it should be just enough time to pull on his suit and get himself looking semi-respectable for Bricktop's.

Chapter Twenty-One
Bricktop's

He burst into the restrooms, grabbed the handle of the first cubicle and quickly bustled himself inside. He threw the suit bag over the mirror and kicked off his trainers, pulling off his jeans then his t-shirt swiftly after. He realised with a pang of regret that he'd forgotten to pick up some respectable-looking shoes while at Madame Bertin's tailor shop earlier, and was now faced with no other option but to don his mangey looking New Balance trainers with the shiny maroon suit he had rented. It was too late to head back downstairs and try and rent some fancier ones with the dwindling pile of Shekels he had left.

He unzipped the bag and pulled out the suit, admiring the fine tailoring once more before quickly pulling on the shirt and the fitted trousers, and slipping back into his scabby trainers. Finally, after an eternity of fumbling with the buttons, he'd managed to do his shirt up and now he picked up the jacket and slipped inside the smooth velvet interior. It felt silky and expensive and he admired himself fleetingly in the mirror before swinging back out of his cubicle and plunging his hands under the faucet.

He pulled his wet hands through the lose trills of his hair until it sat nicely out of his face. He paused for a moment and assessed the reflection staring back at him.

This was it. The nerves hit him all at once like a bass player strumming jazz music on his electrical systems. His arms and legs had gone tingly like his limbs were awakening from some deep slumber. The blood was coursing through his veins and captivating his senses. He felt alive, even though he knew he was dead. With one last heartening look at himself, he hurried back out into the hallway and made for the stairs.

The rain thundered against the turret windows of the tower as he approached the staircase. It was unusual for the rain clouds to reach this far up the building, but today was the exception and the relentless pounding of the storm outside battered the glass ceaselessly. The two-hundredth floor seemed to be about cloud level he'd noticed. The rooms on the ten to fifteen floors above and below that level looked out into continual cloud cover, and the floors below that were constantly battered with rain, whereas the floors above enjoyed pleasant blue skies. Thankfully, the House of Numbers was only a single floor down and he took the steps two at a time, noticing just before he left the restrooms that he had seconds until noon.

Alice was already waiting for him when he reached the bottom of the stairs. She looked magnificent, like the angel she would one day become. She was wearing a white gown that shone like it had been made out of pearls and her sleek blonde hair was pulled into an elegant formal updo. She was smiling at Tom as he tumbled down the last set of stairs and arrived at the bottom, cheeks burning red and panting like a dog.

"I see you remembered to get the matching shoes then," she said playfully, noticing the relaxed manner of his footwear.

"Yeah… I kind of dropped the ball on that one," Tom replied glumly. "So where are we going then?" he

195

asked, briskly changing the subject.

"You'll see," she said mischievously.

She led Tom back towards the elevators and hit the arrow call button. Tom watched curiously as she took her time before revealing which floor the mysterious Bricktop's was housed on. She hovered her finger over the shiny steel wall of buttons, smiling impishly as she feigned forgetting the secret location's floor. Tom waited patiently as she made a show out of hovering her finger over certain buttons then changing her mind and switching to somewhere completely different. Eventually her finger came to rest near the top of the board, moving slowly over buttons 498, 499, 500. She pressed her finger gently onto the button for the five-hundredth floor and Tom gasped in horror. He vividly remembered what had happened the last time he'd trespassed onto the five-hundredth floor. They'd been caught red-handed by Raphael and swiftly escorted down to the dungeons to see Mastema, who had taken Tom on his first very memorable school trip down to the fiery mountains of Purgatory.

"The five-hundredth floor? Are you sure?" Tom asked nervously as they waited for the doors to close.

"Quite sure," she replied confidently.

The silver label next to the button for the five-hundredth floor clearly stated, '*off limits to students!*' Tom eyed it uneasily as the elevator began to ascend smoothly up through the tower. It reached its destination in no time at all, seeing as they were already on the four-hundred and seventy-ninth floor.

As the doors pinged open, Tom looked hesitantly at Alice. The risk of being caught up on the five-hundredth floor again had made his palms start to sweat and his grip felt slippery as he clutched the wooden railings. Despite the mounting fear, there was the slightest hint of excitement growing in his stomach. The twinkle in Alice's eye when she turned to him, told him that he should trust that she knew what she was doing. He tried to relax as he wiped his palm on the velvety material of his suit trousers.

The five-hundredth floor was dark and deserted as they stepped out of the pristine elevator onto the cold flagstone floor. Tom looked at Alice expectantly and she reached out and took his sweaty palm in her own.

"This way," she said conspiratorially, leading Tom in the direction of the doors to the left.

Tom wished silently that he'd given his palm a more thorough wiping on his trousers, but the silky material didn't provide for the easiest of surfaces to transfer the moisture. Thankfully Alice hadn't seemed to notice (or at least if she had, she'd been polite enough not to mention it). The feeling of her tiny hand in his was blissfully sweet. Her delicate fingers clutched around his, as she pulled him around the first bend in the hallway and they continued along the dark corridor.

The rooms they passed as they moved all seemed dark and void of activity. Tom remembered what Mary had told him about the mirror that was kept on this floor, the one that they used for the final exam. The mirror that, when you pulled off its covering, showed you a window into hell. Tom couldn't imagine what seeing something like that must do to a person. Especially since you were expected to stand there alone in this room, with the window to hell open in front of you, until some creature crawled out of it, and you then had to battle this creature into submission somehow while presumably being observed by the Heads from some hidden vantage point. The thought terrified him, and he could feel his hands starting to sweat again as he gripped to Alice's fingers.

"Not far now," Alice said as they rounded another

bend in the hallway. The only sound other than his own heavy breathing was the slapping of their footsteps that provided a shrill staccato rhythm against the drum of the torrential rain, thrashing against the turret windows that they passed at continuous intervals as they walked.

"It's over there," she said finally, motioning to a doorway near the end of the corridor. Tom followed as she led them towards the rickety wooden door and turned the handle. Next to the door was a small wooden sign that read: *'Enter ye in at the strait gate: for wide is the gate, and broad is the way, that leadeth to destruction'*.

As she opened the door, Tom could hear the distant sound of music perforate the silence. Alice smiled at him knowingly as she slipped through the entrance and pulled Tom along after her.

Behind the door was a small passageway that led to a narrow stairwell that spiralled up into the darkness. It was clearly in a turret of some sort that angled off the main body of the tower. Alice moved silently towards the stairs and slid her hand behind her back so she could continue holding onto him as they moved single file up the staircase.

The music was getting louder now. Tom could hear laughter and merriment from the floors above as they climbed. The stairway circled around on itself four whole times before they finally reached the doorway at the top. There was a man there. His tall frame fit tightly into his dark suit and his grey hair was parted neatly at one side. Tom felt his eyes judging them as they approached.

"Good evening, Miss Albright," he said as Alice arrived at his feet. The man was so tall that she barely reached up to his navel. He grinned down at her as she handed him her invite and he waved it away without looking.

"Thank you, Bill," she said as she stepped aside to allow Tom's approach.

"Your invitation, sir?" The man named Bill said as he glared down at Tom with his sceptical eyes. He had a stern look about him that made Tom suspect that he'd probably once been law enforcement.

Tom fumbled into his breast pockets as he tried to remember where he had stashed it. He found it eventually in the back pocket of his trousers, crumpled into a ball. He unfolded the wrinkly invitation he'd received from Professor Newton and handed it to the man. The man grabbed it with a large baseball mitt palm and proceeded to read every word of it studiously. Eventually, after much careful scrutiny, the man handed it back to him.

"Have a good day," he said, stepping aside to reveal the entrance to the club. Alice grinned widely as she led them across the threshold.

"Friend of yours?" Tom asked, once the doorman was out of sight.

"Who? Bill?" she laughed. "No, he's just a nice guy. He used to be FBI y'know. And he was a bodyguard for Bobby Kennedy. He punched the shooter twice, then helped wrestle him to the ground on the day he was assassinated."

"Who's Bobby Kennedy?" Tom asked.

"You know… RFK?"

"You mean JFK," Tom corrected.

"No RFK," she insisted. "Robert Francis Kennedy - JFK's little brother!"

"They were *both* assassinated?"

"Yup… Afraid so. Anyway, come on, I've just spotted Isaac!" she said, motioning to the corner of the room eagerly.

Tom was struggling to see anything at all. The room was extremely dark, and the ceiling was low. He could just make out a stage at the far side of the room where a dark-skinned woman sat atop a piano singing some jazzy number to the delight of the patrons. There were little alcoves and hollows scattered into the periphery, and there were crowds of people bustling around in the centre, laughing and conversing in huddled groups. There was a bar directly in front of them. The two men perched at it seemed to be sipping at the same bright purple concoction that was being poured from the taps. Alice had pointed to the alcove next to the bar where he could now see Newton sat intimately amongst a small group of associates.

"Let's go say hi!" she shouted to him over the music. By this time, she'd long since dropped his hand and Tom nearly lost sight of her as she squeezed through the crowd to reach them. He followed the glow of her pearl dress that shone in the low lights from the ceiling, sending sparkled reflections into the hazy swirls of the room like a disco ball. He couldn't see the faces of the people he barged past to reach her, but they grunted and moaned, and someone even spilled a purple libation onto the lapel of his jacket as he passed them.

Alice had taken her seat next to Newton when Tom finally arrived. The seat next to her was occupied by a woman with short dark hair who was smoking a cigarette. Alice turned to him as he approached and motioned for him to join them. She pointed to an empty space on the other side of the table that Tom felt dubious about his ability to squeeze into.

"This is my friend, Tom Woolberson," she said to the group as he awkwardly squashed himself into them.

The group eyed him as one as he raised one timid hand in hello.

"Welcome to Bricktop's!" Newton smiled at him

from across the table. He picked up his glass and took a delicate sip of the same purple concoction that had stained his suit jacket.

Alice noticed Tom staring at the liquid enquiringly as the older man sat his glass back down on the table.

"It's manna wine," she said, answering Tom's unspoken question.

"Fermented here in the tower," Newton added, "by none other than Mister Enoch. Although I must say, I've not been the biggest admirer of this month's batch. It's usually much sweeter but has a decidedly bitter taste this month that doesn't suit my pallet at all."

Tom eyed the dense purple liquid again; it looked like grape juice except with a much thicker consistency.

"I would offer to purchase you a glass my dear boy, but I'm afraid you fall short of the legal drinking age here in Vilon."

"Don't worry," Alice interjected. "I'll grab us a few glasses of manna juice - it's much nicer anyway." Alice disappeared to the bar and left Tom alone with the table of strangers. He took a covert glance around the group in hope of spotting a familiar face but was sadly disappointed. The woman next to Newton with the cigarette flicked her ash carelessly over her shoulder. Her hair was cropped into a short, almost boyish, style and she wore a loosely fitting blouse that resembled more of a polo t-shirt than a feminine garb. She appeared to be around Professor Newton's age, which is to say almost certainly pushing middle aged, but the sullen expressions she wore made her seem older somehow, whereas Newton's light-hearted charm had the opposite effect on his appearance.

Next to this woman was a short balding man who wore heavy-framed spectacles and a smart looking pin-striped suit, that had clearly been tailored to a much higher standard than his own. The way he crossed his legs and held his own cigarette, with his wrist flopped loosely to one side, gave him a distinctly camp demeanour. The martini glass he sipped from was filled with the same purple manna wine as Newton's.

Next to this man was a young voluptuous African woman with a large flower in her hair and expensive looking pearls at her neck. Her embroidered dress was embellished with jewels.

Next to her was a handsome young man with tight dark curls and a pencil thin moustache. He was deep in conversation with the young woman to his right who wore her hair in ringlets and nodded along timidly.

Seated next to Tom were three men in heated discussion who had yet to notice his arrival in the group. Two of the men were lean and tense looking with dark hair and thin moustaches, and the third man was older with a balding head and neatly trimmed white beard.

The man sat closest to him was the elder gentleman whose suit had a timepiece tucked into the inside pocket; the man next to him wore a black frockcoat with a matching cravat that was tied somewhat loosely; and the third man wore a tightly-fitted grey suit and held a tissue to his face as if he were overly conscious of contracting some airborne illness.

Alice arrived back at the table quickly holding two tall glasses filled with manna juice. She reached over the table and handed one to Tom, which seemed to break the discussion that the two lean men next to him were engrossed in.

"How rude of me, I do believe I have neglected to introduce everyone," Newton said, helping Alice back into her seat. "You know young Alice here, of course, and the fine woman sat next to her is Nelle, and the

gentleman next to her is Truman, and next we have
Eleanora, and then there's George and Mary, and then
finally we have Nikola, Edgar and Sigmund," he said,
gesturing to each member of the group in turn. "Young
Thomas here is new to my Laws of the Universe class. He
still has lots to learn about the mysteries of creation, but
don't worry, we won't spoil any surprises!" He took
another long drink from his glass and wiped his mouth
with the sleeve of his tunic.

The woman who had been singing on stage had now
finished her number and was slinking her way through the
crowd in the direction of the bar.

"Ada my dear!" Newton called to her. The woman
stopped in her tracks, then beelined her way across the
dancefloor to their table. "Let me introduce our host!"
Newton said loudly as the woman arrived behind him.
"Thomas Woolberson, I would like to introduce you to
Miss Ada Bricktop, who is the proprietor of this fine
establishment, and procurer of the splendid elixir that I'm
drinking!" Ms Bricktop smiled at him warmly.

"Pleasure to meet you, Thomas," she said. "This
your first time?"

Tom nodded at her from across the table.

"You're in luck, we have a very special guest taking
the stage later," she said placing her hand on the shoulder
of the woman called Eleanora with the large yellow flower
pinned in her hair. "Be sure to stick around," she said
throwing him a playful wink.

Tom now suspected that there was some secret
among his companions that he wasn't a party to, but he
grinned enthusiastically anyway and watched as Ms
Bricktop lowered her ear to indulge in a more private
conversation with Newton, who was all too keen to win
back her attention. After a while, she kissed him on the
cheek and walked off towards the bar.

Tom picked up his tall glass of manna juice and sipped at it; it tasted sweet, like lychee juice, or something akin to that, except with a very distinct and unexpected effervescent aftertaste that tingled on his tongue as he lowered the glass back to the table. As he licked his lips and savoured the last of the sensation in his mouth, he began to feel strange, a sense of profound peacefulness stole over him and he felt instantly more relaxed about being seated amongst these strangers. He leaned back in his chair and sighed contentedly, he could feel himself start to grin in spite of himself. The man next to him called Sigmund observed him humorously.

"I see the manna juice has started to take effect!" he trilled in heavily accented Angelican.

Tom stared at his glass on the table and was suddenly suspicious that someone had spiked it.

"Not to worry!" Sigmund continued. "The juice of the manna fruit is known to have many desirable effects. Primarily, it works as a presynaptic releasing agent of the neurotransmitters serotonin, norepinephrine and dopamine, that are responsible for feelings of tranquillity, pleasure and reduced anxiety, thus explaining the heightened sense of well-being you are experiencing presently."

Tom's eyes widened in amusement as Sigmund explained the science involved in the consumption of his manna juice. Then, for no good reason at all, he burst out laughing and fell back into his seat in hysterics.

Edgar and the man next to him named Nikola, both laughed with him, then raised their own glasses and drank deeply.

"Unfortunately for you, the effects are short lived," Sigmund said once the laughter had subsided. "They should taper off ten minutes or so after consumption.

Whereas manna wine," he said raising his own glass and smiling, "lasts much longer."

Tom took another long drink from his own glass and felt the immediate resurgence of peacefulness steal back over him.

"However, I would err on the side of caution if I were you," Sigmund said guardedly. "The juice of the manna fruit has been known to cause hallucinogenic effects when drunk to excess."

"It can make you hallucinate?" Tom asked perplexed.

"Precisely," Sigmund confirmed. "Of course, whether you consider this as a good thing or a bad thing is entirely up to you. As is whether you consider the perceived pleasurable benefits to outweigh the potentially negative side-effect of hallucinations. It is, as they say, your call my dear boy."

Tom lifted his drink again and looked at it calculatingly. Then with a Devil may care shrug, he raised it to his lips and took another drink.

"That's the spirit," Sigmund winked at him. "So, how about this young lady then?" he said, nodding towards Alice.

"Oh, she's just a friend," Tom replied bashfully.

"In my experience, there are only the pursued, the pursuing, the busy and the tired; so, you'd better get right to it or somebody else will."

Tom stared blankly at him for a moment before conceding that he was absolutely right.

The people huddled out on the dancefloor had grown silent as someone new was about to take the stage. Tom craned his neck to try and get a glimpse of the figure who had emerged from the wings. He could see the top of somebody's head as they approached the microphone and greeted the exuberant crowd. The piano started softly as the crowd began to soothe, then through the thinnest of windows that opened between the shifting heads, he could see the big yellow flower that had been on the head of the woman sat across from him just a moment ago. Tom darted his gaze across the table and saw the space where she had been. Evidently, the woman called Eleanora had taken to the stage.

The crowd cheered as Eleanora purred her first few sumptuous notes as the pianist caressed his keys and a gentle saxophone began to play from her other side.

"Lady Day, she sure can sing!" Sigmund cried as he lifted himself from his seat to get a fuller view. Tom followed suit and stood up next to him.

"Who is she?" He asked as Sigmund stared transfixed to the stage.

"*Who is she*? You must be joking my boy! That's Billie Holiday!"

Eleanora swayed softly to the tinkling of the piano and Tom took another long sip from his glass, feeling the manna juice tingle on his tongue and relax him further. Eleanora finished her first song to riotous applause from her onlookers. Sigmund, Newton and the young man called George whooped and cheered while the rest of the table clapped politely. Sigmund excused himself and made his way to the bar, followed by Edgar and the man called Nikola. Newton had pushed off towards the stage to get a closer look at Eleanora as she dived into her next number. Tom saw the empty seat next to Alice and she motioned for him to join her. He made his way clumsily around the table still reeling from the calming effects of the manna juice.

"Enjoying yourself?" she asked, as he plopped into the seat next her.

"I am!" Tom replied enthusiastically, the grin on his face unmistakable.

"Shall we get another?" she asked, seeing Tom's glass was just about empty. He nodded and they politely excused themselves before pushing their way through to the bar. Tom extracted the purse of shekels from his jacket pocket, spilling the contents into his hands and frowning at the few measly coins left.

"Don't worry," Alice said comfortingly, "it's not expensive."

Tom counted what he had left, seeing the sum total at just over four shekels. He'd almost completely exhausted the funds he'd received from Uriel and he mentally noted the urgency of finding some gainful employment at the earliest possible opportunity. They arrived at the bar just as Sigmund and his friends were leaving. Alice hopped onto a bar stool and ordered them two more glasses of manna juice.

"Four shekels," came the reply from behind the bar. The barman was a short Scottish man who wore a long white lab coat style jacket.

Tom reached over the bar top and dropped the four coins into his hand. The man pulled two glasses from a hanging stemware rack above his head and poured them two glasses from a tap before placing the drinks neatly in front of them on napkins.

"Thanks, Harry," Alice said as she accepted her own. She turned on her barstool and stared out over the crowd towards the stage. Eleanora was just completing her second tune and the applause was breaking across the room. Tom grabbed a seat on the stool next to her and took a sip of the sweet purple nectar in his glass.

"You've just been served by the inventor of the Bloody Mary," she said, leaning across to him. "He owned his own bar in Paris called 'Harry's New York Bar' that boasted all sorts of high-profile clientele. The President and the King of England were even said to have drank there on occasion. Now he runs the bar at Bricktop's. I imagine he's gotten used to serving history's A-listers over the years here as well! Do you want to get some fresh air?"

Tom was puzzled by the question. "What?" he yelled back at her, just as the music had started to break again into a particularly raucous tune.

"Come on, follow me!" Alice shouted back, as she sprang from her seat and led them towards the dancefloor. Tom put his half-finished drink back on the bar top and hurried after her. She slid through the crowd, gracefully avoiding contact with any of the flailing dancers or bustling onlookers, a feat which Tom found almost impossible to replicate. He ambled his own way through, receiving sharp glares and wounded cries as he bumped into people and stood on their toes. To the right of the stage there was a passage to another room, almost completely hidden from sight by the masses of people crowded on the dancefloor.

Tom saw the room was blissfully deserted as they moved further in. Eyes moving upward, he realised that half of the ceiling of this room was missing. It opened out into a perilously situated rooftop terrace that was only partially shielded from the more than adverse weather that still pounded the tower walls.

The heavy storm clouds outside hung just above eye-level and formed a seemingly impenetrable blockade to whatever was beyond them. It was like the sky before them had a dark ceiling that loomed just above, almost within touching distance. Alice led them beneath the shelter, then without turning back, she continued out to the railing that bordered the terrifyingly high terrace and was immediately soaked by the thundering storm outside.

Tom hesitated before following. The dangerously

inadequate railing rose just above her navel and it seemed one good gust of wind could sweep her clean over the edge, sending her plummeting down the five-hundred floors of the tower before smashing into the marshland below. She looked like she was peering over the backend of an ocean liner as she leaned over that hazardous ledge and threw her head back in delight, letting the rain wash over her and immerse her completely.

She was lovelier now than she'd ever been. The pearl dress was saturated and clung tightly to her skin, revealing her shapely figure and the slightest hint of nipple at her bosom. She'd taken out the pin that had held her updo in place, letting her sleek blonde hair fall freely to her shoulders. He watched as she whipped it from her face, sending the loose tendrils spiralling into the air.

"Are you coming?" she shouted back to him.

Tom stood motionless beneath the shelter, unable to take his eyes from the angel balanced against the railing. Wild horses could not have pulled his gaze away from Alice at this moment in time. He felt captivated by her beauty and was terrified that his slightest movement would break the spell that had been cast over them in the last few seconds. At long last he let his legs break from their shackles and he followed her out into the rain.

"Isn't it amazing!" she cried, the exhilarating ripple of her voice punctuating the air.

"We're going to get soaked!" he yelled as the wind and rain battered him from all sides.

He joined her against the railings and grinned wildly as the rain drenched his rented suit and flattened his hastily styled hair against his head. Never before had he felt a more palpable sense of place than he did now. He knew that, at this moment in his existence, this was exactly where he was meant to be.

Alice leaned towards him slowly, blinking as the

water from her hair dropped large beads into her eyes. His dream seemed so close now that he could hardly fail to grasp it. Tom inched himself closer, stopping only when their noses were mere inches apart.

"I wish I could read your mind..." she said sorrowfully.

"Believe me, I think you'd find my mind pretty unappealing," Tom replied.

She faltered there, inches from his face, water drops trickling down the passage between her eyebrows then falling off the ledges of her lashes as she blinked them away. Tom took her hand in his own and stared at her fingers as they intertwined around his. He brought his eyes back up to meet hers then they both slowly closed them as they reached in and closed the gap.

Her soft lips were hesitant at first as they pressed against his, then their mouths parted slightly, and Tom felt her tongue move gently against his and electricity jolted through his bones. She wrapped an arm around his back and moved him closer until they were a single entangled silhouette, cast against the storm clouds behind them.

Chapter Twenty-Two
Clouds of Witness

When they finally re-joined the group, Alice suggested they leave the club early and take a wander down the tower to find somewhere to be alone. They quickly bid their companions farewell after Tom mentioned how lovely it was to meet them all, and Sigmund had mentioned that he hoped to see Tom join them at next month's soiree. As they pushed their way towards the exit, Tom thought he caught a glimpse of a familiar face at a table in the corner. The sleek black hair, muscled physique and pointed nose were almost unmissable. He was clearly trying not to be seen. The hood of his cloak was pulled low over his face and he was bent over in fervent discussion. It was Raphael, he was sure of it.

It was dark, but he was almost certain that he'd recognised his face. He hadn't recognised the man with whom he'd been conversing, however, it was too dark to tell. Although the back of the man was almost certainly that of a man and not that of a boy (say a certain boy whom he'd followed into the garden terrace earlier).

As they approached the door, Tom stole one final look in their direction, no it wasn't him. It wasn't that creepy kid who had followed him into the elevator. It was someone else talking to Raphael. They raced down the spiral staircase and when they reached the bottom, Alice

211

pushed Tom against the stone wall and stole another passionate kiss that was as desperately sweet as their first. She grasped his hand and pulled him out of the small wooden door back into the dark hallway of the five-hundredth floor. The corridor was deserted, much as it had been when they had arrived. The rain still pounded the windows and the only sound they could hear was its rhythmic drumming as it echoed along the hallway.

Their arms swung gently as they walked hand in hand back towards the elevator. One of the panes had a crack in it and the water had started to pool beneath the window in an ever-expanding puddle that was stretching across the hall. Tom pulled Alice to one side as they tip-toed around it, feeling the action was somewhat unnecessary seeing as they were both creating tiny puddles from their own dripping clothes. They rounded a bend and Tom almost slipped on his back when he saw who was standing down the corridor. As he lurched them to a halt, he managed to regain his footing and ducked them behind the wall before the scuffle could alert the stranger to their presence. He pressed his arm across Alice's chest and held them both against the wall. Alice made to protest but he threw his finger to her lips sharply and said, "sshhhh!"

Alice scolded him wordlessly as he silently explained that there was someone down the corridor. He inched towards the edge and peered around the bend, confirming what he'd suspected all along. Raphael had brought that creepy kid to the five-hundredth floor with him after all. He watched as the boy used a key to silently unlock a door then disappeared through it.

"Who is it?" Alice fumed, clearly enraged at having been remanded so hastily.

"It's him," Tom replied.

212

"Who's him?" she chided.

"The boy! That boy! The one who's all wrong."

"I don't know which boy you're talking about," she sneered.

Tom was in no mood for explaining himself. He was certain that he was just about to have all his suspicions about the boy confirmed and they were moments from catching this beast in the act of something unspeakable.

Once he was sure the hallway was clear, he motioned for Alice to follow him as he crept soundlessly towards the doorway. Alice, who was still clearly agitated, looked to be humouring him at the very least, if only for the entertainment of watching Tom creep around like a veritable imbecile. As they approached the door that Tom was sure he'd seen the boy disappear through, Alice seemed to perk up suddenly.

"What are you doing outside that door?" she asked.

"Ssshhhh!" Tom reminded her.

She rolled her eyes and continued in a reluctantly softer tone. "What are you doing outside that door?" she repeated.

"That's the door he went into," Tom whispered back.

"He went in there?" her voice growing louder again, despite Tom's advances.

He nodded then fixed her with a puzzled expression. "Why? What's in there?" he asked.

"That's where they keep… the mirror," she said ominously, covering her mouth with her hand as if appalled by the prospect.

Tom's eyes widened as they stared at each other in silence. He knew all about the mirror of course. His discussions with Mary had conjured disturbingly vivid images of what had crawled out of it in the past. He'd yet to see the thing for himself of course, but he was no less

213

horrified by the thought of it sitting just beyond this door to his left.

He also suspected that Alice had never had an attempt at the final exam due to her expressed desire to stay on as a prefect when she reached the required twenty-five-year mark, so he was doubtful whether she'd seen the mirror either, even though she'd been at St Michael's for just about twenty years. If that were true, then neither of them knew what they were really dealing with behind this door, regardless of who may or may not be in that room with it.

He was pretty sure that it'd been this door that he'd seen the boy disappear through, although now he knew what lay beyond it, he would rather he was positive before turning that door handle.

"What are you doing?!" Alice whispered sharply as Tom reached towards the door.

"I need to see," Tom replied hesitantly. His hand hovering inches from the handle.

"But… you'll get expelled!" Alice exclaimed, almost flabbergasted that someone would take such a risk.

Tom's hand grasped around the cold brass handle. He could hear Alice's sharp intake of breath as he began to turn it slowly in his hand; each twist accompanied by a corresponding spike in his heartrate, until finally it was twisted completely. He leaned forward on the door and felt the anticlimactic force of the bolting mechanism nullify his motion. The door was locked…

Alice seemed to breathe a desperate sigh of relief as he released the handle. The failed attempt at the door had been silent, but if somebody on the other side had been watching the handle, then they'd know that someone was trying to get in. Alice put her hand on Tom's shoulder and made him turn towards her, but Tom twisted away.

"Are you sure you saw somebody go in there?" she asked, dropping her outstretched palm to her side. "That manna juice can cause hallucinations y'know if you're not used to it. It can make you see things that aren't really there..."

"I know what I saw," he said assuredly.

He'd told her he was sure, but was he really sure? He'd never had a hallucination before, not that he could think of anyway, so he wouldn't know just how lifelike some hallucinations could be. It had certainly seemed real, but *was* it real? The boy was there down the hall in front of them as they rounded the last bend in the corridor; he had keys in one hand, he watched him unlock it, then he disappeared through this door in front of them. The only problem was this door was locked.

Why don't you knock? asked the voice in his head. *If you knock, then we can know for sure.*

But what would I say if he answered? Tom asked his own questioning mind.

You could ask what he's doing? He is on the five-hundredth floor after all, and I didn't see him in Bricktop's... did you?

Tom quickly shook off the idea. *No that's ridiculous*, he told his subconscious. *I'm not doing that, it's stupid.*

Well then, you'll never know... his subconscious breathed in final retaliation. Tom reached his clenched fist towards the door, but Alice grabbed it and spun him away.

"What are you doing?" she fired, voice well beyond a whisper. "You're mental, you know that?"

Tom stared at the door, eyes unblinking and mouth hanging ajar. He was about to protest when Alice pulled his arm and spoke.

"Come on, let's get out of here."

Tom followed reluctantly.

Back in the elevator, Tom was cursing the opportunity that had just slipped through his fingers. He knew that boy was up to something. Something that had Gabriel on edge and Michael kept in the dark. He'd just had the chance to catch him at it before it was all too late, but he'd scunnered it like everything else he'd ever tried to do. Raphael was in on this too, of course, he knew that in his bones. Wherever there was Raphael, there was that boy never far behind him. His sinister shadow, concocting whatever sinful delights he pleased as he moved unseen around the tower. He was like a cancer that lay dormant under the skin, quietly metastasising into nearby cells until he'd polluted enough body tissue to unleash his contagion onto everybody else. By which time it would likely be too late and there would be nothing anyone could do, and old Tom here had missed his one chance to stop it before it had reached stage four terminality. He knew why he was in that room of course. It was plain as day. A room with a window looking directly into hell, would be a fine point to summon whatever unholy army may be lurking on the other side of it.

Alice wasn't speaking. The romance that had kindled so passionately on the roof terrace had dampened to sodden ashes. He was too riled up to care about it at this point but a voice at the very back of his mind told him that he would deeply regret this fact later. She stared blankly at the shining metallic board of buttons without pressing anything and Tom felt the guilt start to creep over him.

"Sorry," he said timidly.

"It's fine," she replied, without turning.

"Where are we going then?" he asked.

"I'm probably just going to go back to my common room," she said coldly.

"Oh…" Tom mumbled. "Do you want me to walk

you back?" He tried, not really expecting her to agree to it.

"If you like," she replied indifferently.

Well there was one tiny consolation at least, if he had managed to ruin things completely with Alice, at least she would allow him the honour of accompanying her for the minute or so that it would take to walk from the elevator to the Numbers common room.

"What boy were you talking about?" she asked suddenly. "You said you saw a boy go into that room with the mirror. A boy who was 'all wrong' or something like that?"

"It's just this kid I keep seeing around the tower," he replied vaguely. "He's been up to something bad and we almost caught him back there in the hallway."

"Which kid?" she asked again.

"I don't know his name," Tom conceded, "but he's got black hair and a crooked nose, and his skin is really pale. He wears odd clothes that don't seem to fit in with anyone else's."

"You mean Daniel?" she asked plainly.

"Who?" Tom uttered, stunned by the response.

"I think you're talking about Daniel," she said again. "He's in my House."

"You know him?!" Tom gasped, gaping at her.

"Sure," she replied casually. "He's actually really nice, once you get speaking to him. Most people avoid him because he seems a bit weird, but that isn't his fault."

Tom gawked at her incredulous. He couldn't believe the words he was hearing. *She knew this kid? He was nice? She talked to him?* He didn't want to believe it. He quickly explained to Alice about the conversation he'd overheard on the Astronomy floor between Gabriel and Raphael, and how he suspected that the conversation had been about this boy Daniel.

217

"No, they can't be talking about Daniel," she said after a moment's hesitation. "He's from Cleveland. His parents were Amish. His dad was a Bishop, which is sort of like a pastor in their religion I think, and his mom definitely didn't kill him. He was hit by a truck on the highway and dragged for nearly a mile."

Tom was stunned into silence. They'd yet to press a button on the elevator wall and the doors still hung open, looking at the same dark section of the five-hundredth floor. There were noises down the corridor now. Loud noises. Laughing and shouting. Clearly more people leaving Bricktop's; their merry cries echoed along the long hallway towards them. Alice reached forward and pressed a button before they could make it to the elevator doors - they were in no mood for company. The doors pinged closed and the lift sank down towards the House of Numbers and everything that Tom thought he knew sank with it.

When the doors pinged open again a few seconds later, Alice turned to him with a resolute look on her face.

"Look, I like you okay," she said simply. "But you just can't be running around taking risks like that. Especially up on that floor. Something like that could get you expelled and I'm not going to risk getting myself in trouble by associating with someone who would do that."

She was right. He had been brash. Trying that doorknob had been a massive risk and he was already regretting doing it, especially as Alice had been with him at the time. She had been so good to him since they'd met and acting like that was no way to show his gratitude.

"You're right," he said, letting out a long, protracted sigh of regret. He made to take her hand in his own, but she flinched hers away. Then after a moment's deliberation, she reconsidered and wrapped her fingers around his.

"You're going to be more careful now, right?" she prompted.

"I am," he replied solemnly.

She grinned at him and he felt the fire between them start to slowly rekindle.

Chapter Twenty-Three
Men Without Women

After bidding Alice a brief goodbye and promising to be better behaved, he made his way back down to the Revelation common room. It was getting late in the day now and classes would start up again in a few hours. He still wasn't accustomed to not having sleep to break up his days, but he supposed he would get used to it eventually. Without the need for sleep, his time seemed to meld into one endless day that lasted for eternity. There was no yawning and waking up in the mornings, and there was no yawning and settling down at night, there was pretty much no yawning whatsoever since his new life had begun at St Michael's.

He was starting to admit to the fact that he may have hallucinated seeing that boy disappear into that door back up on the five-hundredth floor. Maybe the manna juice had had more of an effect on him than he'd realised at the time. Had he imagined kissing Alice? He really hoped not as it was the single greatest moment of his existence to date.

He was also starting to believe that this Daniel kid really could be as innocent as Alice made him out to be. After all, what had he seen him do really? Everything he'd suspected him of had been surmised in his head through the possible mistranslation of one overheard conversation. Since then, the idea had snowballed in his head at an uncontrollable rate and if it had kept going at that pace then he probably would've started suspecting this kid was behind 9/11 and the 7/7 bombings in London as well. Now he knew the reason that the kid dressed so weird was because he was Amish, and his mum hadn't killed him; he'd been dragged for a mile along the highway by a truck according to Alice. *Poor kid*, he thought as he bustled through the door of the Revelation common room.

He looked around hopefully for any sign of his friends. Without him there he guessed Finn would probably be hanging out back in his own common room, doing whatever it was Finn did when he wasn't around, and if Mary weren't here then she would most likely be in the library so that would be his next port of call. Thankfully, that wouldn't be necessary, he had just spotted Mary sitting alone in a chair in a location he'd never seen her in before. She was sat way off to the west side of the common room, far and away from their usual armchairs. He approached her cheerfully, relieved to see her after his long day away. She glanced up as he approached but didn't smile or close the book she was reading.

"Hey!" he said cheerily.

"Hi."

"What are you up to?" he continued.

"Just reading."

"What are you reading?"

"Nothing you'd know," she replied.

"Is something wrong?" he tried feebly, a little hurt now by her bluntness.

"Why would anything be wrong?"

"It's just you seem a little funny with me that's all…"

"Why would that be I wonder?" she replied.

"Because I was with Alice?" he guessed.

"It's a free country," she said. "If you want to see Alice then see Alice, but don't come back in here looking like the cat that got the cream, then expect me to be all nicey nicey about it."

Tom didn't know what to say. He could clearly remember the scene in the hallway earlier that day when Alice had met them outside the common room and Mary had disappeared through the door before he could even get a word in. She was clearly upset. He couldn't lie to himself, he'd always known this would happen. There was no point acting shocked now that she was taking it like this when this is exactly the way he would be acting if their roles were reversed. He couldn't have his cake and eat it too, it just didn't work like that. He had a struggle on his hands here and that was putting it lightly.

"Look…" he said, pulling up a chair next to her. "I wanted to tell you something. I met my brother in the garden terrace earlier today. He's here at St Michael's. He's been watching me the whole time I was here, but Uriel told him not to intervene with me right away or something like that. Apparently, she wanted me to find my feet first before she'd allow Scott back into my life."

"How nice for you," Mary chided coldly.

"Don't be like that Mary," Tom pleaded. "You're my best friend in this place… I need you okay?"

"You've got Alice now, apparently. Why do you need me?" she scorned.

"Look, I'm not sure what's happening with me and Alice okay? But whatever that is doesn't come between what me and you have…"

"And what do we have exactly?" she asked.

"We're mates, aren't we?" Tom replied.

"Just mates?" she asked dolefully. "I thought it might have been more than that."

"So did I…" Tom conceded, in spite of himself. He was so confused by all this. Fifteen-year-olds weren't made to deal with this many emotions. There was a limit to the emotion that one boy could knowingly withstand, and that limit was fast reaching capacity.

"But now it's ruined," Mary declared sadly, seeing the pained expression on her face for the first time.

"I guess it is," he conceded again. "Who knows, things might not work out with Alice…"

"So, then I'd be your backup?" she scolded.

"No, not at all!" Tom begged, pleading with her now. "It's not like that Mary. I hate being in this position. I don't want to lose you!"

"Well you should have thought about that before you started this business with Alice," she said with some finality. And with that, she re-opened her book and turned her chair away from him.

*

Tom left the Revelation common room feeling broken. Things with Mary were not good, and he really didn't want to lose her as a friend. Why couldn't he just have all the things he wanted, and everyone just be happy for him? It was clear that he was going to need to give Mary some time. Maybe she would never come around. He prayed that wouldn't be the case.

He made his way soberly back to the elevators. Maybe Finn would have something cheerful to say if he could find him. He stepped into the lavish wooden elevator and hit the button for the House of Deuteronomy. He'd been meaning to take another visit back to that neck of the woods but hadn't got around to it again since the first time he was there. Maybe a look at some gruesome old artefacts in the curiosity cabinets would cheer him up.

He really hoped Finn would be in the Deuteronomy common room; one thing he'd noticed about life after death was the glaring hole left by the modern technology that they were all so used to having access to back on Earth. For instance, he could no longer just text his friends and find out where they were; he physically had to go looking for them and just hope they would be hanging around their usual haunts, otherwise he hadn't a chance in hell of finding them. It's like what arranging to meet somebody back in the nineties must have been like. If they didn't show up at the time you'd agreed to meet them, then you just had to go home and hope for better luck next time. Your only option was to go on somebody's word that they would be at a specific place at the specified time that they'd agreed to be there. This was pretty much how things worked at St Michael's and Tom was quickly learning that arranging to meet somebody here was a substantially more problematic task than he was used to. He was also missing the habitual use of social media; although he suspected that was more out of habit than an actual physical need for its existence.

He exited out into the dark and grimy looking hallway that led to the House of Deuteronomy. The hallway was crowded and there were kids lurking in huddled groups at every corner. The animated chatter seemed to be particularly fervent this evening he noticed as he pushed past a large group of boys at the doors to the staircase. They all seemed to be eagerly debating the same topic, which Tom was catching fragments of as he made his way down the corridor.

"Haven't you heard?" asked one boy. "It's all anyone's talking about."

"I heard they hadn't been seen in three days," replied

another.

"I bet they've just gotten lost in the garden terrace or something," countered a podgy girl dubiously.

"Or locked themselves in one of the rest rooms," added someone else.

Tom arrived at the doors to the Deuteronomy common room and prayed that he would find Finn on the other side of them. He pushed through the heavy doors and went to walk out into the shadowy depths of the cavernous room, when the girl sat behind the table to his left barked at him.

"Excuse me! You need someone to sign you in before you can go in there, I'm afraid!"

Tom, who had forgotten about this particular hinderance, replied, "oh, I'm just looking for someone."

"Well you'll have to look from where you're standing. I can't let you inside without someone from Deuteronomy signing you into the book," she ordered.

Tom was at a loss. He had no one to sign him in. He remained where he was standing and perched onto his tiptoes to try and catch a glimpse into the far reaches of the common room. He couldn't see Finley anywhere. Even if he'd been seated in an armchair relatively close to him, he probably still would've missed him as it was too dark to make out anything in the room anyway. He made to turn and leave, feeling deflated, when the heavy doors to the common room burst open again.

"Finn! Thank God!" Tom could have hugged him.

"Hey, what's happening?" Finn said, seeing Tom standing precariously at the entrance. "What are you doing here?"

"I was looking for you," Tom said quickly.

The girl at the table seemed to be losing patience with the blockade they had formed by the doors. "Are you going to sign him in?" she asked, exasperated.

"Yeah yeah, calm your horses Tiffany," Finn replied scathingly, making his way to the small table and quickly signing Tom into the book.

"So, where've you been all day?" Finn asked as he led them to some free armchairs in a corner.

"With Alice," he replied, taking a seat in a blood red armchair by a large fireplace that was burning away brightly in their corner.

"Are you going to tell me where?" Finn prompted, plopping himself into his own armchair.

"I'm not really supposed to," Tom said nervously, "but what the hell. We were at Bricktop's."

"Where?"

"It's like a nightclub," Tom explained, "or a day club I guess you'd call it here."

"In the tower?" Finn asked, perplexed.

"Yeah, five-hundredth floor," Tom replied.

He wasn't sure why he'd told Finn this fact when he hadn't told Mary. Somehow it had just rolled off his tongue without really realising he was saying it.

"You've been up on the five-hundredth floor?" Finn asked, highly sceptical.

"Yup…" Tom replied flatly.

"So, you're telling me, that there's some secret nightclub up on the five-hundredth floor that you were invited to in your first month at this school, and I've been here for two years and I've never even heard of it?"

"Afraid so." Tom replied bashfully.

"Unbelievable," Finn replied, chucking the pencil he was playing with into the fire. It flickered and burned then was quickly consumed as the thriving flames engulfed it. "So, you and Alice then, yeah? I'm impressed."

"Yeah I guess," Tom replied, feeling uncomfortable.

"Does Mary know?" he asked, uncharacteristically curious.

"She does, and she's not speaking to me," Tom replied dolefully.

"It's 'cos she's got the hots for you," Finn jibed, throwing another small object into the fire.

"I'm not sure what to do," Tom admitted, watching the new object burn up and wither.

"She'll come around eventually," Finn replied. "Probably just needs some time to get used to it. I wouldn't even worry about it if I were you. It's a case of mind over matter, if you don't mind, then it doesn't matter."

Tom nodded his agreement, but he didn't feel as hopeful. The way Mary had turned away from him so coldly back in the Revelation common room was particularly worrying. It was if to say *'that's it… I'm done with you'*, and she wanted nothing further to do with him. He'd been forced to walk away miserably, his tail between his legs and much more that he still wanted to get off his chest.

Mary had been like an island for him since he'd arrived at St Michael's; like a safe haven he could retreat to whenever he was feeling lost or down. Would it still be like that between them? Or would it be different now? Would she be a different person to him entirely now she thought that he'd chosen Alice over her? He didn't even know if that were really the case, he hadn't chosen her over Mary, it was simply a matter of taking the opportunities that were presented to him, and there'd never, as far as he could remember, been an opportunity to take things further with Mary.

Truth be told, it was probably because Alice was a lot more experienced in these situations than either Mary or he were. She'd leaned in and kissed him with an ease that

227

showed just how naturally things like this came to her; a practice most definitely gleamed from experience. *Just how many boys had there been since she'd arrived at St Michael's?* he wondered. *And how many boys before that while she was down on Earth? Maybe she wasn't even a virgin anymore?* Maybe she'd been with dozens of boys and would laugh at him when she learned just how inexperienced he was?

Finn noticed that Tom had drifted off into his own silent reverie. He decided to break the silence by throwing another small object from his pocket into the fire.

"So, did you hear?" he asked.

"Hear what?" Tom replied.

"About those kids that've gone missing?"

"What kids?" Tom blurted.

"Two kids from my House. A boy and a girl. They've been missin' for three days and no one can seem to find 'em anywhere," Finn explained.

"So that's what they were talking about in the hall…" Tom muttered almost to himself.

"You reckon it's got something to do with that creepy kid?" Finn asked.

"His name's Daniel," Tom clarified, "and no, I don't think so anymore."

"Well you've changed your tune," Finn exclaimed. "That kid was all you could talk about for the past week. What's happened?"

"Just something Alice said…" Tom replied. "She knows him. Says he's alright when you get talking to him."

"Well that doesn't prove anything," Finn interjected.

"She also said he died when a truck hit him, so he wasn't killed by his mother," Tom continued.

Finn went quiet and seemed to consider this for a moment, then he shrugged and fell back into his chair.

"So back to the drawing board then," he said, dejected.
"I guess…" Tom replied, equally as disappointed.

Chapter Twenty-Four
To Have and Have Not

Two weeks had gone by since Bricktop's, since those kids had gone missing and since Mary had last spoken to Tom. The classes they shared together had been particularly awkward. Mary seemed to race for the door at the end of every class before Tom could get a chance to speak to her. Things most certainly hadn't gotten better between them; if anything, they'd gotten worse. Maybe this was because she'd had more time to think it over and had decided she was even more mad with Tom than she'd initially thought, or maybe it was because Tom had started walking around the corridors hand-in-hand with Alice and had started spending all of his free time with her since he'd last spoken to Mary. Finn had even started joining them as they walked between classes, and so had some of Alice's giggling cohorts that she was usually never seen long without. Tom suspected Finn's motivations lay in the girl called Nettie, who he'd started trying to strike up conversations with as the awkward group roved clumsily through the tower. On occasion, they'd pass by Mary in the hallway, and she'd storm by at a hundred miles an hour without looking up at them. She'd even stopped spending time in the Revelation common room during the day, which Tom was slightly relieved about as Alice and her friends had started joining Finn and him there after classes finished.

The chances Tom got to talk to Mary were now few and far between, and he was beginning to worry if they'd ever be friends again.

One particularly rainy afternoon, while this new makeshift group were sat together in the Revelation Common room (Tom, Finn, Alice, Nettie and Alice's other friend called Truly, who rarely spoke a word and who caused Finn to break out into a chorus of Chitty Chitty Bang Bang whenever someone mentioned her name), some news came to light about the two kids who had gone missing. It was Nettie (a pretty but rather loud girl, whose blonde hair was plaited into an immaculate braid) who had overheard the news, and Finn hung desperately on her every word as she elucidated the tale.

"So, I heard in Celestial Botany today that Liu Shiohama and Yevgeny Volkov - those kids that went missing from Deuteronomy - were last seen talking to some kid from Numbers called Scott."

Tom perked up at her words. "Scott Woolberson?" he asked.

"I don't know. How come?" Nettie replied.

"He's my brother…"

It was true, Tom hadn't seen his brother as much as he'd hoped to since he'd first ran into him in the garden terrace. Scott had visited Tom only twice in the Revelation common room, and it had always been while he was alone. He had seemed strangely distracted to him, like there was something on his mind that he wasn't letting Tom in on. He was still to introduce Scott to both Alice and Finn, and whenever he'd suggested they all do something together, Scott had always insisted he was busy. He'd said something about being behind in class and really needing to study for the end of year exams, but they were still months away and Scott had never been much of a studier back down on Earth.

Later that evening, just as they were preparing to get to class, a bulletin was issued around the school for all students to attend an emergency assembly in the library immediately. Gabriel's voice rang out over the antiquated tannoy system and the group stared at each other in bewilderment.

"THIS IS AN URGENT ANNOUNCEMENT: ALL STUDENTS AND STAFF ARE REQUIRED TO MAKE THEIR WAY TO THE LIBRARY IMMEDIATELY FOR AN EMERGENCY BRIEFING. THANK YOU."

Tom looked over at Alice who was staring at him intently, eyes wide as headlights. He cocked his eyebrow questioningly and Alice shrugged back at him.

"What's going on?" Tom asked, bemused.

"I don't know," she replied. "This has never happened before."

"Surely it's those missing kids," Finn interjected.

"Maybe they found them?" said Nettie.

"We better get down there," Alice prompted, making to leave.

Back out in the hallway the elevators were swarming. The mass exodus out of the common room had resulted in a blockade at the doors to the stairway.

"Oi!" Finn barked as someone shoved him from behind.

The mob had ground to a halt at the doorway and it was clear to Tom that no one was getting into the elevators anytime soon.

"What do we do?" Alice moaned from behind him. She was pressed so closely that he could feel her warm breath on his neck as she began to hyperventilate.

"This way," Tom said, pulling her arm as he shoved his way to the wall.

The elevators, unfortunately, were no longer an option, and since they were up on the three-hundredth floor, neither were the stairs, unless they wanted to arrive at the library sometime tomorrow afternoon. Normally he would have suggested just going back to the common room and waiting until this mad rush subsided, but this time things were different. After what Nettie had said about Scott being the last person those two missing kids were seen talking to, getting to that assembly had become priority number one. If Scott had somehow been involved in all of this then he wanted to know about it, and he didn't like their chances of having to stand and wait until they could get into the elevator, especially when the same mad rush was probably happening all over the school right now. The elevators were more than likely a disaster waiting to happen, and he didn't want them to be in the middle of it.

Tom could think of only one other option, and it was something he wasn't entirely comfortable asking. The female rest rooms were said to contain a few more creature comforts than were available to the males; one such comfort they enjoyed was access to a service elevator that connected some of the rest rooms to a store closet. It was this very service elevator that Mary had used to get down to the rest rooms on the first floor on the day he'd first met her, while waiting outside the enrolment office. He remembered asking her later what she was doing all the way down on the first floor that day, when there were so many other rest rooms in the tower to use. Apparently, she'd taken the service elevator down to the first floor so she could pinch some of the rubbing alcohol (which was supposedly great for cleaning leather-bound books with) from the store closet, located just along the corridor from the enrolment office. If they could just make their way through this crowd to the rest rooms on the other side of the hall, then maybe they could use that service elevator to escape down to the first floor.

Once they were safely against the wall and out of the rabble, Tom explained his plan to Alice. She nodded her agreement but grimaced at the thought of making her way back through the bustling masses. He caught Finn's attention and signalled for him to push his way through to the girls rest rooms. Finn frowned at him confused but turned to Nettie and Truly and beckoned for them to follow. After much pushing and jostling and one elbow to the ribs, they eventually made it safely to the other side of the corridor and to the door of the girl's rest rooms.

"Feeling a little gender confusion?" Finn asked, when Tom and Alice reached the others.

"Shut it," Tom replied, in no mood for frivolity. "I just remembered something Mary told me once…. There's a service elevator in some of the girls rest rooms that could take us down to the first floor." He eyed Alice warily as he mentioned Mary's name; she'd been a bit sensitive of late to the fact that Tom was hurting over another girl. He'd explained that they'd only been friends, but she refused to see it that way.

"I hate to burst your bubble, but you need a key for that elevator," Nettie said contrarily.

"Don't look at me," Alice said shaking her head to indicate that she didn't have one.

It was Truly, the quiet girl with bunches, who turned out her pockets and presented the tiny silver answer to their problems.

"Nice one, Truly!" Alice said, beaming at her.

Truly shrugged and replied quietly, "I use it to get

paint brushes sometimes."

Alice led them inside the girls rest rooms, which were mercifully deserted. All the cubicle doors hung limply and Tom and Finn both scoffed enviously at the pristinely ornamented facilities.

"That's not fair!" Finn griped through gritted teeth. "We don't get…"

"Ssshhh!" Alice scolded, cutting him off mid-sentence.

"It's over there," Nettie pointed, indicating the silvery service elevator door at the far end of the room.

The group made single file towards the backend of the rest rooms. Nettie reaching the door first, pointed to the small key hole located next to the call button. Truly stepped forward and slotted her tiny key into the hole. When she turned it the lights on the call button illuminated and she pushed down on the arrow button as the rest of them waited.

Inside, Tom was struck with a sense of déjà vu, recalling the service elevator Mastema had used to escort them down to the underground lake. It wasn't nearly as primitive as that contraption had been thankfully: there was no polished wooden hand rails or luxurious oak panelling, but there was also no rudimentary lever system to operate the thing. There was a wall of buttons, similar to the lavish elevators of the main building, but there were only five buttons as opposed to the five hundred they were used to, and the buttons weren't marked with the little silver labels that normally accompanied them either.

Apparently, this service elevator was highly selective about which floors it stopped at. As well as the first floor and the three-hundredth floor for the House of Revelation, the elevator also made stops at the Houses of Numbers and Deuteronomy, the five-hundredth floor and floor three-hundred and thirty-three, which peaked Tom's curiosity as they waited for the doors to close behind them. Nettie reached out and pressed the button for the first floor and they waited in silence as the elevator plunged through three-hundred floors worth of tower in remarkably quick time.

They exited out onto the first floor down a little side passage that housed the store cupboard. They passed Uriel's enrolment office, which was empty from the looks of things, much like the rest of the floor.

"I remember sitting in this corridor fifteen years ago," Nettie said, as they walked by the row of chairs.

Tom realised after she'd spoken that he really didn't know much about Alice's friends, but now wasn't the time for questions. They had to make it to that assembly quickly before Gabriel started and they still had a long way to go.

"To the elevators then?" Finn asked, as they exited onto the plateau by the stairwell.

"No dummy," Nettie replied scathingly, "they're all full remember?"

"Oh yeah…" Finn muttered, downhearted.

They made their way over to the staircase and started the long climb reluctantly, with Finn bringing up the rear. The library was on the twenty-third floor and that was a lot of stairs to climb in a very short amount of time. Again, Tom was reminded of their trip down to Purgatory, and the staircase to him was just starting to resemble the jagged peaks of Mount Purgatorio, as they rounded the bend onto the tenth floor. They weren't the only ones who'd resorted to the manual climb either, with teachers and students alike taking to the stairs along with them, as they slowly ascended through the floors.

"That's it… I'm done," Finn gasped, as they turned

onto the fifteenth floor.

"Come on slow coach, only eight more to go!" Nettie taunted, slapping him on the head as he reclined onto the top step.

Tom grabbed him under the armpit and grudgingly helped him to his feet.

"Come on mate, not far now," he said encouragingly, feeling his own motivation start to wain slightly.

When at last they made it to the twenty-third floor, the staircase was besieged with pupils that were pushing their way to the library doors. Tom grabbed Alice by the hand and squeezed them through the first group, then ducked around the next, gradually forming a path on which the others could follow them. At the top of the staircase he could have sworn he got a glimpse of some soft red curls just as they disappeared into the crowd. The shuffling mass of students were now moving as one towards the library doors and Tom clung tightly to Alice's hand as they broke out into the large hall.

It was a spectacle the likes of which he'd never seen before. Nearly three thousand people crammed onto the terraces of the library. Each of the three floors were swarming with students and as he peered up, he could see them pressed against the golden bannisters that ringed the room like bracelets. The hoard that was pouring through the doors was met by an even bigger hoard staring back at them. Every last inch of floorspace was taken up by the chattering and anxious-looking crowd that eagerly awaited Gabriel's announcement. They came to a standstill not far away from the doors as the masses that had poured in ground to a halt. Alice squeezed his hand nervously and looking back, he could see that Finn and the other girls had been separated from them by at least ten feet of cramped angry students.

At long last, Gabriel walked out onto the stage and

the crowd slowly but surely started to quell. She ushered with her hands for silence and even from where he was standing, Tom could see her eyes as ferocious as ever.

"EVERYONE PLEASE," she boomed. "I realise you are all uncomfortable, but I have a *very* important announcement to make."

At that moment, the doors to the right of the stage burst open and Michael and Raphael strode out to join her, their long cloaks snapping as they strode powerfully towards their sister. Tom could see that some of the faculty were assembled near the bottom of the stage and they were all staring up at Gabriel anxiously as she continued.

"As many of you may know," she went on, "two students from the House of Deuteronomy have been missing from this tower in the past couple of weeks. Liu Shiohama and Yevgeny Volkov have both not been seen since they disappeared thirteen days ago. I can now tell you, with deep concern and regret, that a third student has gone missing as well…"

The thousands of students packed into the library burst into raucous discussion.

"I WILL HAVE QUIET!" Gabriel boomed. "Now… a student by the name of Scott Woolberson of the House of Numbers, has not been seen in nearly three days. Please rest assured that my fellow Heads of House and I are doing everything within our power to find these three missing students, and we are increasingly confident that we shall do so. However, if anyone here has *any* information regarding any of the missing students, then they should make their way to the stage immediately."

The eyes of the room darted around expectantly. Everyone waiting with bated breath for somebody to start pushing their way forward through the crowd towards the stage. Gabriel kept silent and scanned the room, allowing a full minute to pass before speaking again.

"Very well," she said emotionlessly. "Until these three pupils are found safe and well, we will be introducing additional security measures around the tower."

The doors to the right of the stage burst open again, but this time a platoon of fearsome looking warrior angels marched out onto the stage. Their footsteps echoed loudly around the room as they marched, coming to a halt in a regimental line behind the Heads. They wore matching white cloaks and thick leather boots, and their legs were bound with tight leather straps that matched those worn by Michael and Raphael. They were gruff bearded men with lean muscular frames and wild untamed manes of hair. Each of them was armed with a long wooden spear by their side, the business ends of which gleamed menacingly in the light.

"Unfortunately, this measure has been deemed necessary," Gabriel continued. "No more students will go missing under my watch, and I promise you, those who are lost *will* be found and the culprits will be dealt with swift and brutal retribution the likes of which they'd never dreamed. Sentry angels from Michael's Tenth Legion will be posted on every floor of the tower, as well as based on the doors to all common rooms and at the base of every staircase. A curfew will be instated immediately. When classes end at five o'clock every morning, every student will be required to return immediately to their common room. This curfew will *only* be lifted at such a time when myself and my fellow Heads of House have deemed this school to be safe once more. It is with deep regret, these measures that we are imposing today have become necessary, but I will not risk the safety of anyone at this school and the forces of evil will not prevail within these walls, not now and not in ten millennia from now. St Michael's will *always* be a place of refuge for the righteous and noble descendants of Michael, and that is my promise to you."

Gabriel stormed off the stage swiftly, accompanied by her brothers and the platoon of sentry angels.

*

The next morning when classes had finally ended, Gabriel's promise to the school was manifest throughout the tower. After the assembly had disbanded, it had taken hours for all the students to get back to where they needed to be. It was so bad that it wasn't until fifth period that Tom had finally found himself sitting in a classroom. Upon leaving Immortal Moralities with Professor Hume, they were immediately met with a burly looking sentry angel standing at the end of the hallway. He reminded Tom of one of the Beefeater guards at Buckingham Palace in the way his fixated gaze was entirely unaffected by the movement in his periphery. His eyes were fixed icily on the walls in front of him. Tom walked past him apprehensively as he made his way alone to the Revelation common room.

Mary, who was still not talking to him, had dashed for the exit as soon as the bell had rung, and Tom had watched her leave with the mounting regret he'd become accustomed to feeling whenever she was near. He dragged himself sluggishly to the elevators and was met with another brawny sentry angel once the doors had pinged open. He didn't even blink at the rabble of students as they squashed in around him; he simply gazed head-on with the same icy cold glare as the guard in the hall.

There been no chance to talk to anyone after the assembly had finished. No chance to talk about how he was feeling or to talk about the fact that his brother was now listed among those who were missing. Ever since he'd been reunited with Scott that beautiful day in the garden terrace, his brother had been like a ghost to him, appearing only for the most fleeting of instances, then disappearing without a trace, impossible to track down. There had been something going on with his brother in the weeks before he went missing, and now whatever that something had been was likely the reason he'd not been seen in three days.

Back in the common room, some obnoxiously loud eighties kids had commandeered their usual armchairs. There was no sign of Finn, Alice or the other girls, but he supposed that now the curfew was in place they would have to return to their own common rooms after classes had ended. Mary was sat in her new place across the far end of the room and Tom noticed her glance up, then quickly return to her book as he walked through the doors. It struck him that there was probably not going to be a better time to try and break ground with her again. Swallowing his pride nervously, he walked across the room and sat in the armchair across from her. She hadn't looked up again of course, but he'd expected as much, he was well aware that he would be the one taking the punches in this particular bout.

"Hi Mary," he said assuredly, looking to catch her eye over the top of her book.

She frowned into her pages but returned his greeting anyway with the least possible enthusiasm. He inched his chair forward, forcing her to interact. She was still pretending to be deep in her book, but he could see that her eyes were no longer moving back and forth over the lines.

"Mary…" he said again, defiantly.

"What is it Tom?" she said abruptly, slapping her book closed.

"We need to talk…"

"I've told you before, there's nothing to talk about," she spat back.

"There is though," he insisted. "You don't know the whole story."

"Well by all means then, tell me," she replied.

"Things with Alice…" he began, "it's not how it looks."

"It looks pretty black and white to me."

"It's not though," he countered, and at that moment, he let his guard down completely and allowed the whole sordid affair to spill out onto the table. "I didn't choose Alice over you. It wasn't a case of me choosing anyone. Things just sort of fell into place and I got swept away in it, and before I knew it things were completely different. I couldn't help what happened any more than you could. You can't punish me for something that happened naturally with Alice. There's no reason why we can't still be friends. I really like you… a lot… And maybe things could have gone further with us and I would have wanted that, but it hasn't happened that way, and we can't change the past or rule out anything from happening in the future. You're still my best friend Mary and I miss spending time with you…"

"But you spend all your time with Alice now…" Mary lamented.

"It doesn't have to be like that," Tom argued. "I can make time for just you and me. We can do anything you want to do, and no one will bother us."

"But as soon as Alice calls, you'll go running off with her," she challenged.

"No, I won't, I promise you that," he said. "Give me the chance to be your friend again Mary. You owe me that much at least."

She was silent for a long time as she considered Tom's words. He watched her chew on the skin of her bottom lip uncertainly, as the thoughts were debated, and reservations wrestled inside her head. Tom sat patiently as he was scrutinised, until finally, with a sigh that signalled her surrender, she let go.

"Friends?" Tom tried tentatively.

"Oh, what the hell," she smiled at last, "I've already given up on myself twice, third time is the charm."

"Best friends?" Tom grinned.

"Don't push it," she grinned back.

Chapter Twenty-Five
Helter Skelter (Part One)

It just so happened that the first class they had the next evening was Laws of the Universe. Finn walked into the magnificent starlit room and nearly fell flat on his face when he saw Tom, Mary, Alice and Nettie all sitting together at the circle of tables. He stood there, slack jawed at the doorway, eyes as wide as pancakes, before finally taking his seat next to Tom.

"Have they gone plum crazy?" he whispered into Tom's ear.

"I'll explain later," Tom whispered back.

The uneasy dynamic that had formed between Mary and Alice was one of necessity rather than desire. Neither liked the other, it was obvious to Tom, but each was pleasant and accommodating and by all accounts it seemed like it was working (well in Tom's presence it did anyway). Finn was baffled by the whole thing. He tailed behind suspiciously as the group made to leave at the end of class; untrusting of this new uncomfortable alliance and expecting it to implode at any second.

"So, what's the deal with this then?" he said to Tom as the others went on ahead. "Are you dating both of them now?"

Tom laughed and shook his head. "No just Alice," he assured him. "Mary is just making an effort to be a part of things I guess."

Now it was Finn's turn to shake his head. "This is going to end badly for everyone," he said sceptically. "Just wait and see. There's no way in hell that Mary is going to sit and play tea party with Alice and Annette."

"You don't know the whole story," Tom replied mysteriously. "It seems there's some history there... between Alice and Mary I mean. Apparently, it was Mary who took Alice under her wing when she first arrived at St Michael's all scared and alone twenty years ago. They used to be friends, according to Mary anyway."

Finn gaped at him dumbfounded. "Mary told you this?" he asked eventually.

Tom nodded. She had told him this much, but she'd also neglected to mention how they'd stopped hanging out in the first place. He suspected it was probably a touchy subject and the last thing he wanted to do was incense her further. Maybe he would bring it up again at a later date, but right now the risk of upsetting her again was too high. So, Tom had gone along with it unquestioningly and Alice had seemed perfectly welcoming when he had walked over to her with Mary by his side earlier that afternoon. He was under no illusions that this truce was going to last indefinitely. He knew that things like this were tolerated at times of necessity, and one day soon Mary and Alice would go right back to how they were before he'd arrived on the scene. For now though, he was happy to have both of them by his side, even if it was destined not to last.

Back out in the dark corridor of the astronomy floor, the sentry angel was stationed woodenly by the doors to the staircase. This one was a particularly mean looking specimen and his arms and legs were littered with scars the way Salathial's had been on Mount Purgatorio, which gave him the battle-hardened look of a Roman legionnaire. Thankfully, the social experiment they'd embarked upon was issued a brief reprieve when Mary excused herself to the library for free period. The rest of the group headed down to the Revelation common room which was still open to visitors during free periods at least.

Sat in their usual armchairs five minutes later, the topic of Tom's brother was back on the table.

"I'm sorry, but your brother was weird," Nettie blurted, unable to hold in her opinion any longer.

Tom noticed how she was already using the past tense and he bitterly resented her for it.

"He was always hanging around with this boy called Christian. I never saw him talk to anybody else."

"Who is this other kid?" Tom asked, a little too harshly.

"He's as creepy, if not creepier, than your brother. He always seems to be smiling about something. If you ask me, those two were a Columbine in the making. I always avoided them like the plague. I didn't have any classes with them thankfully, but if I saw either of them in the common room, I'd make for the exit fast!"

Alice looked up at Nettie and frowned.

"Do you know this boy? he asked Alice.

Alice shook her head, "I've seen him around, but I don't *know* him. Besides, I think Nettie might be exaggerating a little…"

"What about you, Truly?" he asked the quiet girl who seemed to be completely distracted by something happening at another table.

"Yes, I know them," she said shyly, still staring off into the distance. "I have Heavenly Art class with the taller boy. He's very handsome, and very good at painting."

"You're weird, Truly," Nettie said smugly. "Those two give me the creeps and that's all there is to it."

Tom knew that Scott was extremely tall, but he also knew that his brother was terrible at painting - that particular talent had been bestowed upon him alone within the Woolberson household. Scott was always the one good at sports and Tom was the one who liked drawing and painting. With this in mind, he was safe to assume that Truly hadn't been speaking about his brother.

"Have you seen this Christian guy since my brother went missing?" Tom asked, turning to Nettie again.

Nettie shook her head lazily. "I haven't actually... although he's not listed as missing, so somebody must've seen him."

"Where could they even go?" Alice asked, looking rather disturbed. "I don't understand how someone could even go missing in this place. It doesn't make any sense."

Tom's thoughts turned again to the mirror on the five-hundredth floor. That was a possible exit for sure, although the destination on the other side of it wasn't exactly desirable. However, if someone had been actively manhandling kids through it, then he supposed that kid wouldn't have had much of a say in the matter either way.

"There's always out the top exit," Finn piped up suddenly. Alice looked at him puzzled. "Like I've said before," he went on, "my friend George said there's a whole world for exploring above the five-hundredth floor."

"You mean the place you were trying to take us to the last time we got caught up there?" Tom asked, remembering the occasion vividly.

"Exactly," Finn replied, swinging his legs up over the arm of his chair. "If someone could get up there, then they'd have no problem disappearing. Sounds like a fine idea if you ask me..."

247

"Well we weren't asking you," Nettie sneered at him. Finn shrugged, putting his arms behind his head and reclining deeper into his chair.

"No, I think he's right…" Tom said suddenly.

"What?" Nettie scoffed.

He'd started to recall a chapter that he'd skimmed over in the library that day when Mary had given him A History of St Michael's to read while she got on with her shift there. The chapter had been on the topography of the school, and although he couldn't remember the whole thing, there was definitely something about the tower being so big that it stretched beyond the first heaven and into the second heaven, (whatever that was).

"I read it in this big book in the library called A History of St Michael's. It said something about the tower stretching out of the first heaven and into the second heaven, and how the five-hundredth floor is like the cut-off between the two."

The group stared at him like they'd all suddenly realised he was a few sandwiches short of a picnic basket.

"We need to get down to the library and read the rest of that chapter," Tom said resolutely.

*

Five minutes later, Tom, Finn and Alice (and the sentry angel) were in the elevator descending through the tower to the twenty-third floor which housed the library. Nettie had elected to return to her own common room, instead of embarking on a wild goose chase she considered a waste of her time, and Truly had agreed to join her (although Tom suspected that she would've much rather come to the library with them). They made their way past another sentry angel at the doors to the library who didn't blink an eye or move a muscle, even though Alice, the most beautiful girl in the building, was passing right under his nose.

The library had returned to its usual peaceful self after the madness it had hosted during Gabriel's assembly. There were only a handful of students quietly picking through the bookshelves and curled up on the couches in the many private alcoves of the library's three floors. Finn spotted Mary near the back of the ground floor sat quietly at a desk by herself. Tom felt bad disturbing her when she was so clearly in her element, but he was worried that what was in that book might have something to do with his brother's disappearance.

"Hi Mary," he said warmly, as the three of them approached her.

"Oh, hi!" she said embarrassed, quickly closing her book and turning a rosy shade of pink.

Tom was curious as to what exactly she had been reading but thought better of asking at this time.

"We were just wondering," he began, "if you could tell us where to find that book you showed me a few weeks ago? The one called *A History of St Michael's*?"

"Oh…" she replied puzzledly. "Sure… It's up on the first floor in the *'Authenticated History'* section. I can show you if you like?"

"We don't want to disturb you," Alice interjected.

"Really, it's no bother at all," Mary insisted.

Mary led them towards the spiral staircase in the corner that wound magnificently through the three floors like some kind of giant ornate bottle opener. Tom stroked his palm across the golden handrail and marvelled as the cool metal gleamed between his open fingers. The room looked like an opera house fit for the heavens, and he supposed that in some ways it was. The first floor provided for a spectacular panoramic view of the interior; the intricacies of the designs sculpted into the walls and the innovative engineering involved in the construction of this architectural spectacle was clearly evident from this vantage point. The bookshelves were designed so they amalgamated into the curvature of the walls and some of the books seemed to defy gravity as the shelves they were stashed in leaned precariously forward, making Tom wonder if they were in fact glued to the shelf at the spines. The whole room just seemed to flow seamlessly like it had been carved from one single lump of gold and any bits that were extra were used to make the tables and the chairs, so nothing went to waste. It was so satisfying to look at that it almost demanded the casual observer stop in their tracks and marvel at it with childlike wonder. It wasn't hard to see why Mary liked to spend most of her time here – the room was a masterpiece, the likes of which mere mortals could only dream of.

Mary guided them expertly through the various stations of the first floor; passing countless leaning shelves and alcoves and comfy looking couches and beanbag chairs that were scattered neatly around the immaculate crimson carpet. They arrived eventually at the section marked '*Authenticated History*' and Mary used the set of golden sliding ladders to propel herself along the bookshelf, stopping with her hand when she arrived at the appropriate subsection. She pulled out the heavy book and passed it down to Tom, who'd hurried along to catch her.

"Thanks," he said, using two hands to bear the weight of the cumbersome volume.

*

Mary decided to join them as they huddled around a small table in the neatly situated alcove to their immediate right.

"Can I ask what you're looking for?" she said curiously, as Tom skimmed the long list of contents.

"Topography," he replied simply, finding the required chapter at pages 50 – 65.

They all leaned over his shoulder as he flipped the pages to the chapter they were after. He arrived at page 50 and reread the initial paragraph he'd seen a few weeks before.

St Michaels School for Watchers is located in the Fields of Vilon, also known as The First Heaven - situated between the realm of Purgatory and the Second Heaven. The tower is so big that it stretches beyond the First Heaven and ends approximately five-hundred cubits into the Second Heaven…

"See," piped Finn, "I knew George wasn't lying."

"Wait," Tom pressed, "there's more."

Since St Michaels has so many floors, only the first five hundred reside within the First Heaven. The remaining floors are in Rakia (known as the Second Heaven), which falls under Jurisdiction of the Archangel Raphael. It is forbidden for any uninitiated student at St Michaels to enter the Second Heaven, since it is home to John the Baptist and to Jesus of Nazareth.

"I told you!" Finn cried gleefully. "I knew there was something up there! You all said I was stupid for wanting to exit out the top, but who's laughing now?"

"Would somebody shut him up?" Mary grumbled to Alice, who chuckled appreciatively. "It says clearly right there that the remaining floors are forbidden to students. So even if you could get out up there, you'd be caught before you could even get past the elevator doors!"

"Well, where else are all these missing students going then, do you suppose?" Finn challenged.

"What about the mirror?" Tom asked suddenly. Alice and Mary both stared at him strangely.

"Excuse me?" said Alice, unsure she'd heard him correctly.

"The mirror," Tom repeated. "The one on the five-hundredth floor that they use for the final exam."

"Once again," Mary said, "the five-hundredth floor is off limits to students!"

"That's not entirely true..." Alice offered, timidly.

"What do you mean?" Mary fired back.

"Well, there's a club up on the five-hundredth floor that teachers and students both visit once a month, and the Heads usually turn a blind eye to pupils being up on that floor on that day, if they're accompanied by a teacher and have an invitation..."

"What club?" Mary spat at her. "There is no club."

"It's true," Tom said, rising from his chair and standing next to Alice. "I've been there..."

Mary stared at them speechless; her eyes revealing the internal battle raging behind them as she desperately clung to her own perception of reality.

"Well, there you have it," Finn said finally. "There's plenty of people up on that floor and I'm sure, if one of them wanted, they could easily sneak off to this Rakia place."

"Or through the mirror," Tom added eagerly.

"That's not how it works, Tom," Mary said reprovingly. "You can't just jump through it, it's not a doorway."

"But I thought you said that…" Tom began, before Mary cut him off.

"I said it was a window - that you could see through it, not go through it!" she corrected, exasperatedly.

"So how exactly do demons come through it then if it's not a doorway?" Tom challenged.

Mary shook her head wearily and took a seat back at the table beside Tom, as if she were about to explain to a toddler why it's wrong to run with scissors.

"Demons don't come *through* the mirror Tom," she began slowly. "It's a mirror, when you look into it, it shows you your reflection."

"I'm not following," Tom frowned.

"Let me explain," she said hesitantly. "The demons in the mirror don't come from hell. The mirror isn't some doorway between St Michael's and the underworld that people can just pass through. When you look into the mirror, the mirror reflects back the demon inside of you. It shows you the absolute worst of yourself – your *inner demon*. Everything you hate about yourself and all the evil that exists inside of you."

Tom screwed up his face, starting to feel frustrated by the direction this conversation had taken. "So, what exactly is the point of the final exam then?" he asked at last.

Tom could feel Alice and Finn lean in closer as Mary continued. "In the final exam, the student has to face the mirror alone and the mirror manifests the evil inside each of us. All your greatest fears and everything that you hate and despise about yourself, and everything that you've

253

bottled up and prayed to God that no one ever found out about you. All that evil inside of you is manifest into the entity staring back at you - your own reflection. Except, it's not you at all; it's the very worst of you. In the final exam, you have to defeat that evil before it consumes you."

Tom was lost for words. Not even Finn managed to crack wise about this one. He stood there behind Mary, staring blankly at the back of her head, as if he too were struggling to process what she had just said. Mary's eyes were blurring as she stared back into Tom's. He could see the strain on her face as she struggled to fight back the silent tears threatening to pour from her eyes. He knew what this meant for her of course. Mary had twice been faced with the evil inside herself and twice she'd failed to overcome it. The next time would be her last time and if she couldn't find the will to defeat it then, she would be cast out of St Michael's and she really didn't know what would become of her after that. Tom watched these emotions play like silent movies in her eyes as they blurred to the point of bursting.

*

Five minutes later, as the group gradually settled, Tom turned his attention back to the book on the table and Mary, it seemed, was more than willing to capitalise on the distraction. She got out of her seat and walked around the table and they read the next paragraph together.

The Second Heaven (also known as 'Rakia') was fashioned by God on the second day of creation. It is home to the sun, the moon, the stars and the constellations. Both the First Heaven and the Second

Heaven are composed of natural phenomena, the likes of which can be found on Earth and are listed on an Earthly chart known as the 'periodic table'. The Archangel Raphael, who holds dominion over Rakia, separates his time between the First Heaven and the Second Heaven; much like the Archangel Michael separates his time between the First Heaven and the Fourth Heaven, where he holds dominion. The Archangel Gabriel is the only Head of House at St Michael's who resides exclusively within the First Heaven (where she holds dominion).

When it is time for a young Watcher to ascend from the First Heaven to the Second Heaven, they will be led to the upper floors of the tower, which reside within the Second Heaven. On these floors they will find, amongst a host of other departments; the deed office, immigration control and the wingery. On the very top floor they will find the entrance to Rakia, which is guarded at all times by two sentry angels, and only the initiated Watcher may pass through it. Once in Rakia, the new Watcher's wings will be put immediately to the test as the doors open at a lofty five-hundred cubits above the ground. As well as offering a means of weeding out the weak, this also prevents any uninitiated students from attempting to enter into Rakia illegally.

"Look at this," Tom said, interrupting the conversation that had started between Alice and Finn while the other two had been huddled around the table.

The group clustered around him again reluctantly with Alice throwing Mary a hesitant glance to check whether she'd gotten over her brief flurry of emotion. Clearly, she'd been uncomfortable when it'd looked like Mary might have started to cry, so she'd resorted to striking up a conversation with Finn to distance herself from it.

"It says here that the top exit is five-hundred cubits above the ground. So even if someone wanted to leave that way, they couldn't, not until they're 'initiated', whatever that means," Tom said, highlighting the text with his finger.

As Alice and Finn both read the passage over his shoulder, Tom was caught tightly between Alice and Mary at either side of him. He smelt the sweet fragrance of both girls meld together to form some new alluring concoction that was both familiar and foreign to him. The vibrant and confident notes of Alice were complimented by the timid and sweet scents of Mary. Alice put her hand on his shoulder to balance herself as she leaned closer — or to remind Tom of which girl he belonged to.

"It sounds to me like no one is leaving from up top without having graduated from the school first," Mary said resolutely, sounding more like her old self again now.

And as usual she was right, the text was quite clear. The only exit above the five-hundredth floor into Rakia was one that required you to fly away from.

"We all seem to be forgetting about another exit from the school that I thought would have been obvious, especially to you two," she said gesturing to Tom and Finn.

Tom had no clue as to what she was alluding to, or why it should've been so obvious to both Finn and him.

"Where?" he asked puzzledly.

"The service elevator in the dungeons of course! Have you forgotten already?"

"Oh yeah!" Tom cried, baffled as to how he could have forgotten about that particular exit already. It had been nearly seven weeks since Mastema had taken them down into the fiery depths of Purgatory, but the memory was still as crisp as ever.

"I don't suppose anyone could get out down there though," he offered, considering the option. "Not with Mastema standing guard in the dungeons."

"Wouldn't be hard to sneak past that old bat," Finn piped, taking his own seat at the table. "She most likely locks herself in that office and sleeps all day."

"She won't sleep," Mary said, rolling her eyes.

"You know what I mean," Finn replied. "All I'm saying is, she's most likely in that room at the end of the dungeon with no idea of what's going on in the rest of the place."

"It's possible," Tom offered optimistically.

"Possible, but unlikely," Mary chided.

"I'm sorry, but what service elevator are we talking about? And where does it go exactly?" Alice cut in puzzledly.

Tom quickly filled her in on the specifics of their day trip to Purgatory at the behest of Mastema, who had been their sickeningly enthusiastic tour guide for the day. Her eyes grew wider to the point that Tom thought they might pop, as he expounded their account of the underground world. The fact that there was a service elevator to Purgatory within the tower hadn't seemed to bother her; it was the fact that Tom had been there already on his first day at the school that had irked her incessantly.

"You're full of surprises, Tom Woolberson," she said at long last. "Anything else I should know about you while we're at it?"

Tom shrugged defensively and Finn muffled a snigger into his fist.

258

Chapter Twenty-Six
Helter Skelter (Part Two)

As the group scattered for Third period, it was obvious to Tom that Alice was decidedly unhappy with him. Her customary kiss on the cheek, that had become a welcome tradition whenever they parted, had been coldly mislaid. Tom watched her walk away with a burgeoning sense of rejection. Finn too said his goodbyes as he parted for Heavenly Art, and he was even polite enough to give Tom a quick kiss on the cheek before Tom shouted "*Geerrrofme!*" with Finn walking away in stitches.

Mary and Tom made their way together to Professor Wilde's Notable Literature class. Mary had perked up considerably since her near breakdown in the library and Tom was feeling just about the opposite: dejected and hurt by Alice's cold dismissal of him. Tom walked silently to the elevators while Mary chatted happily about 'De Profundis,' which was an exceptionally long letter written by Professor Wilde himself during his incarceration on Earth, that they were currently reading through in class. The letter was named after the Latin for 'Psalm 130' from the Book of Psalms, which just happened to be one of the Psalms traditionally recited in times of communal distress – *a fitting parable,* Tom thought to himself grudgingly.

As the doors opened onto the forty-sixth floor, Mary had moved on to talking about Alice and how she thought that she wasn't right for him. Although Tom resented the unnatural progression of conversation topics, he had noticed Mary seemed to be handling the situation a lot better than she had been initially, even if her opinion on the matter had remained somewhat unchanged.

Out in the dark corridor, they quickly made their way around the calculating bends to room 33C - seeing as they were late, and the rest of the class had already taken their seats. As they approached the door, Tom could have sworn he heard muffled voices coming from around the corner at the far end of the hall. He looked over at Mary and her face confirmed that she had heard them too. They looked at each other curiously while Tom placed his hand on the cold brass handle and waited before turning it to see if he could make out what the disembodied voices were saying. Suddenly, Tom's face turned violent. It was Scott. No 'ifs' or 'buts' about it. That was his brothers voice, he would've recognised it from a mile away. He dropped the handle, turned on his heel and sprinted down the corridor towards the voices. As he approached the bend, Mary grabbed him firmly by the wrist, causing his arm to jolt painfully in its socket as he was ground to a halt.

"What are you doing?!" she seethed through gritted teeth.

"That's Scott..." Tom uttered back to her. "It's my brother!"

He turned away and made to move again, but she clung to his arm tightly. He reached on his toes and peered around the corner, seeing Scott standing in a shadowed alcove, muttering furiously at some unseen figure. He looked terrible. His hair was matted and plastered to his forehead and his eyes were ringed with sunken impressions. He looked as if he were in the final stages of a short but vicious battle with radiation sickness. His clothes were stained black with soot and ash, and there were smudges on his cheek and forehead where he'd been wiping the sweat from his brow. Mary let go of his arm and peered around the corner with him, gasping as she saw the state of the sinister figure muttering heatedly in the shadows.

"Who is that?" she breathed silently over Tom's shoulder.

"That's Scott…" he said plainly. "That's my brother."

The two of them watched as another boy pushed gruffly by Scott and made his way hurriedly up the corridor and out of sight, leaving him alone in the shadowed alcove. Tom made his move. He stepped out from behind the bend and rushed silently towards his brother.

"Scott?" he said slowly, seeing he'd now sank to the flagstone floor and was holding his head between his hands looking defeated. Scott looked up immediately, stricken with panic.

"Tom?" he uttered, disorientated. "What are you doing here?"

"Where have you been?" Tom said, throwing himself to his knees beside him. "The whole school is looking for you! They say you went missing and haven't been seen in three days!"

Scott frowned as he wiped a fresh smudge of soot across his forehead. He considered his younger brother disparagingly, before his head finally sank back into his hands and he broke down in tears.

"What is it?" Tom urged, placing one hesitant hand on his shoulder.

261

"It's me…" he said finally, through a flurry of tormented tears. "I'm the reason there are kids that're missing. I took them."

"What?" Tom uttered, perplexed. "What are you talking about? You can't have…"

"It's true," he sobbed again. "Look, there's things I need to tell you. Things you don't know about me. There's so much you don't know. I'm not good Tom."

Tom heard movement behind him, and Mary pulled up at his shoulder. Scott stared up at her through wet, bloodshot eyes and then he shrugged and dropped his head again. Mary sat down beside Tom as Scott slowly looked up at them and finally, for the first time in his existence, he bared his soul for all to see.

"It was my first year at Foxden when I met them," he began hesitantly. "Phase one of training had ended and we'd been shipped off to join our unit at the barracks in Norfolk, not far from Brundall near the Broads. I was bunked with a boy named Jason who was strange but friendly in an odd kind of way. Jason had these older friends who'd finished training and were part of the Royal Logistics Core; two guys called Dean and Tristan. We all knew about what'd happened at Foxden before we got there. The stories about the murders were all anyone could talk about in the last weeks of red phase. We knew how there'd been two recruits who'd died mysteriously on the camp, and how no one was coming forward or saying anything to the officers about what'd happened. The first boy, called Stephen Belson, had gone off on a lone patrol of the perimeter one night and had never reported back the next morning. They found his body at the edge of the woods, stripped naked and covered in dirt with seventeen stab wounds in his chest. He'd been stripped of his rifle and all of his gear as well, they looked for weeks but it never turned up.

"Next was a girl named April Fincher. She was found with a single gunshot wound to the head, two hundred metres from her abandoned guard post. The army coroner listed the death as suicide, but there was talk around the camp that she'd been killed by some cult. None of the officers ever caught wind of it though and neither did anyone else. As far as they were concerned, she'd killed herself and that's all there was to it. It didn't matter that she'd been naked when they'd found her and stripped of her rifle and her pack and the rest of her gear, the same as the Belson boy had. When we arrived at Foxden, the barracks were already national news. Then, what happened next, only made it worse…

"It was Jason who introduced me to 'em – Dean and Tristan I mean. They had this sort of buzz around them which instantly attracted you to them. Like they were celebrities or somethin'. They were just back from Afghanistan and they were full of stories about the gruesome stuff that had happened over there. They didn't seem to be bothered by all the death and devastation they saw. It was like they were glamourising it, as if it were scenes in some action movie as opposed to actual people being killed. But they made me feel like part of the gang y'know and it was nice. It's not easy being the new guy on the camp. Last thing you want to do is end up being somebody's chew toy, so when these guys took me in, I was grateful.

"One night we were sitting around in the bunks where all the new recruits were situated, and Dean started talking about this club I should think about joinin'. He said I'd be perfect for it and it'd be a great way to make some new friends around the camp, which was somethin' you were always looking to do in those places. I asked him what it was, and he said I should come along one night and see for myself. Jason said he'd come too, so I agreed.

"I remember the next day we had this ten-kilometre run across the broads and I was absolutely shattered when we got back to the barracks. We got some grub then hit the showers and then when we got back to the dorms Dean and Tristan were there waitin'. 'It's time,' Dean said to me, so we followed him out the back door of the mess hall, and he led us off base and into the woods, which we thought was a bit strange but we just went with it as these were Jason's mates and we didn't want to look like a pair of pussies in front of 'em. We kept walking through the woods in near total darkness for what seemed like hours. Jason busted his knee up pretty bad tripping over this log, and I laughed and helped him to his feet again. Looking back at us then we seemed so innocent. Just two idiots tryin' to make friends and stay out of trouble.

"So, we kept walking in the dark and eventually Dean stops and points to this light up ahead of us, it was some kind of fire in a clearing in the middle of the trees. We got closer and we could see all these figures huddled around the fire with their hoods up. I remember looking at Jason and telling him this was a bad idea, but he didn't seem phased by it, so I pretended like I wasn't either. I asked Dean if this was some sort of devil worshipping cult and he told me to keep an open mind, so I kept my mouth shut from then on and just listened…

"Sat around the fire, Dean talked about social Darwinism and police-state authoritarianism, which didn't mean anything to me at the time. He said that humans are instinctually predatory, and things like lust and carnal desire are an essential part of human nature. He criticised religion as a man-made construct and said we needed to question everything we've been taught in schools and by our parents. Things like 'good' and 'evil' were arbitrary concepts and the only thing that mattered was that you '*do unto others as they do unto you*'. So, if someone ever treated you poorly, you should respond viciously.

"After that first meeting, everything changed for me. Dean got me into bands like Mayhem and Burzum from the Norwegian death metal scene, and he gave me books to read as homework like *Atlas Shrugged* by Ayn Rand and *The Satanic Bible* by Anton LaVey. I was sceptical at first but once I really got into reading those books, I found I really connected with what they were saying. I had so much anger in me that I didn't know what to do with. Years of fighting with mum and dad and the teachers at school and feeling like I was useless, and nobody wanted me around.

"Until that point in my life, I'd never considered the fact that I should've been putting myself first, then maybe I would get along better in the world. So that's what I started doing. I started loving myself at the expense of everyone else. I started doing everything in my power to get what I wanted out of life. We'd drive into town every night and were indulging in sex and drugs and booze. It was incredible, and I felt liberated for the first time ever. But then things started to get really dark. I found out things about Dean and Tristan that I really didn't like. I wasn't taking this whole thing as literally as a lot of the other guys were - including Jason. They told me about what they'd done to those recruits that'd died on the base. It was them. It was Dean and Tristan and the rest of them. They said sacrifices were necessary so we could continue to be free. They said that no one was truly free unless they could embrace death as a natural part of life, and that we are all animals and to deny our predatory instincts was to be bound by the chains of society.

"I started having these terrible nightmares every night when I went to sleep, and I realised I was getting quite disturbed about the whole thing. I told Jason I was thinking of getting out of this business with Dean and Tristan and maybe getting out of the army all together and applying for college or something, but he didn't take it very well. It went to fists right there in the dorms, and when I went to the mess hall for lunch after cleaning up my bloodied nose, I realised right away that Jason had told Dean and Tristan about what I'd said to him. I was scared and I panicked and grabbed a seat at another table by some other recruits and as soon as I did that, I knew I was in trouble.

"That night, lying on my bunk, the three of them came into my room. They said I was coming with them tonight and I didn't have a choice about it. We went out into the woods again and they were all dead silent – nobody spoke a word as we walked through those trees. I remember the snapping branches beneath our feet, and it had been raining for days so my boots were sodden and flooded with water. When we finally got to the clearing, I saw what they'd done. There was a boy there; he was tied with his hands behind his back and they'd gagged his mouth with some tape, and he was lying there on the soaking wet ground staring up at me. That look in his eyes, I'll never forget it.

"Dean turned to me. He didn't speak. He just stared at me with his black unfeeling eyes and then he pointed at the boy on the ground and said *after tonight, you'll be one of us*. I looked at Jason desperately trying to see fear behind his eyes, but he just stared at the ground and didn't say a word. Tristan walked over to the boy on the ground and he pulled a handgun from his belt and he shot him twice in the head. I remember Dean turning to me and he was

266

actually smiling; he said '*now you're one of us…*' They told me that I had to drag his body back to the camp and dump it by the perimeter fence. That way it was supposed to look like he'd been on a lone patrol and had shot himself. Only we would know the truth.

"I broke my back dragging him through that forest. It took me most of the night. The next day, nobody said a word and I saw the three of them in the mess hall for breakfast as usual, and when the alarm was raised about the recruit that'd been found dead, none of us even blinked. I had to live with that. I had to live with knowing what we'd done to that poor kid and it was the worst time of my life.

"It was during the next few weeks that I started learning more about Jason and his past. There were stories about him going around the camp that I wouldn't have believed when I first met him. Apparently, Jason had been something of a local celebrity in his hometown of St Ishmaels in Wales. He'd even made the local newspaper one year when a little girl of five had washed up on the beach and Jason had been the one to find her. It'd been his neighbour's young daughter who he'd taken out for a walk along the sea path. The official report based on police interviews with Jason was that she'd fallen over a cliff edge while they were out walking. Jason had been too far away to grab her, and it'd been too dangerous to jump in the sea after her. He found her an hour later - the current had dragged her out to sea then washed up her body on the beach when the tide came in. Of course, the story around the barracks was that the girl had been pushed and Jason had been the culprit. It was all just talk but at that point I was starting to believe it.

"I was certain then more than ever that I needed to get out of those barracks and away from the army and put as much distance between me and the rest of them as possible. I went to the Sergeant and told him I wanted to be discharged. Since I was still in training, I only needed permission from my CO if I wanted to leave. He said, it wasn't a good time right now with all the media around the barracks again, but if I still wanted to leave in a month then I could go.

"So, I went back to normal army life and kept my distance and kept my head down as best as I could. The death of that recruit Luke Greyson was listed as another suicide. It was unbelievable. The urge to come forward and tell somebody what'd really happened was almost unbearable. I still shared a bunk with Jason at night and he started looking at me all suspicious like he was just waiting for me to break and go to the Sergeant.

"Eventually, I decided that was what I was going to do. The guilt had consumed me. It was all I thought about every second of every day. I made a plan that after exercises finished that day, I was going to go to the CO and then I was leaving the army for good and never coming back. That was my last day on Earth.

"When we got back to camp after our hike that day, Jason was stood next to our bunk with Dean. I walked into the room and asked what they were doing, then Tristan came out from behind the door and hit me with the butt of his rifle. I blacked out. When I woke up it was dark, and I was in the woods again and I was tied up exactly how that other recruit had been. They'd gagged my mouth but left it loose enough so I could still talk. I spat out the cloth and cried out as loud as I could. Dean was sitting alone by the fire and I could see Jason off in the distance by the edge of the clearing. My head was throbbing, and I kept on slipping in and out of consciousness at first - anything I could see was all blurred and hazy, and I was so close to the fire that the heat was burning my eyes when I tried to open them. I cried out again, but it didn't do any good. The last thing I ever saw on Earth was the blurred form of Tristan standing over me with his handgun. Then, it was over…"

Chapter Twenty-Seven
A Handful of Dust (Mea Culpa)

Scott held his head between his knees in resigned indignation as Tom and Mary silently processed what they'd heard. Tom looked at his brother – he looked weak and tormented, like he'd been through hell and back to get to where he was now. All those years of not knowing what'd happened to him, and all the anger and resentment that had spawned because of it, had now finally been reprieved. This was Scott's story. This was the answer to the question that had plagued him for four long years. At last it was here. Listening to Scott tell his tale had been one of the most painful experiences he'd ever had to endure. He felt like he was there beside him at every moment of it, as if he'd lived through those years with him, and as if he too had been gagged and tied by that fire in those woods at Foxden.

Now it was all over, he didn't know how to feel about the whole thing. Was he angry at Scott? Was he relieved that he'd finally come clean about it all? One thing that he was sure of was the guilt that had gripped him for four torturous years was now slowly starting to release him. Tom wasn't the enemy in this story, and neither was Scott. It was clear that the real evil had been within two young army recruits by the names of Tristan and Dean, who had been responsible for the deaths of at least four young men and women at the Army Barracks at Foxden, near the Norfolk Broads. He scolded them silently as his brother slowly stirred. There were still questions that remained unanswered.

"Scott?" Tom said gently, careful not to invoke any needless rebuttals. Scott looked up and met his eyes again hesitantly. "Scott, who were you talking to just now when we found you? And why were you saying that it's you who's behind the disappearances here at St Michael's?"

Scott dropped his eyes again and flinched, as if ashamed to even hear those words spoken aloud in front of him.

"I was talking to Jason…" he said, holding Tom's gaze consistently for the first time since they'd found him. "He arrived at St Michael's the year after I did…"

*

Jason? Tom thought bizarrely. *How can it be Jason?*

"What about Christian?" he asked, beside himself with confusion. "Everyone say's you're always seen around the tower with that boy Christian?"

"Christian *is* Jason…" Scott explained painfully. "He goes by his first name now, Christian Jason Little."

Tom and Mary stared at each other in horrified disbelief. "It can't be…" Tom muttered almost to himself. "But how…?"

"Jason isn't like you and me," he explained carefully. "He was so consumed by the whole Satanism thing that it's all he believes in now. Everyone else is just a pawn in his mind for him to manipulate and move around as he wants. He doesn't see them as people with feelings and emotions, only pieces on a chess board that're there solely to be played with.

271

"After Tristan and Dean were done with me and dragged my body back to the barracks and set me up like just another suicide, life had gone on as normal for them. That was until twelve months later when Jason was chucked out of the army. He received a dishonourable discharge on the grounds that witnesses had come forward saying that they'd seen him arguing with Luke Greyson on the night before he'd turned up dead. They could never link any physical evidence to him, but the witness testimony was enough to put him under heavy suspicion from the officers and they had him thrown out of the army for it. When he got home to his mother, she'd argued with him about the reason he was discharged and even she suspected that he'd had something to do with the death of that recruit. I guess she decided that she couldn't live with what she'd brought into this world, so the next day she brewed a pot of tea using hemlock from the fields beside their house and served it with dinner. Jason wound up at St Michael's like me and his mother went to hell for his murder and her suicide..."

This time it was Mary who seemed to take issue with Scott's story, "but that doesn't make any sense!" she fumed, as Scott looked up at her strangely. "Jason *was* behind the murder of that recruit and he *was* behind your murder too! He should've been sent to hell, not his mother! He doesn't belong here at St Michael's!"

Scott seemed to understand her frustration. "It looks that way," he said in agreement, "but Jason never *actually* killed anyone... it was always Tristan who pulled the trigger."

Mary open her mouth to reply but she couldn't seem to muster a solid enough argument, so she fell silent.

"So..." Scott continued, "when Jason arrived here and I saw him sitting across from me in Ancient History one day, I'm ashamed to admit that I was almost relieved to see a familiar face."

"But he had you killed!" Mary fumed from over Tom's shoulder.

"It's true," Scott professed, "I should have been mad at him, I should have hated him for what he'd done to me."

"Then why?" Tom asked, perplexed.

"My life at St Michael's didn't get off to the same rosy start that yours has, little brother. I picked right up from where I left off at Bridlington High. I was in trouble with the teachers nearly every day and it was hard to make friends because of it. I ended up lonely, skipping classes most nights and spending my days in the dungeons with Mastema. When Jason arrived, he shook me out of the rut I'd gotten myself into. He was articulate and polite and charming, and the teachers seemed to like him, so I started tagging along with him and I got myself back on track and out of the dungeons. Before Jason came along, I was close to being thrown out of St Michael's and God knows what would've happened to me then. I was almost grateful that Jason had arrived and changed all that for me. I've spent the last three years at this school, getting on with my work and, for the most part, staying out of trouble, and I have Jason to thank for that."

Mary's blank face staring back at him was not one of understanding but of utter frustration. Tom, however, knew his own brother a lot better than she did. He'd seen him make all these mistakes before back on Earth and now he'd started making them all over again at St Michael's – but this time instead of the police, he had Gabriel and Raphael to answer to, who could sentence him to something a lot more sinister and eternal than a juvenile detention centre. Then it struck him, like a bolt of supercharged electricity - this was the person he'd been

273

looking for! The person who'd had Gabriel so afraid in that overheard conversation on the astronomy floor and had launched this Agatha Christie-like pursuit in the first place! It all came back to this one missing link in the chain, the link that had a hand in Scott's death and now it seemed had been manipulating him like a chess piece since he'd arrived at St Michael's. It'd been Jason the whole time!

"He came to me a month ago," Scott carried on timidly. "He said he'd thought of a way for us to get out of this stupid school. A way for us to truly go back home, where we'd never have to answer to anyone ever again. As it turned out, he'd gotten the idea while watching the two of you one day."

"Us?" cried Tom. "You were watching us?"

"Of course. Like I told you, I was watching you from the very first day you arrived, and sometimes, Jason came with me."

Mary gripped her fingers around Tom's arm again and squeezed his skin tightly. Tom's feelings were mutual, he felt sick. This guy Jason, the psychopath who'd driven his own mother to murder him, had been watching them since day one at St Michael's. He felt a shiver rattle his collar bones, then reverberate down his spine and his intestines clenched tightly like a fist.

"It was your first day actually," Scott continued. "Raphael escorted you down to the dungeons to see Mastema, then she took you somewhere completely unexpected, somewhere completely off the grid, and you were gone for most of the night. We took that shaky little service elevator down to that underground lake to follow you, but when we got there you were gone and there was no boat for us to follow. Jason was furious. He wanted to know where that gangly old hag had taken you and where that cave system led to, but we were stuck. Our only option was to go back up to the dungeons and wait for your return. When you finally got back, exhausted and covered in dust, Jason and I gave Mastema the slip. We crept back into that service elevator and headed down to the lake, and this time there was a boat there waiting for us."

"You went to Purgatory?!" Tom asked, in disbelief that anyone would go to that place willingly.

"Only briefly at first," Scott replied. "We didn't leave the boat. Once we realised where we must be, we turned back pretty quickly."

"Oh," Tom muttered, slightly relieved.

"But," Scott continued, "what I didn't know at the time, was that Jason was secretly planning on going back there without me, and he did - more than once from what I can gather."

"Why?" Mary blurted from Tom's other side.

"He was planning something," Scott replied mysteriously. "You see, what Jason found out is, there's more than one way out of Purgatory. In fact, there's three. The one from the caves which we used, then there's the bridge at the top of the mountain which, from his best guess, he thinks might take you to paradise or somewhere similar, then there's the gates..."

"The gates?" Tom said sceptically. "What gates?"

"You know, the gates that lead to that other place, the place where Jason's mother ended up. Hell."

Tom shifted uncomfortably on the cold flagstone floor as his brother continued.

"So, like I said; a month ago he came to me. He told me about the gates. He took me down there again and he showed them to me."

"What do they look like?" Mary asked, unable to help herself.

"Old," Scott replied strangely, "like really old, and rusty. I'd say they were in desperate need of replacing - like one good shake and they'd crumble into dust. Definitely not as sturdy as you'd hope the gates to Hell would be."

"What's on the other side of them?" Tom asked, finding himself curious in spite of himself.

"Nothing," Scott replied, "just the same that's in Purgatory - rock for as far as the eye can see. I guess it must go somewhere though as there's a path leading away from the gate."

"So, what *is* Jason planning at the gates?" Tom pressed, the fear in his voice apparent now.

"And why did you kidnap two innocent students from the school?!" Mary added, with an admonishing glower in Scott's direction.

Scott had his head in his hands again. He looked utterly defeated. "He manipulated me," he said defiantly. "He made me feel like I was in his debt and I had to help him with this. The way he spoke to me it was like I didn't have a choice in the matter. He said without him, I would've been chucked out of St Michael's already. I felt like I owed him this. He changed things for me here. I didn't want to end up back in that dark place I was in three years ago. Can you understand that?"

Tom stared down at him pityingly. He couldn't condone what his brother had done, but in some bizarre way he had to admit that he understood it. Scott's habit of getting in with the wrong crowd had plagued him his entire life. There was no malicious intent in his actions, he wasn't capable of it. It was clear to Tom that his brother had been motivated by a mixture of sheer desperation and stupidity, a lethal combination when placed in the wrong hands, (like Jason's).

Mary was scolding Scott as he slowly raised his eyes to meet theirs. "Where are they?!" she fired at him as he stared back at her pathetically. "What've you done to them?"

"They're down there," he conceded pitifully. "We tied them up outside those gates."

For a second, Tom was sure that she was going to hit him. She pulled her hand back as if to slap him but stopped herself at the last moment, collapsing back onto the floor. "You'll be expelled for this," she said finally, glowering at him with a mixture of loathing and pity. Despite what he'd done, she couldn't bring herself to hate him completely, his story was too sad. What'd happened to him at the army barracks and then falling prey to the same deranged psychopath for a second time when he'd arrived at St Michael's, was just too tragic to merit her out-and-out contempt.

"We need to tell somebody," Mary said jumping to her feet. "We need to go to Gabriel and let her know that they're down there!"

"It's too late!" Scott challenged, finding a modicum of his temperament again. "Jason is already on his way back there. They'll never stop him in time!"

"What's he going to do?" Tom asked, rising to his feet with the rest of them.

"Ritual sacrifice, just like Dean and Tristan did at Foxden. He believes that since while he was alive, he failed to make one himself, he won't be allowed into hell, so he's going to sacrifice those students at the gates as an offering to the Devil."

"But.. that's insane!" Tom cried.

"I know!" Scott agreed. "But like I told you, Jason isn't like other people. He doesn't care what happens to me or to you and he sure as hell doesn't care about what happens to those students!"

"We need to get down there!" Tom cried, now feeling like he was partially responsible for all of this as it was *his* brother who'd kidnapped them in the first place. Mary nodded decisively and together they bolted towards the elevators with Scott in tow.

*

"Look out!" Mary cried, as the classroom doors burst open and chattering students ambled out into the corridor. It was only then that Tom realised that Scott's recanting of his tale had taken almost the entire hour they were supposed to have been in Notable Literature. A girl cried out as Tom shoved into her and he apologised hurriedly while trying to squeeze past the jabbering groups and get back towards the stairwell. He grabbed Mary's hand and pulled her behind him, eventually managing to spill through the doors as they were dragged with the tide.

As they waited for the elevator to arrive, Tom realised there were whisperings from the students around them. It was Scott. People were nudging their friends and pointing at him.

"Is that him?" one girl whispered to another. Tom had completely forgotten that Scott's re-emergence into the school might cause a stir. He did his best to ignore it as Scott shuffled uncomfortably by his side and did *his* best to look inconspicuous. He looked down at his hand and realised that Mary's sweating palm was still clutched inside his own. He gripped it tightly, anxious for the elevator to arrive. Of all days it had to choose today to start taking its time. Usually it was here within ten seconds.

Finally, it arrived and the doors pinged open to reveal the stoic-faced sentry angel inside. Tom pulled Mary in by the hand and Scott followed them nervously. People were still staring at him as the tiny room jammed quickly to capacity. Mary's hand was trembling in his own as the elevator made several precursory stops on its way down to the dungeons. It occurred to Tom that they'd soon have to give Mastema the slip which was a prospect that made his own palms start to sweat, her rotted smile flashed before his eyes as they descended through the tower.

When the elevator doors opened once more, they were the last remaining occupants, save for the ever-present sentry angel who stared out blankly from behind them. Thankfully, it seemed that Gabriel had neglected to give the sentry angels any sort of description of what the missing students might look like, so the unfortunate chap with them had no idea that he was standing inches away from one.

Outside the dungeons, another sentry angel stood steadfast at the entrance.

"What do we do?" Mary whispered frantically.

"Just follow me," Scott replied.

They walked past the guard as casually as they could, but they needn't have bothered, like an empty suit of armour, his vision remained transfixed on the hallway behind them, paying no notice whatsoever to their passing.

"What is it with those guards?" Mary whispered, when they were safely out of earshot. "I'm beginning to doubt whether they'd be any use at all in a crisis…"

*

The dungeons were as dark and as dismal as ever as they slid down the crooked stairway into Mastema's lair. Tom had been set on never laying eyes on the grotesque dungeon-master again, and he had no intention of breaking that promise to himself now. A loud clang broke his chain of thought; Scott's finger shot sharply to his lips and they froze as a loud clatter rang through the dungeon. Tom's heart thudded unevenly in his chest as they waited with bated breath for the fallout that would surely come after. But strangely, it never came.

"What was that?" Mary whispered, verging on panic. Scott looked at her and shrugged. They waited a moment more in the stairwell - ears taut, ready to run if they had to.

"Ok," Scott said finally, signalling with his hand for them to follow. He crept out into the open dungeon, only meters from where the line of cells began and in full sight of the grim doorway at the end of the room where Mastema was surely lurking. The service elevator was to their left and Tom dashed towards it without so much as glancing at the rest of the dungeon. Scott watched him with antipathy as he zipped by him, then grudgingly made his own dash towards the elevator. With only Mary left to make the crossing, Scott beckoned urgently for her to follow. Mary looked sick as she reluctantly crept across the cell line, pausing with each creek on the cold cobbled floor, before finally joining them at the service elevator.

Scott had already begun pulling back the rough iron grate that formed the makeshift elevator door while Tom looked on nervously with Mary at his side. He opened it just enough for the three of them to squeeze through a gap; once it was wide enough, he slid himself through, followed by Mary and then Tom.

With all of them inside, they stared at the rusted yellow lever apprehensively. Tom knew that as soon as that lever was pulled, the rickety old service elevator would shake itself to life and the noise would undoubtedly alert someone to their presence. With a self-assuredness that surprised him, Tom watched as his brother heaved back the lever and thrust it into place, followed instantly by the rattling of the grate door and the rough iron floor beneath them.

As the elevator shook itself to life, Tom waited anxiously for the unsightly cell keeper to come careening from her office and hurtle herself disjointedly across the nave of the dungeon to thwart them. Mary had grabbed his hand again, her face was ashen and twisted with anxiety. It seemed that she too was awaiting the inevitable tirade that would surely follow now they'd kicked up such a racket.

Once again, the storm clouds had assembled above them, but the rain never came. It seemed the commotion that had rumbled through the dungeon had gone unnoticed inside Mastema's office. Tom breathed a heavy sigh of relief as the elevator made its way down past the dark dungeon floor-line, then past the twelve floors of slabbed stone and into the wet bedrock of the tower. It was too late to turn back now; they were on their way to Purgatory again and it seemed no one could stop them. The lack of even a whisper of opposition had been somewhat disconcerting and Tom didn't know if he should be thankful or worried by such an unexpected turn of events.

The long ride down wasn't the most comfortable. The noise made by the rattling of the cage door was so loud that he could hardly hear himself think, so talking was out of the question. He found this more than a little irritating as it was the perfect time for them to be formulating some kind of plan of action for when they arrived at these gates Scott had described. It looked like they would have to 'wing it', as Finn would've put it.

Tom found himself wishing that his friend were here with them, he could use a joke or two to lighten up the mood at this point in time. The prospect of what lay ahead was more than a little daunting. First they would have to take the boat through the caves, then they –

"Wait a minute!" Tom cried over the deafening rattling of the elevator. The other two stared back at him worriedly when they saw the look of utter panic on his face. "What about the boat?! If Jason is already down there, then he'll have taken the only boat!" Tom saw Mary's eyes widen as she made the same realisation, (Scott was slightly slower on the uptake, but the point hit home once he'd fully processed Tom's words). They were twenty or so minutes into the forty-five-minute journey when Scott heaved on the yellow lever again and ground the old elevator to a halt. The lift was silent at last and Tom could hear himself breathe again for the first time in ages. His breaths were heavy and laboured from a mixture of the thin air inside the tiny compartment and the recent over-exertion at trying to raise his voice above the rattling.

"What do we do now then?" Mary seethed - clearly frustrated that they'd all failed to realise this rather obvious impediment before they'd jumped in the elevator in the first place.

"We've come too far to go back," Scott said pensively.

"But there's no point in going any further if we're just going to be stuck down there is there?" Mary fumed.

It was Tom, who had remained silent until now while he tried to catch his breath, who made the final decision on the matter. "Let's keep going," he said firmly. "Jason might still be at the beach, and if he's not then we can wait for him there."

The other two nodded reluctantly. Scott heaved back the lever and the old elevator shook itself to life again, sending dust and gravel from the bedrock smattering to the floor. The second half of the journey was exasperatingly long now they knew they'd most likely be trapped on the small island of sand that circled the elevator door.

When the vast underground lake finally came into sight their relief was replaced quickly by confusion, and then fear. Mary gasped and clung to Tom's hand while Scott took a horrified step backwards. Jason was there waiting, but he wasn't alone.

Chapter Twenty-Eight
To the Lighthouse

Jason stood on the banks of the black lake staring coldly at the three of them through the rough iron grate of the old service elevator as it made its final descent through the open elevator shaft. On each of his shoulders was a firm hand from the two sullen-faced sentry angels who had him apprehended. Just to the right of the sentry angels was the gleeful grin of Mastema, and the pious scowl of Raphael. Next to Raphael, and most worryingly of all, was the cloaked apparition that Tom recognised from his very first moment at St Michael's – it was the Headmaster.

It seemed that the group had been awaiting their arrival – no doubt information gleamed after a firm grilling of Jason who could have given them as much.

As the old service elevator stopped by the sand, one of the sentry-angels stepped forward and with one swift jerk that appeared almost effortless, he pulled the rough grate away, thrust Mary and Tom aside and grabbed Scott by the shoulder. Scott cried out in protest, but his struggles were futile, the angel pulled him from the tiny compartment and out onto the beach with the use of a single hand (the other still gripped around his wooden spear). He carried Scott off to stand beside Jason, who had watched Scott's apprehension with an emotionless glare. Raphael stepped forward next and stood before the

284

two perpetrators. He assessed them with a satisfied grimace, while Scott stared solemnly at the sand by his feet.

"Well…" he said sarcastically, almost enjoying himself, "it seems we have our perpetrators at last! You stand accused of breaking not only our rules at St Michael's, but the commandments of the Lord God Almighty. How do you plead?"

Only Jason looked Raphael in the eye as he spoke, his unblinking gaze was as deceiving as it was indifferent.

"Well?" Raphael shrieked, his voice echoing around the low ceilings of the caves. "What do you have to say for yourselves?"

"If I may…" Mastema interrupted from his side, "perhaps what they need is some gentle coercion. Our beloved Headmaster can be very persuasive when he chooses."

Mastema turned to the Headmaster and flashed her sickeningly sweet smile at him. He was so tall that her crooked frame barely came up to his waist, or at least what Tom assumed was his waist. It was difficult to discern any bodily outline under that black cloak he wore. The headmaster turned his featureless face to Raphael who smirked and nodded his approval.

"Very well," Raphael said, turning again to his prisoners, "perhaps a little coercion is in order after all."

Mary squeezed Tom's hand excruciatingly tight. He looked at her and saw her face had gone pale with dread. He didn't quite understand what was just about to happen or why Mary suddenly looked so petrified. He looked out to the beach again and saw the Headmaster loping slowly towards his brother. He was pulling back the sleeve of the heavy black robe that completely covered his arm and underneath, Tom caught a glimpse of his bony white skeletal finger protruding like a wand. He was raising it slowly towards Scott's head and Scott had started struggling violently in the arms of the sentry angel, but once again his efforts were useless. The vice-like grip of the brawny angel held him firmly in place and his chances of escaping were little to none. The headmaster's outstretched skeletal finger connected gently with the centre of Scott's forehead, and he shrieked a deafening cry of agony that echoed endlessly around the caves.

"Stop that!" Tom cried suddenly from within the tiny elevator. "You're hurting him!"

The rest of the beach's occupants turned to stare at him in bewilderment.

"That is the idea," Raphael said curtly in reply. Tom had gripped tightly around the bars of the iron cage and only Mary's grasp on the tails of his shirt had stopped him from running out onto the beach. "And who do we have here?" Raphael continued, stepping towards the elevator now. "Co-conspirators perhaps? Or two willing accessories to the crimes?"

"No!" Mary cried from behind him. "We were coming down to save the missing students Sir! We wanted to tell Gabriel, but time was running out and we thought Jason might sacrifice them before we could get to her!"

Raphael smirked and fixed her with his patronising gaze. "I do believe my sister would have better things to do than to go running at the whims of a stupid little girl."

Mary shied away into the far reaches of the elevator and Tom could see tears brimming in the corners of her eyes again. Back out on the beach, Scott was slumped in the arms of his captors and the Headmaster had retracted his bony finger and now stood assessing Jason who smirked back defiantly. Mastema had begun shuffling along the sand awkwardly to where Tom and Mary were situated.

"Hello dears!" she careened through her green rotting teeth. "I see you just couldn't resist another turn on my own private service elevator! Was it the lure of Mount Purgatorio that beckoned you?"

"N-no ma'am," Tom stuttered hesitantly. "That's my brother," he pointed to Scott who hung limply at the far end of the beach.

"Oh, how lovely!" Mastema crooned, clasping her spindly green hands at her chest. "The bond of brotherly love is eternal it seems; although, I dare say, your brother has been involved in some rather untoward business, and justice must be dealt my dear!"

"Indeed!" Raphael agreed, motioning with his hand for the Headmaster to proceed with Jason.

"Perhaps," Mastema interrupted loudly, "we would be best served by allowing the prisoners to escort us to their victims before our beloved Headmaster renders them incapacitated."

The Headmaster had his bony finger pointed inches from Jason's forehead, he'd paused in his ominous motion to allow Raphael the chance to respond. Clearly Raphael was incensed by the unsolicited interruption to proceedings, but he consented reluctantly, waving the Headmaster's hand away and rounding on the crooked form of Mastema.

"Very well," he said humourlessly, "let them lead us to their victims. Then we shall have justice."

*

Jason struggled wildly as the sentry angel manoeuvred him into the long boat. They were the last to board, Tom and Mary had joined at the behest of Mastema who insisted there be witnesses to proceedings. The boat sagged ominously as the sentry angel finally took his seat alongside Jason. Whether it had been designed to accommodate such weight was doubtful, water splashed over the side and settled at their feet as Mastema grabbed the oar and prodded them into motion. She twisted her emaciated torso and dug deeply into the water, displaying a surprising amount of strength for such a sickly-looking creature. Scott was still staring at his feet as they slowly began their journey into the fathomless caves.

Much like before, the trip was slow and monotonous. The jagged peaks of the ceiling closed in on them as they travelled deeper into the suffocating darkness. At one point, the entire boat had to actively dodge a stalactite that sliced between them like the fin of an upside-down sail fish. Mary and Tom were sat at the very back of the boat where it narrowed into the pointed perch on which Mastema balanced, their perpetually beaming gondolier. The only sounds were the occasional sobs from Tom's brother, who'd begun to softly weep into his t-shirt.

The mismatch group reminded Tom of the Dyatlov expedition who had met their untimely end in a series of bizarre happenings in the Ural Mountains in the fifties. The group had made camp on the slope of the mountain as night fell, then the next morning were scattered hundreds of meters apart, all dead from trauma and some with fractured skulls and their eyes and tongues missing. No one has ever been able to piece together the exact sequence of events that led the mountaineers to abandon their camp that night and flee into the blizzard, scantily dressed and barefooted. The wounds inflicted on the bodies were such that it was said the force required to cause such damage could only have been imposed by a car crash or something of equivalent force of impact.

The Dyatlov Pass Incident was now infamous among climbers for the strange and unexpected occurrences that can take place on a mountain. Perhaps their group would meet similar ends now they were journeying into the depths of Purgatory, without the red cloaks of St Patrick that were said to protect them from whatever terrors Mastema had alluded to the last time they were down here.

After what seemed like an eternity, the caves finally started to recede and give way to the starless black canopy that enclosed the fiery underworld like a snow globe. Strangely, Tom almost felt more claustrophobic out here than he had back in the caves. The sour tasting air of the caves had been replaced by the noxious fumes of Purgatory. Thick black smoke emitting from mountains that were eternally on fire. Tom, Scott and Mary erupted into coughing fits while the others observed them humorously. Jason too seemed to be strangely unaffected, though he continued to stare off into the distance, oblivious to the hacking noises around him.

Mastema steered the long boat towards the far eastern shoreline, the opposite side from where they had docked during their previous visit. As they approached the shore, Tom and Mary both clung tightly to the side of the boat, remembering last time how they'd almost been slingshot into the water as it beached. As the boat lurched violently onto the sand, only Scott was unprepared for the impact. His face hit the back of the sentry angel in front of him with a dull thud that the burly man didn't seem to notice.

Tom leapt reluctantly over the side of the boat and into the waist-deep water, then held out his hand to help Mary alight too. They dragged themselves to shore then turned to watch as one of the sentry angels lifted Jason like a ragdoll and threw him from the boat. Scott made his own way into the water willingly, though his head still hung to his chest and he refused to meet their gaze. Tom looked on timidly as the Headmaster who had been at the very head of the boat, lowered his tall frame crookedly over the side and onto the sand without getting his robe wet. He could see the fiery peaks burning at the far side of the lake and Mount Purgatorio, the tallest among them, looming like a malevolent Matterhorn at their centre.

Their own side of the lake was flatter and void of the mountainous topography that lined the western shoreline. It featured only gradual inclines and small rolling hills for as far as the eye could see into the dark rocky distance. The exception, of course, was the steep inclination lying directly before them. Like the on ramp to a highway, it was levelled out and smooth compared to the rough terrain around it. It appeared to be cut into the rock as if purposefully built by some ancient civilisation, as opposed to naturally occurring like the rest of the land seemed to be. At the top of this slope was the gate.

The group came to a halt at the foot of this manufactured slope and stared up at the old gates at the top. Raphael turned to his prisoners and, with an out-of-place smile, instructed them to lead the way.

Jason led the group, striding with purpose, while Scott trailed sombrely behind him. As they approached the crest of the slope, the gates materialised forebodingly above them. Scott had been quite right in his description; they did appear to be rather rusted and delicate, certainly not what you'd expect from the gates to Hell. In spite of this, they had a decidedly sinister air about them that gave Tom the chills even though it was sweltering. As the gates came fully into view, they all saw the reason they had come here. At the foot of the gates, tied back-to-back with rope and gagged at the mouth, were the two missing students.

They stared up at them soundlessly with terrified eyes. The boy was pale and slight looking with short blonde hair, and the girl was of Asian descent with her hair tied back tightly into a pigtail. Raphael pointed at them victoriously.

"Guilty as charged!" he roared, signalling for the sentry angels to apprehend his prisoners. Tom watched as they made to stride forward, but before they could make it a single step, they were stopped dead in their tracks. They were staring at Mastema who had squealed in delight and was pointing at the top of the gates with a look of exhilarated understanding. Tom spun on his heels and stared up at the gates too. There, perched at the top like a vulture appraising its next meal, was a man. Except it wasn't a man at all. His feet had been replaced by the talons of an eagle, and his legs were feathered like a bird's. The dark brown claws (that would have been his toes) were clutched tightly around the rusted iron gate, holding him firmly in place. Spread magnificently behind him were his wings. Like those of a bat, they were made of a thick layer of skin that was taughtened like leather and turned Tom's stomach just to look at them. His torso was stained black, as if scorched in a forge and his body was pockmarked with welts and festering lesions. His eagle-eyed gaze was fixed on Raphael and his expression was murderous.

"What an unexpected surprise!" he sang in a high-pitched sing-song-like tenor. Raphael had stumbled backwards a few paces and the sentry angels around him had their spears at the ready.

"Hello, Abaddon," Raphael replied disingenuously.

"You've brought two of your dogs, I see?" Abaddon replied, gesturing to the two sentry angels with one of his claws. "And Azrael too! What an honour it is indeed. The

Angel of Death in my presence! I would come down and shake your hand if I didn't know any better."

"It is strange to see you this far from your nest," Raphael enquired offhandedly. "I'd expect your master will be missing his pet budgie."

Abaddon sneered at the slight but was otherwise unperturbed. "I make special exceptions in situations like these," he replied carefully. "When I caught word that one of *His* highest-ranking angels was personally leading an ill-advised expedition into Purgatory, I had to see it for myself, and here you are! At the gates to the Underworld of all places! Should I tell my master to expect visitors?"

Raphael shuffled uncomfortably. "Not at all. We are merely here to collect two of our own," he said nodding towards the two students who sat wide-eyed beneath him.

"Surely you can't expect me to allow you within spitting distance of my domain without even so much as a snack to take home with me?"

Mary quivered at Tom's side as Abaddon assessed the two bound and tied students at his feet, licking his black lips like a snake who'd just had a pair of field mice thrown into his enclosure. What happened next, Tom would play over in his mind repeatedly for the next twenty years. The precise sequence of events was so exact, so destined, it was like a line of dominos falling over one after the other, each requiring an opposite and equal reaction to trigger the next domino to fall, until the entire line was toppled. While Abaddon and Raphael had been politely sizing up the other, commanding the attention of the rest of the group, the movements of Jason had gone unnoticed. He had crept silently from where he was standing towards Tom and Mary, and in one simple and lethal movement had extracted a small knife from inside his sock and grabbed Mary by the scruff of the neck and pressed the knife firmly against her windpipe. Mary had let out an ear-shattering scream that alerted everyone else, then almost instantaneously, the rest of the dominos began to fall.

Raphael nodded at the closest sentry angel at the exact same moment that Abaddon took off into the air like a kestrel to a car horn. The sentry angel threw his spear above him with military proficiency, then like a javelin thrower at the Olympics, caught it horizontally and in one swift motion, hurled it at the combined forms of Mary and Jason. At the exact same instant in time, Tom and Scott had burst into motion. Tom threw himself towards Mary and grabbed the loose knitting of her oversized blue jumper while Scott, in a completely redeeming act of self-sacrifice, threw himself in front of the airborne spear.

The last three dominoes fell at precisely the same moment. Abaddon's eagle-like talons landed hard on Jason's shoulders, then took off into the air with his prey clutched beneath him, triggering another ear-splitting scream in the process; Tom, who had reached Mary at exactly the right moment, pulled hard on her jumper and thrust her to the ground on top of him; and Scott, who's actions had been instinctual, received the piercing end of the airborne spear through his abdomen then felt it exit quickly out of his back. All of this happened in the space of a moment, and in that moment, everything had changed forever.

Chapter Twenty-Nine
The Age of Innocence

Tom sat on the warm sofa watching the rain lash against the windows of the common room. It hadn't stopped raining since they'd arrived back at St Michael's the night before and the weather, miserable as it was, reflected his mood perfectly. Mary lay across him with her head on his lap and he was stroking the soft curls of her red hair absentmindedly as his mind played over the events from the previous evening for the five-hundredth time. Finn was sat across from them, reclining into his own time-weathered armchair and was mulling over the story that Tom and Mary had just recounted to him.

"What I don't get," he said suddenly, still bitter that he had missed out on all the action, "is where this so called 'white angel' took your brother after it took off with him. He's already dead right? Where else is there to go?"

Tom had been wondering the same thing immediately after it had happened, but later on, when they were back in the boat on the long journey back through the caves, Mastema had clarified it for him. Tom had been inconsolable at the time and had been kept still only by the warm embrace of Mary who had refused to let go of him ever since he'd saved her from Jason.

"Where did she take him?" he'd moaned hysterically as she'd stroked the hair of his head that lay unashamedly on her lap, much as *her* head did now back in the common room. Once the echoes of Jason's cries had disappeared into the distance, and the dust had all but settled around them, Tom had stared in horror at his brother who lay broken on the red dirt in front of him. He wasn't moving and looked to be dead, (again) or unconscious.

Tom pushed his weight onto his elbows and tried to lift himself from the ground, but Mary had pulled him back down again, pointing with her one free hand at the ball of light from above that was descending upon them. It was another angel. An angel encapsulated in light. Beautiful and surreal, much like you'd imagine one to be. It was a girl; a young girl, who looked to be no older than ten. She landed softly beside Scott and knelt at his side, placing one tiny hand on where the spear protruded sharply from his back. Then, the white light that encapsulated her expanded like a dying star in the night sky. It grew until it enclosed the crumpled form of Scott and then it got brighter until Tom had to shield his eyes from its searing white brilliance. Once the light had died away, Tom dropped his arm from his face and the young girl and his brother had disappeared completely.

After that, everything had gotten a little frantic and hazy. Tom had been dragged away from the gates and back onto the boat by Mary and a sentry angel (who had held his wildly flailing body in check), and then he couldn't remember much of what happened after that. His brother had been taken from him for the second time in his existence and this time he'd witnessed the whole thing play out in front of him like some kind of horrifying picture reel that he'd been powerless to stop.

"That was one of the Cherubim," Mastema had told him as he lay grief stricken in the long boat. "The Cherubim are the guardians of *Shehakim* – or 'Paradise' if that's how you'd rather think of it. It seems your older brother has redeemed himself in the eyes of the Lord God Almighty with that one act of sacrifice, saving your young friend there. Do not be troubled by the fate of your brother, for he is with the Cherubim now in Paradise, where he shall remain for eternity."

Mastema's words had brought him little comfort at the time, but now he'd had the chance to calm himself and he could reflect on the words properly, he was grateful that she had given the explanation to him at the time that she had. Scott had redeemed himself and was in Paradise. He didn't have to worry about his brother anymore. He was safe and loved and he would see him again one day if he ever made it out of St Michael's, which he hoped someday he would. Then he'd ascend to Rakia, which is the Second Heaven, and he'd be that much closer to Scott and to his goal of becoming one of the Watcher Angels. He found peace in that thought and he smiled to himself briefly, the first smile he could remember breaking in quite a long time.

It was time for rest now, and perhaps for some time alone to shut off his mind from the thoughts that were whirling like cyclones in his head. He walked out of the common room with Mary at his side and her fingers clutched between his.

Alice was in the hallway, with Nettie and Truly by her side. She stared at him, speechless for a very long moment. Her eyes moving from his, down to his hand that held Mary's, then back up to his eyes again. She never said a word. She turned and walked away with Nettie and Truly in her wake, and Tom pulled Mary by the hand and they walked in the opposite direction. Further down the corridor, he kissed Mary on the cheek, then locked himself in the restroom.

He heard a voice say from above him, "Rest now, young Watcher."